STOCKTON-ON-TEES BOR

A FINE WILL BE CHARGED IF THE BOOK IS
RETURNED AFTER THE DATE ON WHICH IT IS DUE

This book should be returned on or before the latest date
stamped. It may, if not required by another reader, be
renewed on request for a further loan period.

# Love Me Tinder

Nicola May

'Never let a fool kiss you, or a kiss fool you.'

– Joey Adams

# Prologue

The fact that Cali was a bit drunk was probably a good thing. She tentatively reached for her mobile and searched for the required 'love app'. If there was going to be a right time, this had to be it.

A flame logo flickered on her phone screen and she felt a sudden rush of adrenaline. Tinder was the dating app that millions of people used worldwide. Surely there was one man on here who would be a suitable match – if only for a few dates to start with?

Now all she had to do was set up a profile and start swiping...

# Chapter One

'Cali big tits, Cali big tits.'

'Lady P! Not tonight, please!' Throwing her keys down onto her desk, Cali Summers ran a hand through her neat brown bob.

'No, no, no, no, no, no.' The African grey parrot shrieked and started diving around its large cage. It'd been fine in the marital three-bedroom detached home she had shared with her ex, Jamie, but in her pokey, two-bedroom first-floor flat, her feathered friend took up half the lounge.

Jamie had, of course, taught the mischievous bird every rude word it could take in, which more often than not came spouting out of her beak at the most inappropriate times.

'Miss Dumb Bell', Jamie's new 'bird', was apparently allergic to 'real' birds, so Cali had pathetically done as asked and taken this particularly badly behaved one in.

Cali sat back on her small cream sofa and looked around. What did she have to show for all the years she had worked and wasted with Jamie?

Yes, she owned her own place, but all that surrounded her was a bird cage, an untidy desk and a TV with a remote control stuck together with duct tape.

She lay back on the sofa and rested her tired feet on the wooden coffee table in front of her. A couple of family photos stared back at her. Josh, her handsome younger brother, sporting his Red Cross jacket in Nepal, and her parents, Sue and Duncan, with a giraffe looming behind them while on safari in South Africa.

Bless her lovely dad; if it wasn't for him she wouldn't have this place. Despite being so settled with Jamie back then he had suggested she use her grandfather's inheritance as a deposit on a flat, as an investment for the future. She wanted to put it in her wedding fund, but he had been insistent and now she was eternally grateful. Luckily the tenants had been nearing the end of their year's stint when her break up had occurred, so it had all been ironically convenient.

She had initially just turned all of her wedding photos around, but now they were shoved in a box in the spare room; smiling reminders of what now seemed like an unbelievable farce. There wasn't even any divorce settlement coming her way. The marital house wasn't in her name and there was no equity in it anyway, as they had installed a brand new kitchen straight after the wedding. Her best friend Annie had said she should fight for money out of him, but she couldn't bear the hassle, and felt that walking away with her head held high made her a better person.

All she had salvaged were her personal belongings and a wonderful ornate mirror they had bought together on a fun day out to Portobello Market.

This past year had been like a bad dream. To everyone else, they were the perfect couple. When they started telling friends that they were divorcing, there was a distinct rumbling of disbelief and a sense of checking their own relationships. If Cali and Jamie couldn't make it work, could they?

But not all of them had taken on a blonde bimbo of a personal trainer to get them both fit. Or a husband with strong abs but a much weaker spine who had run to someone else as soon as he began to feel 'trapped' and 'unsure' of his decision to marry 'so young'.

Cali knew that was an excuse – at thirty, Cali wasn't young, but the sad thing was that at twenty-four, Miss Dumb Bell *was*. She also didn't impose the immediate pressure of creating a family, which was exactly what Cali had wanted, as soon as she was married.

'Bitch!'

Cali leapt up and threw the purple velvet cage cover over the relentless bird. 'Lady P! Stop! Just stop!'

She crashed back down on the sofa as her phone beeped through with a text. *So have you received the divorce papers yet? Be a good girl and get them signed, will you?*

She looked to the envelope of broken dreams, sat dormant on the coffee table for two days, and flicked on the TV.

'Be a good bloody girl! Who the fuck does he think he is, Lady P?'

'Fuckety fuck, fuckety fuck.'

Cali got back up and pulled the cover off her

maddening bird.

'Exactly, Lady P, my thoughts entirely.'

Twelve years she had known Jamie Summers, nearly all of her adult life. What did she have to show for it?

A sad, fragmented heart and one bloody annoying parrot.

# Chapter Two

Putting an empty Tupperware container on her desk, Cali noticed her screensaver was still the one of her wedding day, and thought for the thousandth time that she really must change it. She also must really tidy her desk as her dingy wood-panelled office didn't have room for any clutter.

The one advantage of it, however, was that it looked over well-manicured grounds; she even had a view of the Thames.

Before she even had had a chance to sit down, Louise, the young event co-ordinator at the hotel where Cali was manager of Conferences and Events, began to gabble her not-so-concise handover.

'Ah, Cali ... good, you're back early. There's a wedding show at three thirty and a guy checking out The Red Room for his wife's surprise fiftieth at five. I've finished the contract for the corporate cow at Drake & Co. and we've just had a private lunch enquiry from ... shit, I've forgotten the company name but I've sent you an email.'

'Why are you telling me all this now? It's only two o'clock.' Cali started grouping papers on her desk.

'I asked you yesterday if I could have a half day.

It's my birthday tomorrow, remember, and I'm getting new extensions put in.'

'Oh, sorry Lou, of course you did. My mind's all over the place today.' She didn't think it right to elaborate to the twenty-year-old that the fact she was so nearing the signing of her divorce papers was actually making her physically sick.

'Right, I'm off. Cali, why don't you come along tomorrow? We'll be in The Swan by the time you're done. The more the merrier. It's a mixed age group, so you won't feel too old.'

'Ha! Thanks. I'll let you know tomorrow, if that's OK. Now, off you go. Enjoy the pampering.'

Lou grabbed her coat off the chair and headed for the door. She turned back and smiled.

'You'll be really welcome. And you never know, Cali, the man of your dreams might be in there.'

Cali shook her head and watch Lou go. With her long, wavy hair and sexy little figure, she was the desire of many a man who graced the corridors of the nineteenth century Bridge Hotel – the hotel that had been Cali's workplace for the last five years.

She should go out. She hated walking into pubs on her own, but that was something she needed to get used to now – plus she was getting slightly bored of staying in all the time rowing with Lady P.

Cali logged into her computer. She thought back to birthdays in her twenties. All of them spent with Jamie. It seemed hard to fathom that she wouldn't be spending any more with him. In fact, she was dreading her next one. She would be thirty-one and bloody single. In just a month's time, too.

Marcus Clarke, the General Manager, broke her

train of thought. All six foot four of him, with his neat salt and pepper haircut and classic good looks of a man in his early forties. Cali thought he could step straight into a Mills & Boon novel. He was a true gentleman, too. He treated every guest with kindness and respect. Well, to their faces anyway! The only downside was he had been married to the very beautiful ex-model Patricia for six years and they had two adorable sons.

'On your own today, Cali? All OK?'

'Yes, all good. It's Lou's birthday tomorrow and she wanted a half day to beautify herself. '

'Surprised she kept that quiet.'

'You know what she's like. She's a funny little thing, doesn't like fuss.'

'Unlike this one.' Marcus winked at Cali as a gangly redhead came scurrying by the events office.

'Anyone would think he'd lost a kidney, not mislaid a bloody tie in his room.' Adam pushed his floppy fringe back. 'Cali, Cali, Cali,' he sang, and kissed her on the cheek. 'Ooh, look at you. New blusher, or just because I walked into the room?'

'Adam, not so loud.' Marcus picked up a file that had fallen on the floor and walked back to his office. 'And when you get a sec, could you give the reception phones a good clean? They look grey rather than cream.'

'I signed up to be a receptionist, not a bloody skivvy,' Adam whispered.

Cali smiled at the young lad. She loved his Geordie accent and also the fact that he was so un-PC. He had helped her through with laughter during very dark times.

'Adam. Come on. Just do it, you know he's lovely, really.'

'I'd do him,' Adam laughed. 'And speaking of it, you need to start getting some action soon, too. You'll heal over before you know it if you don't.' Cali shook her head as he started rushing to the door. 'Cover me; I'm going for a ciggie.'

The thought of sleeping with somebody other than Jamie was alien. Another body to discover after so many years of the same one. She wasn't sure she'd know what to do. Sex had been so familiar with Jamie. At the start, young love – frantic and passionate. They would do it every which way, whenever they could. Then, as the years went on, with a deeper understanding of each other.

He was the third man she had ever slept with, the first being a four-month fling at seventeen with Ralph Weeks in sixth form, and the second, a one-night drunken fumble with a goth at university, whom she wouldn't have touched with a barge pole if vodka hadn't been involved.

She had met Jamie a year later and fell in love with him almost immediately. He was studying business. He always laughed at the fact that she was studying events management, as she was so quiet and never seemed to be very organised.

Jamie was her opposite; he was gregarious and he was loud. He had black hair and dark eyes and was very good-looking when she met him. In fact, he still was, at five foot eleven with an athletic body, and always well dressed.

But now, the twenty-something blonde hanging off his arm was reaping the benefits, and it still gave her a dull ache in her stomach at the thought.

He had said the passion had gone between them, the spark. He loved her but wasn't *in* love with her. He was sad but he didn't want to carry on a life with her. Shame she didn't see it coming. He had had the decency – if you can call it that – of promising he had not slept with *her* before he told Cali it was over, but it still hurt. Hurt like a bent arrow through her heart.

The fact that he didn't give them a chance to work through it was what had distressed her the most. His answer was that he couldn't believe she didn't feel that things had changed when they got married. Maybe she was just being naïve, or in denial. But underneath she knew it was because he felt pressured about starting a family straight away.

It was her who had suggested a bloody personal trainer too, as he was worried about not being in good shape for their honeymoon. Bloody ironic, really. She had pushed him into the arms of his future lover. What made it worse was that he had obviously built up a relationship with this woman. It wasn't just a flash in the pan, there was more to it. Adam minced in with a duster in his hand. 'Why have you got a face like a smacked arse now?'

'Just thinking about stuff.'

'Thinking about him, you mean.' He shook his head. 'OK, I have a plan. Tomorrow you are coming to Lou's drinks with me. All you need to do is make sure your phone is charged.' Cali screwed up her face as he continued, 'It's time that I helped you forget the ex and get you some sex!'

12

# Chapter Three

It was late, and not in the mood for a battering from Lady P, Cali gently pulled the cover over her cage and softly tiptoed to the fridge. All seemed quiet on the western front. She poured herself a glass of wine, threw a ready meal in the microwave and put her feet up on the sofa.

She'd had an OK night at the pub with Louise and her friends but, as usual, felt the same sense of not belonging since her split with Jamie. She feared she would never enjoy herself again, but with Adam's continued accentuation of her needing to snap out of it and find some excitement, she knew something had to be done – and soon.

The fact that Cali was a bit drunk was probably a good thing. She tentatively reached for her mobile and searched for the required 'love app'. If there was going to be a right time, this had to be it.

A flame logo flickered on her phone screen and she felt a sudden rush of adrenaline. Tinder was the dating app that millions of people used worldwide. Surely there was one man on here who would be a suitable match – if only for a few dates to start with?

He had told her that all she had to do was set up her profile, then start shopping for lurve. If you saw a man you fancied you swiped to the right, then if they felt the same about you they would too, then bingo, a match!

She bit her lip as she came to the request for photo uploads. Shy of having her photo taken, this wasn't going to be easy. OK ... the one that Adam had taken of her earlier would have to go up. Bright red lipstick and a bit of cleavage on show. She even looked happy. The lipstick was so not her; she rarely escalated to a mid-pink, even on a special occasion, but he had grabbed Lou's newest shade and plastered it on her, uttering, 'Nobody wants a moody, plain Jane now, do they?'

Now, should she put more posy ones up or just 'normal' ones? To be honest, she didn't have many posy ones. And she guessed they should be current photos, but she didn't have many recent ones – none where she didn't look miserable, anyway. She ended up going for one where Jamie had snapped her dressed as a nurse at a fancy dress party and another that a waiter had taken on the beach on their St Lucia honeymoon. Her white halterneck dress showed off her tan, somewhat protruding nipples, and her curvy size ten figure. Her brown hair was long then and her blue eyes looked somehow brighter than today. Maybe all the tears of the past three months had washed some of the colour away. Oh, how happy she looked then, recently married and with the world at her feet.

She had only recently had her hair cut into a chin length bob – a small act of defiance after a big act of treachery. Jamie had always stopped her as he "loved her long hair".

Oh well, if anyone questioned the timing of the photos then she would just be honest. She hadn't changed that much in two years. In fact, people always said she looked younger than her age. She put that down to being a petite five foot two and having always looked after her skin. She may be nearly thirty-one but she was pretty, still had a decent figure and was certainly not past it yet.

Why had she let another human being – one who had done the wrong – make her feel so down on herself? She had to get her self-confidence back, and quickly.

Adam had showed her his profile and suggested she put a few words on there, too. She couldn't believe that this was it. Just photos and a 'strap line' – no hobbies, likes, dislikes etc. But sod it; she had nothing to lose now. And if it wasn't right, then she could just delete the app.

She took a slurp of wine. A short sales pitch about herself, this was hard! She didn't want to give men the wrong impression, but she wanted to at least try and get a few matches. After many deletions she decided on *'Petite, shy but fun brunette, looking for a real life Mr Darcy.'*

Cliché, and she could imagine Adam laughing at that, but she didn't care. He was twenty-three and just looking for fun on the gay scene. She only wanted to attract decent men and hoped the Darcy reference would help her along the way.

She debated what age range she should go for and settled for 28-35.

'Done!' She said out loud, just as the microwave pinged and startled Lady P into action.

'Ping!'

'Evening, Lady P.'

'Big boy, J! Big boy, J!'

The African Grey had never been one for tact.

A tear began to roll down Cali's cheek as she thought back to the fun night she'd had with Jamie when he had taught their wayward bird that new phrase.

Oh, why did life throw so many curveballs?

But Adam *was* right. She'd had enough of heartache. It was time for fun and if it came in the shape of a real life Mr Darcy, then who was she to argue?

# Chapter Four

'So … if you had the choice, what would you rather have – risky freedom or dull security?

Cali sat at her best friend's kitchen table and looked down at her phone. The night before, in her sadness, she had continued to drink, which had led her to swipe right on at least ten men and she couldn't remember what any of them looked like.

'You already know the answer. I'm married to a bloody accountant.' Annie Johnson carried on loading the dishwasher. Her long, blonde hair had been swept back into a ponytail.

'Yes, but if you were in my current single, old maid spinster of the parish situation, then what?'

'Sorry to disappoint you, Cali, but you know me. I worry about bloody everything. I know Rob isn't the most exciting sometimes, but he's an amazing provider, a great dad and I trust him with my life.'

'You didn't mention the word "love" once then.' Cali slurped on her tea.

'Well, we can't all be as much of a romantic as you, can we? Are you working today?'

'Yes, going in at two. I'd better get my act together. The last thing I need is to lose a job as well as a husband.'

'Speaking of the dickhead, have you heard from

him lately?'

'Yep. Just to check I had received the final divorce papers. Probably so he can tell *her* it's all official. You wait; I bet she moves in with him as soon as I sign them.'

'Oh, Cali. You don't know that. But thank God you had the sense to keep your old flat. At least you didn't have the worry of selling up and finding somewhere new.'

'Thanks to my dad, you mean. I just feel empty and a bit lonely at the moment, to be honest.'

'Oh darling, of course you do. You deserved the happy ending with him.' Annie noticed Cali's face drop and her voice lilted. 'But come on, that doesn't mean you won't find another one.'

'I keep looking at the envelope with the papers in, but can't quite bring myself to open it, let alone sign them.' She let out a big sigh. 'Hurts even more that he got it all sorted a year and one day after the bloody wedding! The soonest date he could make it legal.'

Annie squeezed her friend's shoulder. 'I understand, mate, and I'm here for you. But I'm really sorry, I've got to run and get Keira from nursery.' She grabbed her keys off the kitchen worktop and followed her old school-friend out the front door.

'It will all work out OK, honey. And it's not a crime to cry sometimes, you know.'

'I'm fine. Time is a healer and all that jazz, and I've joined a dating site. Well, it's not a dating site as such, it's an app. Adam encouraged me to get it.'

'Aw, that's great Cali. See, you are moving

forward. Pop round for a glass of something after work tomorrow, I'll take a little look at what's on offer.' She winked, got into her car and wound down the window.

Cali's phone pinged.

'I've got a match!' She felt a surge of excitement.

'Time for some risky freedom, eh, Cali?'

Cali got in her car and took a deep breath. Weirdly, she had been worried what Annie might say about her using a dating app, but she obviously hadn't needed to.

There didn't seem to be so much stigma surrounding internet dating any more. In fact, it appeared everyone was at it!

# Chapter Five

'So how's my little vixen this morning?' Adam breezed into Cali's office and put his feet up on her desk.

Cali laughed. 'I've had two matches.'

'Ooh, let me see.' Adam grabbed her phone.

'Michael, 35. Windsor. Ooh, he's hot and just down the road too. Have you messaged him?'

'No. I didn't realise …'

'Cali, are you mental? Do you think you just look at these men and they telepathically know you want to go on a date with them? Message him now!'

'Shouldn't he be doing the chasing?'

'Here, I'll message him.'

'No!'

'Too late!'

Marcus appeared at the doorway and Adam shot up.

'There's a queue three deep at reception. Go on; get back to your post.' Adam scampered off. 'What's too late?' Marcus ran his hands through his salt and pepper hair.

'Oh, nothing. It's not work related.'

'Good, good. And I know we all love young Adam, but we do need to try and keep him under some sort of control.'

Cali made a face behind her manager's back. Her phone pinged.

In response to Adam's *Hey, how are you*, staring back at her were two words – *Nice nips*!

She threw her phone down on the table. Nice bloody nips. What was that about? And then Steve from Eton piped up. *Nurse's uniform, eh? Do you wear that for any other occasions?*

Was romance really that dead? Did men really have to be that basic? She realised then just how long she had been out of the dating scene. She tried to think back to twelve years ago, when she had fallen for Jamie. Had it been instantly sexual? It had taken her at least four dates to let him sleep with her, but she had felt safe and warm with him from the start.

Maybe *this* wasn't the right app to be on? But Adam had convinced her it was. It was all about the chemistry: you could read an interesting, four-page long profile and still not fancy that person. At least by seeing a face you got an element of instant attraction.

Another match and message pinged in. 'So, Jon from Bourne End, what have you got to say for yourself?' Cali said to herself, then took a slurp of coffee.

*Hey! You have beautiful eyes.*

Now, that was better. He had what her mum would call a 'kind' face. Same age as her, cropped dark hair, nice shirt. His other pictures were of him at a rugby match with friends and one on a beach. Good body, too.

She began to type and, within ten minutes, a date

was arranged. She was to meet Jon from Bourne End at The Boathouse in Windsor at eight p.m.

Her virgin voyage to find love – or at least a bit of fun – had just begun!

# Chapter Six

'You're looking nice tonight, Cali.' Rob grabbed a handful of peanuts as he walked through the kitchen where his wife and best friend were chatting over a glass of wine.

'You couldn't just read Keira a story could you, love? I'll come up in a minute. Cali is on her way out.'

'Of course. You have fun now!' He winked at Cali as he headed to the stairs.

'Bless him.' Cali took a sip of wine.

'Yes, I found a good one there. Quick, show me this man you're meeting.' Cali handed over her phone. 'I like the look of him. Now, make sure you're in a public place and don't get in his car and if he asks you to go back to his, say no.'

'Annie! Don't scare me. And even if he does try to charm the pants off me, they are staying firmly on. I can't get hurt again, not after what's happened. Even the thought of getting naked with someone else brings me out in hives.'

'What's his name again?'

'Jon.'

'Jon what?'

'Oh, I don't know.'

'What does he do?'

'Shit, I didn't even ask.'

'Bugger, we can't even Google him to check him out.'

'Annie! What are you like?'

'I'm just looking out for you.'

'I know. I know.' Her phone pinged with a text.

*Looking forward to meeting you, gorgeous girl. I'll be waiting at the bar for you. I'm wearing dark jeans and a white shirt.*

She shared it with Annie and they both 'awwed' in unison.

'Good, well, that's nice. Thoughtful, making you feel at ease. Right, best tit forward, darling, you've got a man to catch.'

Cali parked up in the nearest car park to The Boathouse, checked herself in the mirror and took a deep breath. She had decided on a navy shift dress to enhance her blue eyes and beige wedge sandals with a matching beige bag. 'Tits or legs, not both,' was her motto. And she was showing just enough leg to look sexy. She had stuck with the mid-pink lipstick as wearing red was a bit too 'look at me' for her liking, despite whatever Adam said.

It was a warm April evening and Windsor was buzzing with after-work drinkers and tourists.

Her heart was beating so fast when she reached the riverside pub that she had to stop and collect herself before she walked in. The sunny evening had attracted a crowd and there was a queue at the bar. She looked around – there was a guy standing by a post with a pint in his hand, around six foot, with a bit of a paunch and greying hair. He was wearing a white shirt. She looked past him to see if she could see Jon. As she wandered over to the end of the bar, she felt somebody gently grab her arm.

'Calista?'

How she hated her full name, only ever used by her mother when she was cross with her. But she had decided to put it on her profile, almost to hide from her real self, create an alter-ego as if to pretend she wasn't actually going through with this internet dating 'thing'.

She turned around to see the paunched man smiling at her.

He kissed her on the cheek. 'Nice to meet you. What can I get you to drink?'

'Err, a small Pinot Grigio, please.' She stood back and sneakily checked the photo on her phone while he was at the bar. It was definitely him but there was no way that he was thirty. He looked at least forty.

'Cheers, cutie.' He clinked his glass with hers and she had an urge to vault over the railings of the pub garden straight into the river. *Cutie*?!

Cali smiled politely. 'Quick, those two are leaving. Let's grab their seats.' She walked quickly over to the table and put her drink down. It really was an idyllic setting; swans were swimming contentedly by and the Thames was sparkling with the last rays of the spring sunshine.

'You look great, Calista. Lovely dress, and those *eyes*. So much better in the flesh.'

'Err, thanks.'

'Are you not going to say anything about how I look? Women usually comment at least once about how handsome I am.'

Cali laughed as the deluded one continued.

'I didn't mean that to be a joke. So ... what do you think?'

'Err. Well, I can see a slight resemblance to your photos, but they're not that recent, are they? You said on your profile that you were thirty.'

'Ha! Nobody puts their real age up. And, to be honest, I like younger women, so it's easier to meet them that way.'

Cali took a large gulp of wine. 'But that's not right. I expected to meet somebody younger, who looked like their photo.'

'What, you're saying that I don't? It's not like I'm pretending to be someone else.'

'No ... but ... how old are you, anyway?'

'Age is but a number, Calista. And if the chemistry is right, then what does it matter?'

Jon took a big slurp of beer and lit a cigarette.

'Oh, you smoke? You didn't mention that.'

'You didn't ask. If it bothers you, I don't have to.'

'No, no, you carry on.'

Cali took a deep breath, thinking it would be the only thing that would be smoking between the pair of them – *ever*.

'So what do you do for a living then, Calista?'

'I work in a hotel, in events.'

'Oh, which one?'

'It's an olde worlde hotel around twenty miles from here. Ideal for weddings and small conferences.' God, she had turned into a sales advert.

'Ah, the Bridge in Moulton?'

Cali suddenly realised that she didn't actually want this man to know anything more about her.

'I'd rather not say.' She took another big slurp of wine.

'I understand. But handy for dates that go well, if you get what I'm saying.' He winked at her and touched her hand.

She nervously smiled and laughed. Vile! It wasn't that he was ugly. She had built up a picture of him in her head and she was just disappointed. He'd looked so bloody gorgeous in the photos. And she was annoyed at such a waste of time. The getting ready, the anticipation of it all. If this was what it was going to be all about, she wasn't sure if finding love online was the way forward for her at all.

Jon drained his pint. 'Another?'

'Err …' How did she say she wanted to leave? This was difficult. Was she supposed to stay the whole evening? Was there an internet dating code of etiquette?

She suddenly had a vision of sitting there with Jamie. It would have been so relaxed, so easy. No effort required. The words 'I really must go' spun around her head but for some reason refused to come out of her mouth. Instead, 'Let me get you one.'

'No, I insist. Same again?'

'Yes please, but can you put soda in this one as I'm driving?'

'Are you sure you don't want a large? I could always give you a lift.'

'No! I mean, no thanks.'

Jon came back to the table with drinks and menus. It was getting a bit chilly and the staff were giving out blankets.

'I'm starving; can I get you some food?'

'Err, no, I ate earlier, thank you.' Having to suffer through another drink with this man was like being stuck in traffic.

'So, what do you do, Jon?' She couldn't believe she hadn't even asked him these fundamental questions.

'Oh, this and that. I have three young kids so they take up a lot of my time.'

'Ah, right. I bet they do.' She couldn't even be bothered to ask any more questions. It was a massive lesson that she should chat for longer than ten minutes before spontaneously arranging a date. But she had been caught up in the excitement. She wanted children, but wasn't in a position to have one of her own, let alone take on someone else's.

She glanced at the menu for future reference. 'Ooh, the Thai red curry looks good.'

Jon made a face. 'I don't eat hot food.'

'Really, not even a korma? I love curry.'

'No, I have terrible piles, you see, Calista, so it doesn't do me any favours when it comes out the other end.'

Cali had to disguise her rising laughter with a sneeze.

'Bless you!'

'No, bless you, Jon. That must be very uncomfortable for you.' She drained her glass in one. 'Look, I'm sorry to rush off; I've got an early

30

show tomorrow and really must go.'

'But it's only nine-thirty.' He reached for her hand. 'Maybe a kiss at least?'

He launched at her across the table and all she could think of was her very first kiss at a school disco, when she was fourteen. All tongue, spit and no substance, but now complimented with the added aroma of stale tobacco and beer.

Trying not to gag, she stood up and brushed her dress down.

'Right, best get some beauty sleep, Jon,' she faked a smile in preparation for her escape, 'my virgin dating app date.'

Why had she said that!?

'Ooh, don't get me going with the V word, you little minx.' He stood up. 'Let me at least walk you to your car.'

'NO! No, it's fine. Thanks for the drinks and err … nice to meet you.'

Once out of eyeshot of the pub, Usain Bolt wouldn't have made the sprint to her car faster. Virgin dating app date? Virgin dating ape, more like!

# Chapter Seven

'Well, at least he didn't taste of curry too … you little minx!' Annie was almost wetting herself. 'I mean, who tells anyone they have piles on a first date? Actually, who tells anyone they have piles, apart from a doctor? I only told Rob after Keira was born because he kept asking why I wasn't sitting down to feed her.'

Cali clipped a water bottle onto Lady's P's cage as her friend continued. 'Look, I know it was a bad first date, Cali, but you have to laugh and learn that you need to know a bit more about these men before you meet them. You've got to wheedle out the fakes after just one thing and find the genuine ones.'

'I know, I know. I think lesson one is to make sure their photos are current. Do you want another cuppa?'

'Cuppa, cuppa, cuppa, bitch!'

'Shut up, Lady P,' they both said in unison.

'No, no more tea, ta. Rob's got football tonight and I need to get Keira to bed.' She stood up. 'Just be careful, eh? I'll have a look at some profiles over the weekend with you if you like, but you're not stupid, Cali. Just message them for more than ten minutes next time. Have a quick chat on the phone, maybe?'

Cali, still scarred from the whole experience, carried on. 'He insinuated that I could take men back to the hotel for sex!'

'Now there's a thought.' Annie smiled. 'I mean, if it gets to that stage and you fancy them, how kinky would that be!'

'As if. Can you imagine Marcus's face if he found out?'

'You never know, he might want to join in. I mean, it's a bit of a fantasy thing, isn't it?'

'Annie! You're a married woman.'

'Exactly. Right, I must run. Take care. Let me know when you're around at the weekend. I don't know about you but I'm excited for date two already.'

# Chapter Eight

Recognising Jamie's knock, Cali grimaced, wiped her wet hands on a tea towel, and went to the door.

'Hi. How are you?' Even his bloody voice was sexy.

She could smell his familiar aftershave and had to take a deep breath to compose herself. Her heart was beating far too fast for her liking. Why was love so right in so many ways but so wrong in others? Why, when a heart had been cheated on, could it not change signal and divert to a new track without pain?

'I'm fine, just fine.' She stood looking at him for a second. 'What brings me the pleasure?'

'Um. Just wondered if you've had a chance to send the divorce papers back yet?'

'And this one question constituted a visit?'

'Big boy, J! Big boy J!' Lady P started darting around her cage.

'Good girl!' Jamie laughed. 'So, can I come in then?'

Cali hesitantly let him pass her. She wished she was made up and in a decent outfit rather than her shabby blue dressing gown.

'You've changed your hair.' In Jamie speak, that meant he didn't like it.

He walked into the lounge and noticed the untouched brown envelope.

'You haven't even opened it! Come on, Cali, it's time to move forward now.'

'Maybe for you,' she thought, not wanting to give his ego the satisfaction of hearing it.

'As in you want me out of the picture so you can get *her* fully in it?'

'Sit down and calm down, Cali.' Jamie's voice softened. 'You know I never meant to hurt you.'

This was it, the moment he was going to tell her that he wanted to turn Miss Dumb Bell into Mrs Jamie Summers. She could feel the salt seeping into an already open wound as the scenario she had played over and over in her head was about to become a reality.

Her nostrils flared. 'I don't want to bloody sit down.' Jamie awkwardly swayed from foot to foot. 'I knew you'd want to marry her eventually. But don't you think it's a bit bloody quick? I mean, your husband track record is not exactly a glowing one, is it?'

'We're not getting married Cali. It's just …'

'Oh, for God's sake, Jamie, just spit it out and spare me the drama.'

'Well, Bella won't move in until you and I are officially divorced.'

Lady P spoke for her. 'Bella, Bella, Bella, Bella, BITCH!'

Jamie and his ego tried not to smirk. 'Look, I'm sorry, but I felt I had to tell you.'

They were just moving in together, not the full monty of marriage, but the feeling of hurt that rushed through her was still a shock. In fact, if he had poured a cup of scalding tea right in her face, the pain would have hurt less.

Waving her hand nonchalantly in the air, she walked away to the kitchen.

'Well, great, thanks for telling me, Jamie. Now, can you please leave?'

'Is that all you have to say?'

'Oh, I'm so sorry for my lack of interest. I mean, what were you expecting? A moving in present?' She held back her tears with anger. 'Just fuck off and leave me alone.'

He got to the front door then turned around.

'So, the divorce papers?'

Cali thought she might physically explode into a million pieces, but her inner strength held her tight in a firm grip.

'I need to speak to my solicitor in the morning, Jamie; there could well be some changes.'

'Changes? What do you mean? You said you didn't want anything.'

'Big boy J! Big boy J!'

'And you can bloody take your stupid bird with you.'

Cali clumsily picked up the huge cage, but the already slammed door had caused her beloved Portobello Market mirror to fall off the wall and smash into the same amount of pieces as her heart.

Lady P started pecking frantically at her dried food in fear.

'I'm sorry. I'm so sorry, Lady P.' Cali sobbed, placing the cage gently back on its resting place.

If they were just dating, there was always the

chance that he and the dumb one would split. Moving in might not be marriage, but it was still another level of commitment.

Without care, she stepped over the broken glass and wiped her snotty nose on her dressing gown sleeve. Then, suddenly becoming conscious of Lady P's silence, she looked into her disrupted cage.

The bird poked her little head out of the bars and gently placed it sideways onto Cali's arm.

'Love you, Callerina.'

If it hadn't been Jamie's nickname for her it would have been a very rare, tender moment.

Instead, she ran into the bedroom and threw herself onto the bed and began sobbing again.

Gone were her dreams of a rose-covered cottage in the country, 2.4 kids and a black Labrador. Instead, ahead of her, was a long road to find happiness. And, if her first date was anything to go by, it was going to be a bumpy old track.

# Chapter Nine

'So what are you saying? They *are* moving in together, but only when you're officially divorced?' Annie signalled the waiter to bring over some menus.

'Yes. Just that.'

'Ssh.' Cali rolled her eyes at Annie as a couple sat down at the table next to them.

Deedee's Café was a regular Saturday brunch haunt of theirs and in a small town like Bramley, the gossip train had been known to be an expressway to mortification.

'Morning, ladies,' David, the handsome bespectacled Czech waiter smiled at them. 'What can I get you today?'

'Full English with extra toast, pot of tea and a fresh orange juice, please.'

Annie laughed, 'Blimey, you *are* hungover.'

'Just muesli, yoghurt and a green tea for me, please.'

'*Dobre.* I mean, good.' David, as always, memorised their order and walked back to the now busy counter.

'Green bloody tea, Annie? What's going on?'

'Rob commented on my muffin top this morning. Just jokingly, but you know, I want to be a "yummy" mummy, not one of those "comfy" ones.'

'But Keira isn't even eighteen months! The thought of being all settled like you and a "comfy" mummy, I can't think of anything more wonderful.'

'Even green grass can go brown and die, Cali.'

'Hey, don't you be getting down too.'

Annie smiled. 'I'm fine, just a bit tired. It's relentless having a baby sometimes.'

'It's not always going to be the Cali Summers show, I promise.'

'I know, mate, but you need to get whatever is troubling you out.'

'Well, when he came round yesterday, I was actually expecting him to say he wanted to marry her, not just move in together. But that bloody hurt enough.'

'Oh, darling,' Annie put her hand on her friend's. 'You should have called me earlier.'

'To be honest, I didn't want to talk to anyone after he told me. Even Lady P knew to be quiet. So I got drunk and went to bed.'

'What a bastard.'

'It takes two to tango, Annie. Dumb Bell is young, but she's not stupid. She obviously wants to speed it along to cement their relationship, and you do hear of divorces dragging on.'

With another charming smile, David placed their orders on the table.

'That was quick, thank you.' Annie began to stir yoghurt into her nuts and berries. 'So, are you going to stall on the divorce? Jamie has been an absolute pig, so I wouldn't blame you.'

'I don't know. It crossed my mind, but what's

the point of prolonging the pain? Apart from annoying them both.'

'Exactly,' Annie smiled.

'Oh, I don't know, my head is still muddled with everything. And at best, the solicitor said that it will take a couple of months if I just agree to everything.'

'If you were to be truly honest with yourself, would you really want him back now all this has happened?'

Cali sniffed back her tears, whispering, 'I hate him.'

Annie reached for her friend's hand across the table. 'I know, darling.'

Cali withdrew her hand.

'But I bloody love him at the same time. Annie, how can that be? To still be able to love someone who has blown your life apart? He looked and smelt beautiful yesterday, too.'

'Because there's not an on/off switch on your heart. True love is not a flickering bulb; it is a burning, huge, raging fire of desire that engulfs all of us at some stage in our lives.'

'The dating app logo is a burning flame.' Cali blew her nose.

'Good marketing, then.' Annie took a slurp of her tea and grimaced at its unfamiliar sour taste. 'Look, Cali. Getting over someone takes time, but there's no point sitting in and moping. Do what feels right. And if that's going on a few dates, then great. You don't have to sleep with them. But if you do, just take it for what it is – pleasure between two people.'

'But I don't want to be regarded as a slut.'

'Cali Summers, if you ever think you are a slut, call me for reassurance that you're not. Before I met Rob, I used to be like Aphrodite on acid! Look, you're thirty and you've only been with three men in your whole life. It's time you had a bit of fun. Sex *is* fun.'

David appeared and noticed Cali's untouched breakfast. 'Is everything OK with your food? Would you like me to warm it for you?'

'Thank you, but no. I'm not feeling so great.'

His big brown eyes looked gently into hers. 'I'm sorry to hear that, madam. I will charge just for drinks.'

'See, there are good men around.' Annie got her purse out of her handbag.

'He's quite cute, too.' Cali half smiled.

'Now that's better. Turn the shy into siren and you'll soon be getting as much hot sausage as you can handle.'

'Annie! What are you like?'

'I'm like …' She cocked her head to one side. 'I'm like … Cilla Black on *Blind Date*, God rest her soul.'

Cali laughed.

'And to be honest, I can't wait to start living vicariously through you! Beats dirty nappies, sleepless nights and a part-time job I'm over-qualified for.'

Ping! 'I've got a match!' Cali reached in her bag for her phone. 'Will, 31, Aldershot – ooh yes, I remember swiping right on him.'

'Let me see.' Annie took her phone. 'He's fit,

Cali, and from those photos it looks like he's an officer in the army! How sexy is that? Get chatting, girl. Right, I'd better go and relieve Rob so he can go to the gym.'

When they arrived back at Annie's, Rob was already at the front door; a screaming Keira in his arms.

Annie kissed her friend on the cheek. 'See. Whose grass is greener now?'

'Do you want me to come in and give you a break for a bit?'

'Not at all. Why don't you book a massage or get your nails done? Something for you. I mean, you've got to look good for your date with Will, haven't you?'

'I guess.'

Annie kissed Rob and held her arms out to her red-faced and whimpering child. She waved back at Cali.

'And please do include me from now on. I want a "Hot Sausage" text for a good match, and now let me think … Ha! I know. A "Green Tea" for a shit one!'

Noticing Rob's bemused face, Cali pulled away laughing. Thank heavens for friendship!

# Chapter Ten

Cali only just managed to stop herself saying 'Hot Sausage' out loud as she got out of her Mini and looked into the light blue eyes of Will, 31, from Aldershot.

She had already received a *Lucky cow* reply from Annie on sending the obligatory text.

'Hey, Calista?'

'That's me.' She could feel herself reddening.

'Well, that's a good start. You'd be surprised how many women don't look like their photos.'

Cali laughed. 'And I can say the same for men as well, but you, well, actually, you look far better in the flesh.' Shit, why had she said that?

Will smiled. Good teeth too, Cali thought. Set in a handsome, chiselled face. Blonder than she had expected, but being the antithesis of Jamie could only be a good thing, surely? He fit his jeans well and, at six foot one, ticked many a box. In fact, on looks alone, he was an eight out of ten.

She had struggled with what to wear – as it was such a lovely afternoon, Will had suggested they go for a walk in the park. Finally, she had settled for dark blue jeans, a crisp white shirt and black wedged boots that, although a little bit wintry, gave her legs a little bit of length and tone.

At first she was filled with horror at going for a walk, seeing it as quite a 'dangerous' thing to do. Annie had assured her that if he was in the army and an officer to boot, he would be from good stock. And then jokingly suggested that if he did drag her into the bushes, then by the look of him, lucky her!

She had also suggested that Cali have a brief telephone conversation with him first, after the debacle with Jon. On her announcement that he didn't sound like a serial killer, Rob asked what exactly she expected one to sound like.

Will locked his car and came to walk by her side.

'Sorry if a walk on a Sunday afternoon for a date seems a little weird, but I've been away with the lads on a fishing trip for a few days and I've drunk my body weight in beer and tequila. Could do with the fresh air.'

'No, it's fine. It's such a lovely day. And I was beginning to get cabin fever in my flat, to be honest.'

'Good. Not to the cabin fever bit. You know what I mean.' The officer smiled that smile again. 'I always think that walking and talking is a great way to get to know someone without too much pressure.'

'I hadn't thought of that. I guess it beats staring at each other over a bar table in awkward silence.' She already liked him. Maybe this dating app lark wasn't so bad after all.

'Exactly, and there's always something different to see and talk about.'

'You're a pro at this then, it seems? I'm only on date number two.'

'Ah, right. How was date number one?'

46

'It was worse than awful. The guy didn't look like his pictures and was really creepy. But I'm persevering.'

'Well, I'm glad you did.'

Cali felt warm inside. Will actually seemed a decent guy. 'So how long have you been on the app then?'

'About four months. I split with my girlfriend in Germany just before I came back to work here. I missed her, work was tough and I needed a distraction.'

Two kids on bikes suddenly came careering down the hill in front of them and Will gently guided Cali out of the way.

'So what do you actually do, Will?'

The handsome blond laughed. 'I'm afraid if I tell you I'll have to kill you.'

'Ha! OK, but you're an officer in the army, right?'

'Yes, and it's not all secret stuff. It's not even that exciting, really. I've done two tours of Afghanistan, but now I'm settled at base camp – for nine months anyway, training up some new lads coming in.'

'I admire you for Afghanistan; that must have been hard.'

'It makes you grow up, that's for sure. And I don't sweat the small stuff now, ever.'

'I need to stop worrying so much. Actually, coming out here and seeing how beautiful it is has made me realise that I should start running again. But I think I'd be a bit scared out here on my own, it's quite remote.'

'What exactly are you scared of?'

'Being attacked, I guess.'

'Calista ... never fear anything. It'll restrict you in everything you do.'

'I guess you're right.'

'I am right.' Will's voice softened. 'So how come you're on the app, anyway?'

'More peer pressure than anything. I split from my husband a few months ago, after nine months of marriage. We'd been together for twelve years.'

'Your decision to split?' Will placed his arm gently on hers and she felt a little tingle go up it. 'Look, sorry, you don't have to tell me.'

'It's fine. He left me for the personal trainer we used to get in shape for the wedding.'

'Shit, that sucks. Do you have children?'

'No, I think that was half the problem. I said I wanted them as soon as we got married.'

Cali grimaced. The handsome officer would probably feel safer in a war zone if she carried on.

Will picked up on her awkwardness. 'I didn't realise there was a lake out here. Look at all the swans.'

'They mate for life, you know. If only it was as simple for human beings.'

'The mating bit is easy,' Will laughed.

'Only a man would say that.' Cali poked him gently in the ribs as they walked towards the lake. She wondered what on earth he'd think if she confessed to only properly 'mating' with one man in her life.

All of a sudden the sky turned dark and there was a rumbling of thunder.

'Big storm approaching, by the feel of it. I didn't see that coming. Come on, Calista.'

Will grabbed her hand and they started running back to the entrance.

'I'm scared now, all these big trees and lightning.'

'Hey. What did I say about being scared?'

The rain, initially huge intermittent drops, suddenly became a torrent. By the time the pair of them reached the park gate, they were soaked through.

Cali was conscious of her white bra and protruding nipples on show through her shirt.

As Will's car was nearest, he grabbed an umbrella from the boot and held it over them both.

'And the winner of Miss April Wet T-shirt goes to…'

Cali self-consciously crossed her arms.

'Hey, I was only joking! It was actually those bad boys that helped my decision to swipe right.'

All of this talk was so alien to Cali, but coming out of Will's well-formed kissable lips, she actually quite liked it.

'Right, I'm starving. I'm going to get home, order a pizza, dry off and chill out. It's been one hell of a week.'

'Oh, OK.' Cali was really hoping the date might continue. 'I guess I better go home and eat too, that's the most exercise I've done in months.'

'I can always assist you with that,' Will smirked. Cali blushed beetroot red at the thought. His self-assurance deemed her mute. The rain was still torrential. Will walked to Cali's car, all the while sheltering them with his umbrella.

'Well, thanks for a lovely afternoon, Calista.'

'Cali, please.' If she liked somebody, it didn't seem right for them to call her Calista, she could save that for the men she chose just for 'fun'. 'And yes, it's been great, so thank you, too.'

'Oh, and I hear dipping soldiers in eggs is a good protein/carb combination.' Will smiled, kissed her on the cheek, and casually walked back to his car, leaving Cali sitting in hers in complete turmoil.

So … she fancied Will, really fancied him, and what was that about the exercise and dipping your soldiers comment? He was definitely flirting with her. But there was no mention of a second date. Maybe he was shy like her, just good at talking the talk? She could actually, for the first time in ages, see herself sleeping with this man! Just the feel of his hand on her arm and his soft lips on her cheek had made her feel a bit funny. Why couldn't she have been bolder and just grabbed him and kissed him there and then?

She looked to her phone. She would text him. But what would she text him? Maybe she should wait. She didn't want to appear too keen and blow it before anything happened. He had said fear nothing, though. She started to type and delete, and type and delete. She wanted to let him know she felt it too, but without sounding too rude. This was so hard! And she was so out of practice! She hadn't really found out anything about him, either. Another lesson – ask more questions and keep a bit back about her.

Will pulled up at the Officer's Mess and checked his phone. He bit his lip and shook his head.

*You've given me faith back in this dating app thing. Dinner next time? C x*

A uniformed officer approached him as he got out of the car.

'You're back early, mate. Take it she was a minger?'

'No, the contrary, she was fit, but too bloody nice. I think she's after the long haul, though, and I'd ruin her in more ways than one.'

# Chapter Eleven

'Be careful, Marcus is on the war path this morning.' Louise carried on filing her nails and sipping her steaming cappuccino.

'It's only 8.30 on a Monday morning, what's got his goat?' Cali switched on her computer and winced at the wedding screensaver. Her procrastination really had to be dealt with.

'Adam was late and Miguel phoned in sick. He had to sit on reception for half an hour doing check-outs, he's not happy! Adam is now being abnormally polite for fear of getting fired.'

'And how come you are so early?'

Lou sniffed. 'Oh, Mum was harping on about me treating the place like a hotel, so I thought I'd escape her wrath and do my nails in peace at a real one.'

Cali laughed. 'I do feel for you. It's so hard to get on the property market these days and it's not exactly as if rent is cheap around here.'

'Tell me about it. I'm considering a shared house, but that scares me a bit. I'm quite fussy when it comes to sharing a bathroom.'

'Don't be scared of anything. It'll hold you back.'

Cali's regurgitation of Will's words made her

think of him. In fact, she hadn't stopped thinking about him since yesterday afternoon. Still no reply. But he had said that he was tired and had a busy week ahead of him. Maybe if he hadn't replied by Wednesday, she'd send him another casual text.

'Calisssttaaaaaaa.' Adam came marching into the events office. 'Morning, love. How was your weekend? I doubt there was anything of interest to report, but thought I'd ask to be polite.'

Cali really didn't want to discuss her personal life in front of Louise. 'It was as dull as the colour of your eyes, to be honest.'

Adam laughed. 'What time can you lunch today? I've only got half an hour at 12 as I was late.'

'I've brought sandwiches, so how about I meet you under the big oak tree round the back? We haven't got any outside events on, so we shouldn't get spotted by any guests.'

The wedding season was upon the hotel, so Cali's morning flew by with two show rounds and a meeting with a new cake supplier. Since splitting with Jamie, she actually hated doing wedding show rounds. Firstly because it reminded her of her non-married state and, secondly, indecisive brides and their pernickety mothers (in most cases) drove her crazy.

She usually asked Louise to do the show rounds, but this morning Marcus had asked her to research some new florists, so she was not at Cali's disposal.

By 12 o'clock she was ready to sit in the spring sunshine and let Adam amuse her.

'So your weekend was really that boring? The glint in your eye tells me different, Ms Summers.'

Adam chewed on a stick of celery; his long legs stretched out in front of him.

'Celery? That's not like you.'

'I met a boy at the weekend, he's a model.'

'What, a hand model?'

'Ooh, look at you with the jokes. Now I know you've had a good weekend. I mean, you usually look like a bulldog chewing a wasp on a Monday. And anyway, I can't get fat, he is *so* lush.'

'Oh Adam, you are gorgeous as you are. And if you eat any less you'll look like Skeletor.' She sucked her cheeks in. 'Where did you meet him, anyway?'

'In a club in London. He's called Ryan. Thank God I had a uniform here; I haven't been home since Saturday. I missed the train I was supposed to get, hence being late this morning.'

'Well, at least you live it.'

'Enough about my debauchery. I want to hear about yours. Please tell me you went on a date and got rogered senseless over that dreadful parrot's cage.'

'Err, not quite. Friday was awful. Jamie came over demanding I sign the divorce papers, but I'm done with talking about that. Yesterday I went on a date with an army officer called Will.'

'Oh my God! I love army boys. And?'

'We went for a walk.'

'A bloody walk.'

'It was nice. I really like him. He's good looking; seems genuine and really kind. Made me feel at ease and rushed for his umbrella to shelter me, despite the fact we were already soaked by the time we got to our cars.'

'Kiss?'

'On the cheek.'

'Second date?'

'Well, this is the thing. He seemed to like me. He made a couple of suggestive comments but didn't mention a second date. I texted him straight away, saying I thought he was lovely and maybe dinner next time.'

'Oh, Cali. Too keen.'

'But I liked him.'

'Men love the chase. If you make it too easy for them it'll scare them. Even if you have to sit on your hands for a week, make them run.'

'Says the man who got straight into bed with a model the night he met him.'

'I wanted sex.'

'I fancied Will enough to want to have sex with him, which is a breakthrough in itself. But I want it to be right. I do see him as relationship material, and don't men hate it if you are too easy?' Cali bit into her sandwich.

'I think all these rules are ridiculous. If you fancy someone, go for it. If it's going to work, it will.'

'Patti from *Millionaire Matchmaker* would disagree.'

'Patti from *Millionaire Matchmaker* is paid to make a TV show. She'll say whatever it takes to keep viewers holding onto the perfect romantic dream.'

'I wish I wasn't so naïve.'

'Did creepy Jon get back in touch?'

'No, thank God.'

'Show me this Will.'

Cali reached for her phone and handed it to Adam.

'Blimey. I'd have pushed him against a tree, hitched up my skirt and sung him the national anthem if I was you.'

Cali laughed and then stopped in her tracks as a message pinged through.

'You look, I can't bear it. Tell me if it's him.'

'It is!'

'Aagh! Quick, read it to me.'

Adam's face dropped slightly. He cleared his throat. *'Hey Cali, I really enjoyed our walk in the Queen's garden and I think you're a lovely girl. But, being honest, I think I would hurt you and I don't want to do that.'*

'Oh.' Cali felt like she was going to cry.

'Why don't you reply saying, OK, but maybe you could hurt me just the once?'

'Adam!'

'Look, Cali, being serious, I think that's a lovely message. And reading through the lines he's not after a relationship, just a fling.'

'Then why didn't he make that clear in the first place?'

'Because a lot of men hedge their bets, Cali. Dick first, heart after. He could have strung you along, but he obviously has enough respect for you not to do that.'

'I guess.'

'And he's in the army, maybe he's moving away again. Did he mention that?'

'Hmm, he did say the job he was doing was just

for nine months. But I didn't find out a lot more about him. He was the one asking the questions. Should I reply?'

'I wouldn't, but I know that won't stop you.'

With a heavy heart, Cali sat back at her desk. She had enjoyed the feeling of fancying someone. It had made her feel alive again, had enabled her, albeit briefly, to forget the darkness of her looming divorce. She looked at Will's photo again and with a big sigh, started to type.

*Thanks for being so honest, Will, and I wish you all the best in your search for love.*

She checked the app for any more matches. None. Her heart sank again.

Even the big *X* she got as an immediate reply didn't make her feel better. In fact, it just made her feel more sad and insecure.

Coping with rotters and rejection wasn't an easy process. Maybe she should put this dating lark on hold until her heart was stronger and her mind clearer.

# Chapter Twelve

'Amateur dramatics? Cali, really?' Annie carried on changing Keira's nappy.

'Yes. I need to get out of my shell and maybe I can meet someone the traditional way. Get to know them first. I've always wanted to do it. And it will stop the pattern of me getting in from work and reaching for the wine.'

'But they will all speak really loudly and in verse.'

'Don't be silly. If I'm thinking of doing it, there must be others who are *normal* people.'

'I guess. And good for you. It's easy for me to be judgemental. In fact, I'm a little bit jealous.'

'Well, come with me then. I'm sure Rob will babysit. It's *Romeo and Juliet* too, so romantic. I loved the film with Leonardo DiCaprio.'

'Hmm, maybe. When are the auditions?'

'This Tuesday from seven p.m. Go on, Annie, it will be hilarious.'

'For one so shy I'm surprised you want to do it. And if we both get roles, when are the rehearsals?'

'I've decided I can't be scared of anything any more, Will made me realise that. Um, the rehearsals are Tuesdays and Thursdays, I think.'

'Oh, he has football on a Tuesday.'

'*He* has a name, doesn't he?' Rob appeared from the lounge and kissed his wife on the cheek. He tickled Keira on the tummy. 'What's up?'

'Calista Diaz here is trying to get me to go to amateur dramatics with her.'

Rob laughed out loud.

'Are they looking for Oompa Loompas, then?'

Knowing that many a true word was spoken in jest, her face fell.

'I'm only joking, darling. Go if you want to. We can get a babysitter.'

'Let me think about it, Cali.'

'How's the dating going?' Rob went to the fridge and grabbed a beer.

'Not that well. Half the reason I'm joining a club, to be honest. Thinking maybe I have more chance of meeting new people the "normal" way.'

'Reading the press, I think dating apps are more likely the "normal" way, actually. In fact, one in four people meet through them, which I find incredible. What age range have you put on the app?'

'28-35.'

'OK. Well, that's all right.'

'When did you become the guru of internet dating, husband?'

Rob tutted. 'I was thinking that if Cali had put younger then she was asking for trouble. Most men in their early twenties are after one thing. At least at twenty-eight they might be looking to settle down.'

'Who knows, but I guess you may be right.' Annie sat Keira in her high chair. 'But maybe a fling is what you need, Cali? Don't take it too seriously to start with. Have fun, like I said.'

'Oh, I don't know what I want,' Cali sighed.

Rob was fully involved now. 'So you'd definitely never go higher, say to forty? Us oldies still have a lot to give, don't we, dear?' He pinched his wife's bottom and grabbed a bib from the drawer for Keira.

'Ew, no disrespect, Rob, but no way.' Cali pulled a funny face at Keira. 'I like guys the same age or a bit younger, to be honest. Even thirty-five is quite old for me.'

'It's funny, isn't it, our different tastes?' Annie tied her daughter's bib. 'I've always liked an older man, so you got lucky, Mr Johnson. To be honest, I've never thought twice about our ten-year age gap.'

'Never say never, I guess.' Cali glanced at her phone on the table then put it back in her handbag.

Annie placed a rice cake in Kiera's hand. 'Changing the subject slightly, I was thinking about what you said about being lonely some nights. Why don't you get a lodger? You've got the spare room, and the extra money would come in handy for all the new date outfits you'll need to buy.'

'Really?' Cali turned her nose up. 'I'm not sure if I'd feel comfortable with that. It would stop me slobbing out when I wanted to. And, anyway, Lady P is probably company enough. It would take somebody pretty easy going to put up with her swearing and taking up half the lounge.'

'I thought you wanted Jamie to take the pesky parrot back?' Rob placed a warmed bottle of milk in front of Keira.

'I did, but I'm actually growing to love her a little bit now. At least she makes me laugh.'

'Never say never, as you said,' Rob smiled.

'I guess.' Cali stood up. 'Right, I'm off. The rest of my Sunday consists of cleaning Lady P's cage, and I've decided to open the divorce papers and see what they say. Oh, the joy.'

'Well, that's a positive. Shows you're ready to move on.' Annie put her hand on her friend's shoulder. 'If you need to chat, I'm here.'

'Thanks, mate. I've got to do it. I'll be fine.'

'Dirty bird! Dirty bird!'

Cali laughed at Lady P's ability to learn new words so quickly.

'You're not a dirty bird any more, look at your sparkling cage and you have a sweet potato treat, too. I do spoil you sometimes.'

'Callerina, Callerina, Callerina.'

Cali wished the errant bird would unlearn that one, but reminding her of another one of Jamie's nicknames for her was a good thing to prompt her to do what she had been avoiding.

She had looked online and found out that even a quickie divorce could take a few months, so even without stalling, she would piss Miss Dumb Bell off.

She poured herself a large glass of wine, pulled the form out of the envelope, filled out the necessary boxes, and signed it. Putting it in her handbag so as not to forget to post it in the morning, she sighed loudly.

She topped up her glass, sat on the sofa and

flicked through the TV channels. Staring blankly at the screen, tears filled her eyes.

Annie was right, would she really want him back now? And the thought of getting any money out of him would just prolong the agony. She had to move on. How could she ever trust him again? She would always be looking over her shoulder or never feel good enough for him, and she was a big enough person to know that she deserved better than that.

There was nothing on TV. She had always said that only boring people got bored, but tonight she was bored.

When she was going through the break up, the last thing she had thought about were the lonely nights to follow at home.

When she was married, she hadn't even had to think about amusing herself. The safe and fun company of Jamie was enough. Even if they were just sitting quietly, reading or watching TV, or even one of them was out, there was always the guarantee that they would snuggle up in bed together at the end of the night.

She turned off the TV and reached for the phone. 'Fuck him!'

'Fuck, fuckety, fuck, fuckety fuck!' Lady P trilled.

Fuelled by too much wine, again, Cali opened the dating app, lowered the desired age of her suitors to 25 to 28, and began to swipe.

Annie was right. A lodger could fill a void, but maybe it was the right time for some risky freedom?

If the likes of gorgeous Will from Aldershot didn't want a 'nice' girl and just sex, then maybe just sex Calista Summers would have.

# Chapter Thirteen

'You sound pissed and it's only four o'clock.' Adam's comforting Geordie twang soothed her at the end of the phone.

'What time you on til?' He was right, four glasses of wine down and she was way over the merry mark.

'Midnight, why? Are you OK, Cali?'

'I'm perfectly fine, thanks, baby boy. Is Room 102 free tonight?'

'Err, yes. Baby boy? What? Cali, you sound odd.'

'Is anyone else on reception with you?'

'Nah, on my tod until six.'

'Good, good. Just leave the room key in my desk, can you? And make sure that the fire exit door that leads up to it is open, please?'

'Ah. I know, you've got someone with you, you dirty little cow. Why can't you just shag them at your place?'

'Too many questions,' Cali slurred. 'And not a word to anyone.'

'Mum's the word. I'll do it right now.'

Cali hung up and with Adam's words ringing in her ears, started to get dressed.

A cheese sandwich and glass of milk had sobered Cali up slightly by the time she reached the small market town of Moulton.

She paid the taxi driver and in her little black dress and killer heels (bought during the week especially for dating purposes) sauntered the best she could into the quiet country-style pub.

She immediately spotted the handsome blond in the corner and smiled. Luke was the spitting image of his picture. Twenty-five, hot, and she could tell he was ripped under his tight black T-shirt.

'All right, Calista, what can I get ya?' His East End accent was quite sexy. *He* was quite sexy.

'Something short, please. We're not going to be here long.'

*Did that really come out of my mouth*, she thought, not quite believing what she was about to do.

Luke grinned. 'So you did mean it on your messages?'

'Of course I meant it. Rum and coke will be great, thanks.'

She sat down, revealing far too much of her 34D cleavage, and she could sense Luke's appreciation as he smiled back at her from the bar.

'Cheers.' They clinked glasses.

'So, what's an East End boy doing in a sleepy town like this?'

'Plumbing,' he laughed. 'Good with my hands, you know.'

Just him saying that turned Cali on. What had it come to, when sending a few dirty messages had become courtship? She bit her bottom lip as he

66

continued.

He laughed. 'That's not entirely true. I am a plumber but I live in London. I'm staying with my old man for the weekend, but I needed a little Sunday release, if you know what I mean.'

'So lucky I swiped you today, then?'

'Looks like I'm the lucky one. You're hot. Good pair of tits on ya, too.'

Normally, Cali would have slid under the table in embarrassment but not tonight. Tonight she was Calista Summers, internet dating slut!

Adam had said that the best way to get over someone was to get under someone else, and after signing away her marriage, she wanted to escape. Escape from her head and everything that was going on around her.

'So did you drive here, Luke?'

'Yeah, got my van out back.'

'Well, do you fancy driving me somewhere you can show me just how good you are with those hands?'

She could sense Luke's excitement as they pulled into the back car park of The Bridge Hotel.

'I can't believe you've booked a room here.'

'Only the best for my toyboy plumber.'

She looked around to make sure she couldn't see anyone she knew. Usually the back car park was just used for tradesmen, so on a Sunday she thought it would be safe. With Room 102 being situated at the top of the fire escape and right at the end of the corridor, it was perfect to sneak into. It needed a radiator repair, so she knew nobody would be checked in for the next couple of days.

The rum had topped up her earlier wine intake and she was feeling both tipsy and confident.

Luke came out of the toilet and she could see his jaw drop as she laid on top of the bed, dressed in lacy black underwear, including stockings and suspenders, her killer heels still on.

She could see his cock instantly harden in his jeans.

'Now, Mr Plumber. I think you should get those jeans off right now and inspect my pipes, don't you?'

'It would be rude not to, missus.' He undressed hurriedly.

Cali pointed to a condom she had already opened on the side. 'I suggest you just put that on your cock and fuck me hard.'

Luke thought he had died and gone to heaven. A hot older woman in stockings and no foreplay required.

'Are you sure?'

'Just do it.'

Luke had the softest kiss and the tightest buttocks. She actually thought he seemed like a decent bloke from the half hour she had known him. He gently inserted into her so as not to hurt her and she gasped in pleasure. It had been a long time since she'd had sex and she had almost forgotten what it felt like. She grabbed his taught, muscly back and felt herself getting even wetter. The turn on was amazing, the danger element making it all the more exciting.

Luke was an attentive and good lover.

After throwing her around the bed every which way he could, with cries of 'Fuck me harder' from Cali, he thrust harder and faster until he fell to her side, sweating and smiling.

'Shit I needed that, but not as much as you, I'm guessing?'

Cali laughed. 'Was it that obvious?' She suddenly felt self-conscious and grabbed her dress to place over her nakedness. 'It's a long and boring story. But boy, that was good. I haven't come like that in ages.'

'I aim to please, and I told you I was good with my tools.' Luke leapt up. 'Right, sorry to rush off but my old woman has a roast on the go, so I better not be late.'

'No no, that's fine.'

'And Calista, whoever it is, don't let him take the piss out of you. You're beautiful.'

'Thanks, that's sweet.' Cali looked away to hide her pain.

'Nah, you are. Look, take my number. If ever you're in London town, I'd be happy to oblige.'

With that, he pulled on his clothes and hot footed it down the fire escape.

Cali looked up to the ceiling and tried not to cry. What did she expect? That he'd cuddle up to her and bed down for the night, whispering sweet nothings?

People did this, she had read about it. Just met and shagged and moved on to the next one. A conveyor belt of shallowness.

The worrying thing was that part of her had really quite enjoyed it. Luke was handsome, clean and bloody sexy. He smelt good too! He seemed like a lovely lad. The sex had been safe and toe-curlingly good, plus he wanted to see her again. Flattering and no harm done.

She was just thinking she really must take a shower, when the hotel phone rang.

'Shit! Shit!' She decided to pick it up and remain mute.

'Room service. Are you ready for a maid to come up and clean the mattress stains?'

'Adam!'

He started to whisper. 'I take it he's gone? Good was it, you little slut?'

Her voice started to crack. 'Don't say that. And I don't want anyone to know, you hear?'

'I'm only joking with you, angel. I can't believe you actually went through with it. I mean, the nearest you've had to sex lately is brushing against the filing cabinet.'

'I feel awful.'

'Well, don't. It's fine. You needed to make the break away from that deadbeat ex of yours. Do you want me to whizz up for a chat?'

'No, you're fine. I'm going to tidy up and get a cab home. My hangover is kicking in already.'

She lay back on the bed and took in her sterile surroundings. Yes, the sex had been amazing. Yes, Luke was sweet, but she felt empty now. Empty and alone.

Was she really looking for fun like this? Did anyone really enjoy having mindless sex with strangers? The buzz had been amazing initially. Almost like taking drugs, she assumed. You scored.

You had the high, but was the comedown really worth the fun?

# Chapter Fourteen

'So what are you saying? You slept with him after half an hour?'

'Yes. Just that.' In the cold and sober light of day, Cali couldn't quite believe her own confession. 'It was like I turned into a different person. Gone was Little Miss Prim and out came Calista Summers, big slut!'

'Woah!' Forgetting how scalding a drink without milk was, Annie nearly dropped her mug. 'Bloody green tea. Hmm. I remember now. You didn't text me to say Hot Sausage or Green Tea.'

'I was drunk, sorry, and on a mission. Ssh.' Cali rolled her eyes as David collected their empty cake plates. By the look of his knowing expression, she was sure he had overheard. 'I don't know what came over me.'

'Don't open me up for innuendo,' Annie laughed. 'I'm glad you did what you did. You needed to let off steam.'

'Actually, yes, I did. I signed the divorce papers, I was hurting. I guess I thought I stupidly could forget about it for a minute. And ...' Cali looked to the ceiling.

Annie put her hand on her friend's. 'And ...?'

'I wanted to feel wanted. I know that sounds *so*

stupid. I felt rejected. Rejected from Jamie, even from Will. Even though I know he was just being honest and nice. Oh, I don't know, Annie. It's difficult to explain.'

Keira stirred in her buggy and Annie gently rocked her.

'I get it. I do. You've had a lot of knocks and if this has helped just a little bit, then no harm done.'

Cali smiled. 'I have to say, it was a complete turn on.'

'I bet it bloody was. I'm sooo jealous.'

'He's hot. Look.'

'Shit, Cali, do you think he wants a threesome?'

'Oi, married woman, control yourself. Anyway, I would never do that!' Cali finished off her tea. 'However, I would meet somebody for sex again. I had thoughts of Ana in *50 Shades* as I was undressing, except I was the one in control.'

Keira started to whimper.

'Well, as long as you feel OK, then that's good. But remember, it's just fun. If you can keep sex separate from love and make sure you're safe, then I don't see any harm.'

'Luke was lovely and he was totally open to see me again.'

'I bet he bloody was. Right, as much as I'd like to talk all evening, I best get missy home and ready for bed.'

They paid up and walked into the warm April evening. Annie kissed her friend on the cheek. 'Protect your heart, Cali. Ultimately, you do want love. But if you have to play the field a bit to find it, then there's nothing wrong with that.'

74

'Yes. I hear you. Anyway, when I get the part of Juliet, imagine how many prospective Romeos will be falling at my feet.'

'Ha! Are we still going to the auditions, then?'

'If you can get a babysitter, then of course.'

'I'll sort one. It'll be a laugh and I could do with some excitement. Even if it's in the guise of pretending I'm a Shakespearean actress for a night.'

# Chapter Fifteen

Cali and Annie pulled a chair from a stack against the wall of the village hall as instructed and joined the semi-circle of wannabe actors.

'Oh, Cali, I'm not sure if I want to do this now, it's far too scary.' Annie's whispering was obviously not soft enough as her red-faced, busty and plump neighbour piped up with her very posh accent.

'Scary, scary, don't be so churlish. You're both new, aren't you?'

'Er, yes, we are. That's OK, isn't it? It did say open auditions so I assumed anyone could come along.' Cali was also beginning to think maybe this wasn't such a good idea when a woman shouted out while pointing at them.

'Newbies, everybody.'

Some of the group said 'hi' quietly and raised their hands; the rest continued chatting to each other animatedly. The woman with the loud voice began again. 'I'm Jilly.' Cali noticed the massive diamond on her right hand. 'Welcome, ladies, you can grab tea and biscuits from the back kitchen. We are just waiting for Gerald, then we can kick off. Oh, there's some spare scripts, plus a form to put your details on so we know how to get hold of you.'

With relief, Annie and Cali made their way to the back of the room.

'Blimey, I didn't realise it would be so cliquey. I can't be doing with it, Cali. I'll just watch.'

'Nor did I. But I need to do this for me. Even reading the script will take me out of my comfort zone, and from now on I'm trying not to be scared of anything. Go on, Annie, fill out the form, please.'

'OK, OK. On the plus side, did you see the cute ginger at the end of the semi-circle? He seemed shy, bless him. He smiled at me when the posh fatty embarrassed us.'

Cali peered through the hatch in the kitchen. 'I don't usually go for gingers, but yes, he's all right. Has the kind of face my mother would agree to.'

They scribbled down their details and left the forms on the clipboard hanging on the kitchen door, grabbed tea and scripts, and headed back to the semi-circle of thespians.

'Oh, here he is at last,' the plump, big breasted woman shouted dramatically.

Gerald English was as eccentric as The Mad Hatter. His limbs were as long as the red velvet scarf he was wearing and his wonderful moustache likened him to a younger Poirot. With his jet black floppy fringe, defined features and twinkly blue eyes he had a handsome charm about him.

'Welcome back, darlings ... I've only just recovered from wearing that corset in the pantomime, you know. I had popper marks indented in my arse for two months.'

Everybody laughed. Just as Cali was mouthing 'Gay' to Annie, a match pinged loudly, causing a gasp among the group.

'The first pound of the season towards the new costume fund, well done, dear.' Cali went as red as Gerald's scarf. 'Oh, a newbie. *Two* newbies, how delicious. I'm Gerald. I direct, I act; I pass wind on demand if required for a part.' Laughter ensued again. 'And you are?'

'Er, I'm Cali and this is Annie.'

'Splendid. So ... just so you know, the rules of the Bramley A.D. Society are as follows – no, and I mean no, usage of mobile phones while at auditions or rehearsals, or you will be fined,' his deep voice boomed. 'Such a vulgar invention.' The way he spoke likened him to a sixty-year-old, but Cali reckoned he was late thirties or early forties. 'Oh, and no gum chewing and you must never, ever be late for rehearsals. If you get a part, that is. What are you thinking of auditioning for?'

'Juliet would be nice.'

The group sniggered as Gerald went towards her and put his long-fingered hand on her shoulder.

'Yes, Juliet of course would be nice, but I hate to say, as pretty as you are, you are at least twenty years too old. Maybe the nurse or one of the mothers would better suit.'

Cali wanted the ground to swallow her up. Why had she said that?

Gerald went back to the front of the group, saw Cali's miserable face, and winked at her. 'Sorry, that was harsh. I need a drink.' He pulled a small silver hip flask from the pocket of his beige linen jacket and took a large swig. 'That's better. We are a friendly bunch here really, aren't we?'

Everyone, apart from the cute ginger, let out a resounding 'Yes.'

Cali stood up.

'My goodness, are you that keen to read?' Gerald's voice boomed.

'No, sorry, I feel rather sick.' Cali started to walk fast to the exit, promptly followed by a very relieved Annie.

'Oh, darling, how vile. We will be doing further auditions Tuesday if you do want to come back,' Gerald shouted.

'Let's share a bottle, I feel scarred by the whole experience.' Cali caught the attention of the barman in the pub next to the village hall. 'Red or white?'

'You're driving.'

'It's fine. I'll leave the car and get it before work in the morning. We can get a taxi home.'

'Or I can get Rob to pick us up on his way home from football.'

'Perfect.'

They headed outside with their ice bucket, filled their glasses, and both started laughing at the same time.

'Fuck me, Cali, what was that about? I nearly went back to my roots and gave him a tirade of Scottish abuse. And you know that only comes out when I'm drunk or angry.'

'I actually love Gerald. He's such a character and handsome, in a funny sort of way.'

'Cali, really? He is hilarious, but looks wise I didn't see it at all. Anyway, he's obviously gay and an alcoholic.'

'I actually don't think he's gay, just extremely camp.'

'Hmm, I'd still put it to a jury. I take it you won't be going back Tuesday, then?' Annie took a slurp of wine.

'I would rather join a bowls club. And the mortification of not realising Juliet was a teenager, too.'

'Yes, even I knew that.'

'I did *King Lear* at school and only had eyes for Leonardo DiCaprio when I watched the film.'

'Let's put it down to experience. On a positive, we haven't had a night out for ages. I might even go crazy and get us some crisps.'

'I can't get too drunk, I'm at work for nine.'

'Oh come on Cali, a bottle between us won't even touch the sides.'

Half way through their second bottle, Annie suddenly shrieked. 'Oh my God, you had a ping! Quick, we can chat with him now.'

Cali laughed. 'Look what happened with Luke when I drunk messaged before.'

'All the more reason, then,' Annie smirked. 'You can go into work with a smile on your face for a change.'

'You are so bad.'

'In my mind, dear friend, I am. But I love Rob so much. I would never carry anything through.'

Cali reached for her phone, went to her dating messages and gasped.

'Is he that awful?'

'I don't know yet, but look what Luke sent me.'

Annie put her hand over her mouth. 'No wonder you enjoyed yourself.'

'Nobody has ever sent me a photo like that in my whole life, not even Jamie!'

'Welcome to the world of internet dating.'

'I don't think I like that. Why would a man do that? But you're right, he does have a nice one.'

'He must be drunk.' Annie looked closer.

'He doesn't look drunk.' Cali laughed.

'Did he write anything?'

'I didn't check, hang on.' Cali put her hand over her mouth in shock. 'Oh my God. He's put "*So ... I've shown you mine?*" As if! 'What are men like?'

'Especially as he's seen yours in all its glory already, I should imagine,' Annie replied casually.

Cali made a face. 'Don't remind me. Ew. I mean, fanny photos, really? I'm going to ignore him.' She checked her new message. 'But, hmm. Nigel. Equine Vet. 35. Looking to share his petting skills. Well, he could be eligible for a whole new album!'

Annie took the phone. 'Shame it's just the one photo, and not even face on, but woah, even with a name like Nigel he could sway me for just the night ... no one ever need know. You *have* to message him.'

By the end of the second bottle and after a lot of dating app flirting, a date had been arranged. Nigel the equine vet was going to meet her in the car park of The Station Arms on Monday evening.

Cali staggered as she got up from the table.

'I'm drunk, Annie Johnson, and I blame you.'

'I know, I shouldn't have held you down and

force fed you all that wine.'

Cali laughed. 'It's a shame Luke doesn't live nearer, I'd ask him round.'

'You've changed,' Annie laughed then, holding her phone to her ear, her face suddenly dropped. 'I can't get hold of bloody Rob.'

'Does he go for a drink with the lads after football?'

'Yes, but I texted him earlier and he knows Keira's with a babysitter. It's not like him not to respond. Let's just ring a cab; I need to be back by eleven.'

Cali kissed Annie on the cheek as she clumsily got out of the cab. 'Home sweet home. All alone.'

'Every time you think that just imagine Gerald English with popper dent marks in his arse, that'll make you glad to be single. And you've got Naughty Nigel to look forward to next week, so chin up and sweet dreams, mate.'

Lady P was asleep in her box, so Cali gently pulled the cover over her cage. She sat down on the sofa and looked again at Nigel's photo. It looked a bit staged with his hand on his chin, but he was handsome and his job made him seem all the sexier. She was just taking off her sandals when a text came through. *Thanks for signing the paper, Cal x*

A kiss. Jamie had a put a kiss, why? In fact, how dare he? Tears started to slowly fall down her cheeks. She had been so in love with him, had put twelve years of trust in him. Internet dating may be exciting and different – sex could be on tap if you wanted it – but feeling drunk and insecure, all she wanted was to lie in bed facing the man who used to love her and feel his familiar breath against her cheek.

# Chapter Sixteen

Marcus poked his head through the events office door. 'Happy Monday, ladies, all OK?'

Cali looked up from the email she was writing and smiled. 'Oh, hi. Yep. All good. I'm just doing a proposal for the DEA Systems Summer Party. One hundred people, so that will help towards my target.'

'Good, good. Do they need bedrooms, too?'

'At least half of them, yes.'

'Fantastic. And Louise, how about you?'

Louise, feeling near to death from an impromptu Sunday night drinking session, looked up and smiled, 'Ask me at lunchtime.'

'Out on the town on a school night, eh?'

'Of course not. Time of the month, that's all.'

Without response, Marcus reddened and scurried off as fast as his long legs could carry him.

'Bless you, Lou. Do you need any paracetamol?' Cali scrabbled in her handbag looking for some.

With that, her now green assistant shot up and ran towards the door in the same direction as Marcus, nearly knocking Adam over in the process.

'Where's the bleeding fire?' Adam sat in Lou's chair and put his feet up on her desk.

'She's hungover. Typical for her to be like that

when we're so bloody busy.'

'Hark at Miss Prim Pants. At least she doesn't use the hotel facilities as a knocking shop.'

'Oi, not so loud. That was a one off.'

'Yeah right. I don't blame you if it wasn't. How's the dating going, anyway?'

'No news, Luke sent me a photo of his you-know-what and I've got a date arranged for tonight.'

'Ooh, let me see.'

'Luke or the new date?'

Adam laughed. 'Well, both if you're offering.'

Cali held her phone discreetly under the desk and showed him Luke's naughty photo.

'Bloody hell, Cal, we need a new plumber. Maybe I'll escort him to Room 102, turn the heating up and watch him work.'

'What are you like? No. He can stay on the back burner for now. Nigel seems a far better bet. He sounded lovely on messenger and he's a vet, too. Thirty-five as well, so hopefully not just messing around.'

Adam checked out his photo.

'Bit posey for my liking. And with just the one photo, it's obviously the only and best one he could find.'

'Oh, Adam. Don't be negative. I struggled to find relevant photos. At least he's not stroking a tiger like a lot of the prats on there.'

'I guess. Anyway, I thought you just wanted fun?'

'Oh, I don't know. I felt so empty after Luke. I would rather there was a chance of love than just random sex. Talking of that, have you seen the model again?'

'Model? Oh, Ryan. Yeah, he came over on Friday, but he loves himself more than anyone on the planet and you know it's me who likes to be the centre of attention.'

'Yes, we certainly do.' Adam shot up out of the chair as Marcus appeared at the doorway. 'Get back to reception. Now!' The general manager put some paracetemol on Louise's desk. 'I found these in my drawer. Is she OK?'

He really was the perfect gentleman!

'Aw, that's kind of you. She's popped to the loo, I think.'

'Ah right. Remember what I said about Adam too, Cali. He's got the attention span of a gnat and needs no encouragement to leave his post.'

'Sure, sorry.'

'No need to apologise, he just requires micro-managing. Being honest, if he wasn't so bloody likeable, he'd have been out on his ear months ago.'

'I hear you,' Cali smiled.

'And, Cali ...' Cali took in Marcus's expensive navy suit and perfectly ironed shirt. 'It's great to see you looking happier.' He placed his hand on hers. 'I know it's a bloody cliché, but time is a healer.'

Cali felt herself welling up as she nodded. In the five years she had worked at The Bridge Hotel, Marcus had met Jamie twice. They had got on well. No surprise really, as with Jamie's ebullient personality, he got on with most people.

Marcus had organised a wedding collection and had presented her with some beautiful crystal wine glasses as a present. Which, thinking on it, she should get back from the bastard.

Marcus stood in the doorway. 'My office door is always open if you need a chat.'

She responded with a very quiet 'Thank you.'

'Life is a funny old business, especially where affairs of the heart are concerned. I never judge a book by its cover and nor should you.' He winked and casually walked out of the office, leaving Cali slightly perplexed.

# Chapter Seventeen

Cali had been hesitant at Nigel's initial offer of them sharing a cab home as they were going the same way. But after downing her second glass of wine and telling him that she thought Lady P had a speech impediment, any notion of going their separate ways was a distant memory.

Because his photo had been sideways on, he looked slightly different in the flesh but in a good way. More rugged, definitely broader, and at six foot four, he was a giant. Cali loved that. In fact, she likened him to one of her favourite England rugby players.

'Where to?' The taxi driver questioned as they both took their seats in the back of the silver Mercedes. Nigel gently squeezed Cali's knee.

'Yes, where to, Calista Summers? I mean, it's only ten o'clock.'

'Woodford Road, please, the flats on the corner.' Cali addressed the driver, then turned to Nigel with a smirk. 'And you can call me Cali.'

'Yeah, your full name does make you sound like a porn star.'

Cali whacked her date on the leg. 'Oi, you.'

'Do you have any drink in the house?'

'Yes.'

'Not like a porn star to play hard to get,' Nigel laughed. The taxi driver's ears pricked up. 'And surely Lady P needs to know if she needs elocution lessons or not?'

The taxi pulled up at the main entrance to the block of flats and Nigel looked to Cali questionably.

'OK. OK. One drink and home. It is a school night, after all.'

'Cali big tits, Cali big tits!' Lady P never failed to say the wrong thing at the wrong time.

'Well, she speaks the truth even if she has an impediment.'

Cali opened her mouth in mock surprise. 'And there's me thinking you were a nice boy.'

'Never.' Nigel went over to Lady P's cage as Cali started throwing magazines off the sofa and onto her desk. 'I'd have tidied if I'd known you were going to come back.'

'Ah, that's refreshing. You don't make a habit of this, then?'

'What, bringing strange men back to my place? No, you're the first, to be honest. And how lovely it would be if this app worked and you were the last?'

Luckily, Nigel was still facing Lady P's cage so she missed his pained expression,

Damn, why had she said that! 'So … beer or white wine? Or some awful 40% liqueur I've had in the cupboard for ages? That's all I've got, I'm afraid.'

Nigel turned around and pulled Cali into him. 'It's you I want.' He leant down to kiss her on the nose. 'I think you're hot, Cali big tits.' Cali pulled away. Yes, she fancied Nigel, but she also liked him enough to see herself with him, and like Will, felt she needed to make him wait.

'Look, I really like you, but I have work tomorrow and ... and why a Monday night for a date, anyway?'

'Why not?'

'I guess.' Cali shifted on her heels slightly.

'Sorry, Cali, maybe my bluntness is too much for someone as lovely as you?' She breathed an inward sigh of relief that he wasn't a complete bastard. 'Monday is my teaching day. I teach veterinary studies at a uni in London, so I thought it made sense to get off the train and have a couple of drinks with you, then get a taxi home. It honestly wasn't my intention to come back here. Why don't we sit on the sofa, have a chat, see what's on TV? But if we do, you can get the liqueur out. How's that for a compromise?'

'Deal.' Cali headed to the kitchen to get the drinks.

'Deal or no deal, deal or no deal.' Lady P shrieked and started darting around her cage.

'God, that bird of yours is good. I love cockatoos.'

'Cockatoo? You'll be in trouble if she heard you say that. She's an African Grey.' Cali put their drinks on the coffee table.

'That's what I meant. Or maybe I thought the word cock might spur you into action.'

Cali cringed. There was definitely one cock in the room. Maybe Nigel the vet wasn't quite as hot as she had thought. Maybe she should stop drinking on dates as her judgement was clouded. In fact, she really must cut down her drinking in general as she could feel her clothes becoming a bit tight. And she certainly wouldn't be going back to her old personal trainer to sort it out!

'Down in one, go on.' OK, she would stop tomorrow. 'And another.' Nigel had already got the bottle from the kitchen and recharged their glasses. Cali's head began to spin. 'And one for the road.' They clinked glasses and she downed one more.

Nigel lay down on the sofa and pulled Cali towards him. Without resistance, she flung off her heels and lay on top of him. He began to kiss her with urgency. Then, pushing her skirt right up to her thighs, he began caressing between her legs.

Cali gasped. 'I think we should wait.'

'What for? Your birthday next week?'

She laughed. Nigel pushed her panties aside and thrust two fingers hard inside her.

'Ow.'

'Sorry, sorry.'

'I'm not a bloody horse.'

They both started laughing.

He moved his fingers more gently now. 'We can wait, it's fine.'

'No, no, have you got a condom?' The strong liqueur had put paid to any plans of chasteness Cali may have had.

'Big boy J, Big boy J,' Lady P squawked.

Despite the disappointingly small penis of such a large man entering her, Cali gasped again. 'Harder, harder, harder.'

'Shit, fuck, oh no. Quick, get up.' Nigel had a

panicked look on his face.

Cali jumped up. Was that it? Her skirt still around her waist and knickers now around her ankles, she almost fell over. God, how sex scenes in movies lied!

'What is it? What?' Cali's head was spinning worse than before.

'The condom split. In fact, the bloody thing must have come off inside you. Have you got a shower?'

'Of course I have.'

'Well, go wash yourself and hopefully it will come out.' He was speaking at hundred miles an hour. 'Are you on the pill?'

'No … but …'

'Jesus. Look, here's a tenner, make sure you get the morning after pill first thing. OK, OK. Sorry to shout, but you know. Pregnant after one date. Not good, not good at all.' He pulled on his trousers hurriedly. 'Shit, and it's gone midnight. I must go. So sorry. Call me tomorrow, OK?' And with that he shot out of the door and down the stairs.

Cali, fresh from her hot shower and with the split condom safely located, lay flat out on the sofa. 'Oh Lady P, what am I doing?'

'Fuckety, fuck, fuck, fuck, fuck.'

'Not for a while, that's for sure.' And with that, she promptly fell into an ouzo-induced coma.

# Chapter Eighteen

'You sound bloody dreadful.' Cali could barely hear Annie for Keira's screaming in the background.

'Good. I just phoned Marcus to say I was sick.'

'What's wrong? Hang on a minute, Cal. Shh, baby girl, here. Right, go on, she's got her milk now.'

'Oh, Annie. I've been really stupid.'

'Nigel the vet? Obviously not a hot sausage?'

'Far from it, more like a green potato.'

'Oh dear.'

'Yep, I got drunk, invited him back. Vowed I wouldn't sleep with him, got drunker, and did.'

'Ah, so the main problem is that you invited him back to your house. Probably a little bit early after one date, but it's done now.'

'I wish it were as simple. The bloody condom split. Not sure how as he had a very small willy. A horrible one, in fact. Nearly as wide as it was long … But it did.'

'OK, so go and get a morning after pill. You'll be fine.'

'And what if I'm not?'

'Cali, we'll deal with it, but I know it'll be fine. Now get up and get to the chemist.'

'I feel so ill, we ended up drinking ouzo. I

bloody hate ouzo. He really was quite vile; thrust a ten pound note at me for the morning after pill and hot-footed it off.'

'Have you heard from him this morning?'

'Yes, to see if I'd been to the chemist. But he also was sweet. He said he'd take me out for dinner on my birthday as he felt so bad for rushing off. Said he panicked.'

'*Sweet*?! He sounds like a complete tosser. Please tell me you won't ever see him again.'

'Let's get this little hurdle over with first, shall we?'

'OK. Go do it. And Cali?'

'Yes.' Her voice was getting weaker.

'I know this is really bad timing to ask, but is there any chance you think you could babysit next Saturday? As in stay over with Keira. Bless Rob, he's booked some package which includes a West End show, dinner and hotel.'

'Of course I can. I may need to get the practice anyway.'

Annie laughed. 'Don't say that. And please try not to worry. You get going and I'll give you a call when I'm back from work this afternoon.'

'Harder, harder, harder!' Lady P shrieked as Cali looked in the mirror at her morning-after-the-night-before face and grimaced.

96

# Chapter Nineteen

Cali wasted no time in taking the morning after pill the minute she left the pharmacy and, after a thoughtful drive home, she immediately took herself back to bed. This was not cool, not cool at all. She had to get a grip before she got herself into some real trouble.

In the sober, cold light of day, the more she thought about Nigel the vet, the more she realised he had been after sex and nothing more. And surely a vet would know the difference between a cockatoo and an African Grey? She googled his name alongside the words 'equine vet'. Nothing! It was such a specialised field she didn't believe that there could be that many in the area, and anyway, if there was, surely he would want to have his name out there? The way he talked to her … she should have more respect for herself. That was it, no more random encounters. She would listen to Patti from *Millionaire Matchmaker* and strike up the 'no sex before monogamy' rule.

'Porn star, porn star, porn star.' Perishing the inopportune moment her feisty bird may bring that one out again, Cali groaned and stuck her head under the covers.

And then gave a further groan as a text beeped

on her phone.

*Hey, how you doing, did you get the pill OK?*

'Yes, and I washed it down first thing with a huge gulp of self-respect,' was what Cali wanted to reply with, but instead lied. *No need, my period came this morning.*

The vile one replied immediately.

*Phew, great news and thanks for last night, I'll give you a call about your birthday. Maybe we can have a replay? ;)*

Thinking she would rather watch a replay of a tortoise running a marathon, she deleted Nigel's number and fell into a heavy slumber.

# Chapter Twenty

'Happy birthday to you, happy birthday to you, you look like a monkey and you smell like one, too!' Adam in full song, followed by Louise and Marcus, trailed into the office with a huge chocolate birthday cake on a silver tray.

'Aw, thank you all, it looks delicious.'

'Glad you like it, the head chef wanted to make it special. Well, on my instruction anyway.'

'Marcus Clarke, anyone would think you were up for Boss of the Year.' Cali smirked at him. 'But I really do appreciate it.'

'Right, enough of the niceness, get that candle blown out and a slice cut for me. I've got a board meeting in ten.'

Adam started cutting huge slices. 'What are you up to tonight? My invite has obviously been lost in the post.'

'I'm finishing at four, having my hair cut and then meeting my friend for tea and cake in the café near my house.'

'Tea and cake? What?' Louise wandered to her desk with coffee and plate in hand.

'I'm not up for a big night. It's not a special birthday. I mean, thirty-one is a bit of a funny age. I don't feel young enough to hit the clubs or old enough to have a dinner party.'

'Oh shurrup.' Adam's mouth was full of cake. 'You're not dead yet and I'm not busy tonight. Come out with me.'

'No, honestly, Ads. I'm cutting down on the booze, too.'

'Blimey, you'll be telling me you're becoming a nun next.'

Marcus nearly spilt his tea. 'You're on a dating app? Which one?' Cali was extremely relieved to be saved by the phone.

'Well, Mr Smythe, you're in luck. The Red Room is actually free today from lunchtime, so pop along at two and my colleague Louise Stamp will show you around.' Louise raised her eyebrows. 'Just go to the main reception and ask for her on arrival.'

Cali continued to hold the phone to her ear long enough for Marcus to leave for his meeting and to watch Adam trail back to his reception perch.

Happy bloody birthday. Bloody being the operative word. Here she was at thirty-one, still single and no sign of her period.

Her phone beeped with a text message. Jamie's name flashed up. The name she had once held so safely in her mouth. The name that now often created a taste of bile.

*Happy Birthday, Cali x*

'What part of "we are no longer together" do you not understand?'

What did he expect from her now, really? Maybe he was keeping her sweet until the divorce was finalised. In her mind, if you'd been in love with someone, how could you possibly stay friends? But he was the cheater, not the cheated, and that obviously made a big difference.

'Sorry. What did you say?' Louise, completely engrossed in what she was doing, looked up.

'Nothing, nothing, it's fine.' Tears pricked Cali's eyes. Fine, that misused word.

Part of her never wanted to see her wayward ex ever again. But another part wanted nothing more than for him to beg her to come back and put an end to this misery.

# Chapter Twenty-one

'So she doesn't have a bottle at night now, just her beaker, which usually sends her off. Tepid, full fat milk only. I've labelled all her meals on the top shelf of the fridge and what time you give them to her. Rice snacks are in the kitchen drawer under the microwave. Nappies and cream are all in there.' Annie pointed to the bag on the changing mat in Keira's bedroom. Then she took a breath. 'I'll get Rob to put her car seat in your car in case you need to go out for something. I think that's it. But just call me anytime. My phone will be on, even throughout the night.'

'Annie,' Cali said calmly. 'It will be fine, she will be fine. I've done this before and she was much younger, remember?'

'Yes, OK. Sorry, Cal.'

'Now just go and have the most amazing time. You look stunning. That colour really suits you.'

'Thanks, mate. And you cheer up, eh? We'll have a proper belated birthday drink when we're back, totally on me of course, for doing this. I know it's not a small ask.'

'I'm looking forward to it, actually. Just me, little Kee, and a chilled night. There's loads of good TV on later so I'll probably take myself to the bedroom when she goes down and watch it there.'

'Ah, I forgot the monitor,' Annie gasped.

'I know how it works and I'll make sure it's on at all times,' Cali relayed, as if addressing a child.

'OK, OK. I'm ready. Did your period come yet, by the way?'

'No, but it's fine. I heard that the morning after pill can muck everything up sometimes. Now, stop worrying and go! I can hear Rob pacing downstairs.'

Cali dipped soldiers into Keira's boiled eggs and pretended it was an aeroplane. The little girl shrieked with delight. Eggs and soldiers, ha. It made her think back to Will, the handsome officer. What a shame he didn't want to see her again. She'd have much rather lost her dating virginity to him than Luke or that vile vet.

Keira started bashing her beaker onto her high chair tray. Then she decided to throw it, causing Cali to lose her footing, crash against a kitchen cupboard, and spill a four pint milk carton all over the floor.

'Oh, Keira.' The little girl started to cry, causing the big girl to start to cry too.

Who was she kidding? She wasn't fine at all. She could be pregnant. She was absolutely terrified. And the morning after pill mucking up your cycle didn't help with regards to when she could take a pregnancy test.

Cali wiped her eyes and kissed Keira on the forehead. 'It's OK, munchkin, let me clear this mess up, then you and Aunty Cali can go on a little adventure. I could do with the exercise, anyway.'

Cali had always enjoyed supermarket shopping. Plus, she had always found something rather comforting and lovely about pushing a baby in a pushchair. Today, however, it made her feel sad as she thought back to her wedding and the excitement she'd felt about starting a family with Jamie.

She only needed the milk and a few snacks for herself, so she hadn't had to worry about the intricacies of placing a baby into a trolley as a non-mother. She just hooked a basket on top of the pushchair and got ready to go wild in the aisles. To make the trip even sweeter, Keira had just fallen asleep.

She picked up what she needed and, as the little one was still sparko, decided she would go and browse the books. Maybe a good romance would take her mind off the one she wasn't having.

Making her way through the fresh meat section back to the front of the store she suddenly froze solid. For there, just a few feet away from her was the vet. Not just the vet though, but the vet pushing identical twin boys in a double buggy. If she had been alone, she would have diverted swiftly to the cheese aisle in order to escape. But with a baby on board during a busy Saturday, a three point turn and evasive sprint just wasn't possible.

Praying that Keira wouldn't wake and start screaming, she stuck her head down to the minced beef section and continued to watch him. OK, so the twins could be his nephews, or maybe belong to a friend, like Keira, but no…

BANG!

Here it was, right in front of her eyes ... the evidence that the vet was a complete and utter philandering bastard. The 'vet' was actually a bloody chef, by the look of his black and white checked trousers! The woman who kissed him on the cheek must have been around thirty-five as she handed him a pack of nappies to put in the trolley. Pretty too, with a dark bob not dissimilar to her own. Oh, and what was that on her left hand? A wedding ring? Of course it was.

Cali felt a seething anger go through her. She still had the receipt for the morning after pill in her purse. Maybe she should share that? Or maybe go and put a pregnancy test in her basket to really scare him, vocally out him in the meat aisle of Lidl for the bastard he was.

An obscure photo and 'Monday night is my vet training night'. What a load of bollocks! She really did need to wise up to some of these sharks.

Cali looked down to Keira, who was still sleeping soundly. The vision of her angelic face and sound of her soft breathing centred her. His poor wife was obviously completely oblivious to it all. Why upset her and her kids' lives? She was pregnant too. No wonder he flipped his lid when he thought she might be. Oh God, still might be!

She wholly wished she hadn't put his mind at rest by telling him she wasn't. He deserved the same pain and anguish that she was going through.

Noticing the wife flit to another aisle, Cali stood up and headed the pushchair towards him. She stared right at him, her face contorting.

'Oh, hi, I'm really sorry to interrupt you, but I see you are a chef and I've got this French recipe, you see ... and I was just wondering if I can substitute horse meat for pork?' The vile one looked at Cali, then further down to the sleeping Keira, with an expression of both shock and bemusement; the colour drained from his face as she added, 'A fat, stinky pig with no backbone, perhaps?'

Cali fed and bathed Keira and put her to bed. Once she was sure she was sleeping soundly, she sent a photo of her to ease Annie's mind, set the baby monitor, and crept through to the spare room. She was thankful she had been such a good girl as Cali wasn't sure she could have coped otherwise. It made her yearn to have a baby of her own again. The sweet smell of a child and all that unconditional love.

She looked to her phone and googled signs of early pregnancy. She gently squeezed her boobs; they didn't feel any different. Maybe a bit sore, but that was normal for her when her period was due, anyway. If she hadn't come on by next Wednesday she would do a test. She couldn't bear to think of what she would do if she was actually pregnant. How ironic that she could be in the very state she had longed to be in with Jamie but was now so wishing the opposite. The thought of carrying a being that would be half of that vile man made her feel physically sick.

It was only nine p.m., but feeling sad and depressed, she got undressed and lay in bed in the dark looking to the ceiling. She didn't even feel like watching television. In fact, the peace and quiet, apart from the sleeping baby noises, was very calming. She hadn't been sleeping properly the past few weeks and hoped being in a different environment with no Lady P to disturb her would enable her to get some decent rest.

She thought back to her dating experiences so far. Certainly no romance, or even an inkling of love. Jon was just deluded and smarmy. If he couldn't be honest from the start, he was no use to her as a lover, let alone a partner. She also didn't fancy him one bit. Luke was lovely but it was what it was with him; pure animal passion. Scratching an itch. Will … well, Will was a gorgeous specimen of a human being who was not ready to settle down, but at least he had the respect in not so many words to say he just wanted sex, too. And as for the vile one, at least now her guard would be up for sure. That was if she ever decided to reinstate the dating app again. She started to drift off, and with thoughts of Will turning up at the hotel grounds on a white charger carrying a bunch of long-stemmed red roses, her breathing became deeper and she was soon snoring.

Cali nearly jumped out of her skin as she awoke to loud cries coming from the baby monitor. She picked up her phone to check the time. Four forty-five. She opened her eyes slowly. 'I'm coming, baby girl.' She dragged herself out of bed and put on her dressing gown.

Keira was red cheeked and standing up in her cot. On seeing Cali, she immediately outstretched her arms.

'Oh, baby girl, come here. What's the matter?'

Keira's hot, snotty face pushed into Cali's shoulder. 'Mama, mama.' Then on realising it wasn't her mama, the toddler yelled, 'No!' arching her back and trying to wriggle away.

'It's all right, darling. Let me change your stinky bum.'

Keira screamed and writhed through the whole bum-changing process. When a piece of Keira's poo landed on Cali's right cheek, not only did she feel wide awake, but that maybe this baby lark wasn't quite as easy as she had thought.


She carried the now-clean but still screaming baby downstairs, warmed some milk, snuggled her into an armchair, and put the beaker to her lips.

With a little sigh, Keira started to take her milk, and making an even bigger sigh of complete relief, Cali felt the familiar feeling of menstrual blood seeping into her knickers.

# Chapter Twenty-two

David smiled broadly as Cali and Annie entered Deedee's.

'Ahoy! I mean, hello. Your usual table, ladies?'

'I didn't realise we had a usual, but yes please.' Cali noticed how long David's eyelashes were through his glasses. 'How are you?'

'*Dobre*. I apologise, good, thank you. Busy for a Sunday afternoon. What can I get you to drink?'

Annie rubbed her face and yawned. 'Oh dear.'

'Too much bed and not enough sleep, eh?' Cali laughed. David straightened the cutlery in his professional 'I'm-pretending-not-to-listen-but-I-so-am' guise.

'I wish.' Annie yawned again. 'Black coffee for me, please.'

'I'll have a breakfast tea with milk, please.' Cali sat down. 'Do you want a cake or pastry?'

'No, I'm fine, thanks. Let's hope Keira's afternoon nap is as long as usual. Rob wanted to get some zzz's too. He drank rather a lot of port last night.'

'She's been up since almost five, so she'll be out for the count for a while. It's me who should be yawning.'

'Oops. Did you not manage to get back to sleep

then?'

'I didn't even try. Ms Johnson Jr was having none of it. She wanted her mummy and that was that.'

'I'm sorry, Cali. Thanks so much for looking after her. It honestly is a relief to have somebody I trust with her.'

'It's a complete pleasure. She's such a sweetheart, even when she's screaming her head off. But come on, Annie, talk to me. I'm surprised you didn't want to stay at home and chill after a long awaited night out.'

Annie sighed. 'I think Rob might be having an affair. I haven't had a chance to talk to you about it properly before.'

'No! Really? Out of everyone I know, your husband is the least likely person to hurt you or Keira.'

'They said that about Jamie.'

Cali's defence was shot down in flames. 'Er, OK. But what gives you reason to think that?'

'He literally kept checking his phone all last night, even in the theatre! And remember the night we went out after the Am Dram debacle? His phone was off and he was really late home. He said he was playing cards with the lads and lost track of time.'

'Don't you believe him?'

'I've never had any reason not to trust him, Cal. But what hurt me that night was that he knew we had a babysitter and he didn't even text to check to see if she was OK. And I know he knew he was in the wrong because he crept into bed and went straight to sleep. I'm used to getting a poke in the back when he's drunk.'

'Did you question him about it?'

'Of course, he apologised profusely and said he would be more thoughtful in future.'

'See? It's all right, Annie. We all have wobbles and get fed up. Life's boring sometimes. I know I don't have a child to look after but even as a free agent, the monotony of everyday life gets to me sometimes.'

'It's not all right. When he kept looking at his phone I asked him outright if he was seeing another woman.'

'Woah!'

'I know, I know. I was drunk; I should have thought it through. He said I was being completely ridiculous, that his mate Brian was having "issues".' Annie made air quotes with her fingers. 'And he was "just looking out for him".'

'What sort of issues?'

'He said he didn't feel he could discuss it with me as it was personal.'

'Oh.' Cali slurped on her tea.

'Yes, oh. I know they've also lost a couple of big clients at work so that is really stressing him out. Rob likes to have everything in order. I guess that's why he's such a good accountant.'

'Have I met Brian?'

'No, I don't think so. He's in his mid-thirties, very quiet, quite geeky. I don't think he's had a girlfriend since university.'

'Bless him; has he come out or something?'

'I didn't think of that.' Annie stirred more sugar into her coffee. 'But I'd have thought Rob would divulge that to me. It was so terrible, Cali. I had a go at him about mentioning my weight, too.'

'Rob isn't cruel like that. He loves you, Annie.'

'Don't you remember he asked if I was going for the part of an Oompa Loompa before the auditions?'

Cali tried not to laugh. 'That's just Rob teasing you. He's always been like that. I think you're just being a bit sensitive and took it the wrong way. And it's not as if you're fat, is it? Two weeks sensible eating and a few power walks will sort your problems out. We can do it together now the weather is good. I've been drinking far too much and can feel my jeans getting tighter.'

'OK, that makes me feel better. And yes, we could go to the park, even if I'm pushing Kiera.'

'Cool, well, that's that worry sorted.' Cali yawned. 'Now, going back to Rob. If you're that worried, have you thought of checking his phone? When I began to suspect Jamie I used to do it.'

'I couldn't do that. We've always had such a trusting relationship.'

'So what are you going to do? You can't carry on feeling like this.'

'I don't know. I'll give it a couple of weeks and see what happens. If he keeps acting oddly then I'll have another chat with him.'

'I'm so sorry you had such a shit time.'

'It wasn't all bad, we had a lovely lunch and went back to the hotel room before the theatre.'

'And how was that?'

'Bloody great, better than normal, in fact. We didn't have to worry about Keira disturbing us. But

114

that was before the Spanish Inquisition.'

'Well, that's positive. And if he was up to something, why would he want to make the effort of taking you all the way to London for a weekend away?'

'Guilt?'

'Not Rob. I'm convinced you've got him wrong on this. Just be nice. Ask him gently to divulge about Brian. Make a joke about it, I don't know ... And then, if you're still not sure he is telling the truth, Calista Summers' Detective Agency will come to the rescue.'

Annie laughed and then bit her lip. 'Shit, I'm so sorry, Cali. Listen to me blurting on and forgetting the most important question.'

'It's fine. I came on last night. I can't tell you how relieved I am. And you'll never guess what else happened.'

Annie's mouth remained open in shock as Cali relayed the supermarket incident.

'What a complete and utter bastard. I did think he sounded like a tosser when you told me how he reacted about the condom incident.'

'Yes, a complete loser.'

'And actually, that has made me feel so much better about Rob. Rob is gentle and kind. You're right, I have to believe in him and stop feeling so insecure. It's actually laughable to think of him having an affair. I've never even caught him so much as glancing at another woman. Talking of which, are you still off the app?'

'I am. Although, being honest, I thought about Will last night and how nice it would be to meet somebody like him again.'

'Well, take another look. I think you've scraped the bottom of the dating barrel with Mr Chode.'

'Mr Chode?'

'Didn't you say his cock was as wide as it was long?'

'Er, yes.'

'Well, funnily enough, after you told me about him, I overheard the intern at my office having a conversation about a boy she had met at the weekend with a similarly small appendage. In youth speak they call a willy like that a chode.'

Cali guffawed. 'Puts a new spin on Toad in the Hole.'

'Toad in the Hole?' David placed the bill on the table. 'That's going to be a special here on Monday.'

'In your dreams,' Annie said quietly.

Cali and Annie were now roaring with laughter.

'Sorry, did I say something wrong?'

'No, David, that was just what we both needed.'

Wondering if he'd ever understand the complexity of women, the waiter cleared the table with a bemused expression on his face.

116

# Chapter Twenty-three

'What are you doing here?' Cali was shocked to see Jamie's BMW in her parking space at the flat. 'You could have parked in the visitor's space.'

'I was at the gym and thought I'd pop in and see you. I was obviously going to call first and not just ring your buzzer unannounced.' Cali took in his muscly legs and didn't dare breathe in the scent of his T-shirt. She wanted to be strong and say he couldn't come up, but her heartstrings didn't allow those words to work her mouth.

Once inside, Jamie handed her a carrier bag. 'Food for Lady P.'

'Er ... thanks.'

'I know how you don't want her, and I've put you in a position and I'm sorry. But I think it would be cruel to move her in with me then out again when Bella moves in.'

'It's fine.' There was no way that Cali would say that she couldn't be without her feathery companion now. Let his guilt continue.

'Big boy J. Big boy J.'

They both laughed, something that hadn't happened together for quite some time. Cali suddenly snapped back into reality.

'Anyway, what do you want? I've got things to

do.'

'Well, to bring you the food and say hi and er, to check to see if you had signed the recent forms from the solicitor. In fact, I thought maybe you could sign them while I'm here. I'm dropping mine in on the way home.'

'Bella still not moving in until it's done, eh?'

'It's not fair to discuss that with you, I just want to get everything sorted. You know how I like things to be in order.'

'Whatever, Jamie. But I haven't received anything yet.'

'Oh, OK. I got mine yesterday.'

'While you're here, I was thinking I'd like back some of the wine glasses that work gave us. I keep breaking mine.' She *so* regretted leaving so many things in their marital home. 'And that French shabby chic side table my mum and dad gave us as an engagement present.'

'OK, that's fine. I'll sort it and bring them round to you in the next week or two. There's no point involving the solicitor, it'll hold things up and cost more.'

'Porn star, porn star, porn star.' Lady P charged around her cage.

'What the ...?' Cali was both amused and horrified at Jamie's reaction. 'Don't ask.'

'So, are you seeing anybody else?'

'I don't think that's any of your business.' Cali looked away from his questioning gaze. 'But I may have had a couple of dates.'

'Ooh. Don't tell me you're on Tinder.'

'Er ...' Cali went bright red.

'Loads of my mates are on it. But be careful, Cal. Half of them use it to hook up with girls when they're horny. But saying that, Andy actually met a cracking girl and is already on date three, so it can work.'

'Well, thanks for the relationship advice, Jamie. Being an expert at them yourself, I will of course take note.'

Jamie put a hand on Cali's shoulder. 'Don't be like that. I still care about you. I always will. I mean, twelve years is a long time to spend with someone.'

*And one big betrayal is enough to make me not care about you at all*, Cali thought, tears pricking her eyes. 'Goodbye, Jamie, thanks for the bird food. When that form comes in I'll sign it. I have no reason to hold up proceedings. I hope you and your fake bimbo are very happy together.'

'No need to be like that, Cali.'

Part of Cali wanted to melt into his arms. 'Isn't there?'

Jamie headed for the door. 'Where's the Portobello mirror gone?'

'You smashed it when you slammed the door last time you were here.'

'I didn't.'

'I'm not arguing with you, Jamie, but you did.'

'Oh, I'm so sorry, Cal.' Despite how unmaterialistic his estranged wife was, Jamie knew how much she had loved that mirror.

'Sorry is such a futile word from you, Jamie, just go.' And, without giving him a chance to say anything else, Cali herded him out of the door and shut it behind him.

Despite her intentions not to drink so much, she went to the kitchen and poured herself a large glass of wine.

Why couldn't he just ring or text? Why did he have to keep coming to see her? It made getting over him all the harder, and made her realise just how much she had loved him.

She sat down on the sofa and looked at her new match. With just one sideways photo, Tim from Tilehurst could do one. She wasn't going to fall for that old chestnut again. She pressed delete and flicked on the TV.

'Love you, Callerina,' Lady P said softly for once.

'I love you too, Lady P.'

# Chapter Twenty-four

'Thanks for coming out at such short notice.' Cali flashed her friend a weak smile.

'It's fine, at least it's kick-started our power walking mission. And it's perfect timing, actually; Rob just got in and said he'd sort Keira for me.'

'I need to talk to you about something. Something embarrassing.'

'Go on.'

'It's my fanny. Well … it's humming.'

'You should teach your bum to whistle and you could start up a new band phenomenon.'

Cali laughed. 'Yeah, Cali and the Orifices, great. But joking aside, it's not normal. I'm terrified I've got an STD.'

'Oh, Cal, really? But you always use condoms, don't you?'

'Er, yes, but the Mr Chode incident. That is the only way I could have caught something and I'm sure I'm not the only woman he cheats with, dirty bastard.'

'Well, there's no point worrying, you just need to get it sorted. Either go to the doctors or a clinic.'

Cali groaned. 'I know. But it's so embarrassing.'

'The sexual health clinic is the best and quickest. I'll come with you, it's fine, and everyone there is in the same boat so there's no need to be embarrassed.'

'You're such a love.'

Annie was beginning to become short of breath as they walked faster. 'And to be honest, imagine if you saw Doctor Blake at the surgery and your parents invited him to one of their parties again, you'd be mortified.'

'Fair point. OK, I've got the afternoon off on Wednesday. I'd be grateful if you came with me.'

'It's a date. I'll see if Angie, one of the nursery mums, can have Keira for a couple of hours.'

Cali took a deep breath as she walked into the Flower Unit that was linked to the hospital in the neighbouring town. She had purposely worn jeans and a plain T-shirt that revealed none of her impressive cleavage for fear of anyone branding her as a tart.

Annie took a seat in the stark waiting room as Cali went to reception and collected a clipboard with a form to fill out. When Cali came back and whispered 'Symptoms' in her ear, she laughed. 'Oh God, Annie, what do I put? Fanny smells like Billingsgate Fish Market?'

'Just put "distinct odour from vagina" and whatever else you need to, but I really don't want to know.'

Cali looked around the waiting room; there were two other girls sitting together, both of whom could be no more than eighteen. One of them had been crying by the looks of it. A distinguished-looking suited black man in his early thirties holding a

*Men's Health* magazine close to his face sat nearby, and a beautifully made up woman, who Cali reckoned was in her late forties, shifted in her seat not wanting to catch anyone's eye.

She suddenly didn't feel so embarrassed. Everyone had sex. Everyone made mistakes. The whole stigma was ridiculous, really. Acute bad breath was embarrassing too; just because she was smelly in her undercarriage, why was that so terrible?

A female nurse in her early fifties appeared and called her name. Cali felt relief that it wasn't the male nurse she had seen earlier.

'Hi, I'm Karen. So you've got discharge and an odour? Let's get you sorted out.'

Cali undressed her lower half and got on the bed.

After a thoroughly uncomfortable examination, the nurse said from between her legs, 'The good news is, I think I can tell exactly what it is and it's not actually sexually transmitted. It's a vaginal infection called BV. Basically, the balance of bacteria inside the vagina becomes disrupted. Have you been sexually active recently?'

'Er, yes, more than usual, I guess.'

'That's probably it. A course of antibiotics will clear it up. It does sometimes reoccur, but take this leaflet and you can see how to prevent it.'

'I'm so relieved.'

'Did you have unprotected sex?'

'The condom split. But I'm definitely not pregnant, thank goodness.'

'OK. Here.' The nurse handed Cali a selection of condoms.

'Thank you,' Cali managed a smile. 'And for being so kind.' Thank goodness.

Cali put her hand on Annie's shoulder as they walked to the car park.

'Thanks, mate.'

'It's fine. In fact, I think it was worse for me as I was sitting in the waiting room the whole time. What a relief it's not something nastier.'

'Yes. I've just got the worry of waiting for the results of everything else now. I get a text in around ten days and if not I need to call them.'

'I'm sure it will be fine. It's just good I always make them wear a condom, or one that fits at least.'

'I don't think they make them for chodes, that's the problem.'

In the ensuing laughter, Annie dropped her car keys on the floor. Cali bent down to pick them up and on standing up nearly died of shock, for standing right in front of her was Will, the handsome officer.

'Cali, hi. Good to see you.'

'Will, hi. Er, this is my friend Annie,' Cali started to gabble. 'Got to run, cinema, you see. We always park here, cheaper, less of a queue.'

Will smirked. 'OK. Enjoy yourselves. I'm just picking up some leaflets for the lads from the clinic. Filthy bunch, those young officers.' And with that, he sauntered to the entrance.

Annie opened up the car and they both got in.

'Oh my God, why did you say that? I don't even think there's a cinema here.'

'I panicked, it's the first thing that came into my head.'

'You're right, he is gorgeous.'

'Gorgeous, but there's no chance of me ever having any kind of altercation with him now. He's not stupid.'

'He might be spinning you a yarn.'

'Shit, I didn't think of that.'

'OK, if he does get in contact again – which, by the way he looked at you, I think he might – then just say you were escorting me. Or just say you have a sexual health check every year. He'll think you're really responsible then. I think everyone who has an active sex life should.'

'I don't even want to think about it. But did he really look at me like that?'

'Yes! And you're right, he's hot.'

Ping!

Cali looked at her phone. 'Another match. In my condition I can't even think about another date, but hello, Mario, 31, Formula One Engineer.'

'I thought you'd deleted the app?' Annie secured her seatbelt.

'I did, but got bored the other night and reinstated it again. It's actually a bit addictive, to be honest.'

'Let me look.' Annie grabbed the phone. 'Oh, Cali, you have to. He looks Italian – and he's an F1 engineer! I've heard Rob talking about them, they earn a fortune.'

'He can go on the back burner for now.'

'No. I think you should start chatting at least. You can't let him get away. Shit, here comes the officer. Smile sweetly.'

Cali waved as the officer gave a mock salute to

her in the car, got into his and drove off.

'I would.' Annie put her hand to her heart.

'I might.' Cali laughed. 'Although, bugger, we were running to the cinema five minutes ago. Oh well.'

'It's feast or famine again now, Cal. All you need to do is get everything back in clean and working order for Wonderful Will or Super Mario.'

# Chapter Twenty-five

Mario Milli, face half covered by dark designer shades, got out of his black Audi sports car and sauntered towards Cali.

'I love a woman in red. The same way I love my Ferraris,' he smirked. '*Ciao*.' Cali felt herself going the same colour as her cleavage-hugging top as he kissed her on each cheek. Taking in his sexy demeanour, beautifully cut jeans and highly polished brown leather shoes, she remained mute.

'Outside OK?'

She nodded. Both the light touch of his hand as he led her and his sexy accent already made her feel a bit funny. They settled in a quiet corner of the pub garden and he signalled the waitress over.

'What would you like to drink, Calista?'

'Er. A small white wine, please.' Bugger, she should have said Diet Coke, but she felt she needed some Dutch courage with a man like this.

'Do you have Pinot Grigio, Italian, of course?'

'Yes, sir,' the young waitress responded, trying not to stare at the handsome man in front of her.

'Then one, please. Do you have any energy drinks?' The young girl nodded again. 'Great, no ice. And if you can, be quick. I don't have long.'

'Oh.' Cali managed a sound. 'Are you in a

hurry?'

'You have twenty minutes, Calista. You are the first internet date I have ever had. I know if there is no connection within that time, we say our goodbyes. I am a very busy man.' Mario's sunglasses remained on.

If he wasn't so bloody handsome, had an accent that made her quiver, dressed well, obviously earned a wedge and drove an amazing sports car, she would have got up and walked out there and then. Fickle maybe, but how often did this sort of package get presented right in front of you – with bells on? And she actually loved the fact that he was so direct. And so right in a way. At least there would be no messing about.

The waitress brought over their drinks.

'Well, if the clock is counting down, the least you could do is show me your eyes.'

Mario flipped his glasses up and down quickly and smiled. 'Bit red, I'm afraid. I tell you now, as a Formula One engineer I work very long hours. We are working on the car for the Spanish Grand Prix at the moment. It has to be perfect. Any girlfriend I have ...' He paused for a second. 'Has to be both perfect ... and, how you say, patient too.' He grinned.

'Ah, so he does have a sense of humour? For a minute I thought he was a robot with a very small heart.'

Mario laughed and took a large swig of his energy drink.

'Questions to you, Calista. Quick answers are fine.'

128

'You asked me loads last night, but OK. Can I ask *you* something?'

'Of course.' Mario rubbed his hand over his cropped, jet black hair.

'Do you do anything slowly?'

He smirked. 'If we get through this twenty minutes, then I will show you.' Cali bit her lip. It was like she was under some sort of spell: she already had visions of him gently making love to her. 'Are you ready?' Cali nodded. 'Quick, OK?'

'Yes.' Cali made a face at him. 'Go.'

'You wouldn't tell me if you were single last night. So, are you married?'

Cali thought 'separated' sounded so lame, so she had ignored Mario's questions in fear he may not want to meet her.

'Ah. Er. Um.'

'If it's a yes, then it's a yes. Don't be afraid, Calista.'

'I am married, but I've signed the divorce papers.'

'Good, so you are single and maybe expecting some money, even better for you, eh? Get rid of a bastard and gain a decent bank balance.'

'Something like that.' Cali couldn't be bothered to divulge the whole sorry tale.

'Cali, I chatted to a lot of women this week before I chose you. You look hot, you've confirmed you are single. You have eight minutes left. So far all is well.'

'Next question?' Cali took a sip of wine. It was lovely to feel the May sun on her face.

'I forgot to ask you if own your own place?'

'Yes. I have a flat in Woodford Road, just along from the Primary School in Bramley. Do you know it?'

'No. I flit in and out and stay in a flat in Windsor very infrequently. As you can imagine, I travel a lot with my job.'

'So you go to every Grand Prix?'

'Most of them, that's why I say my girl has to be patient.'

'Well … if something is worth waiting for.' Cali smiled and Mario leaned forward and kissed her on the cheek.

'Exactly.' Cali blushed as he carried on. 'I like you, Calista.'

'I know you do.' Cali rested her elbow on the wooden table and looked directly at Mario's glasses.

'Confident as well as sexy.' Mario signalled the waitress to bring the bill.

'Not that confident. It's just we've been here thirty minutes.'

Mario laughed. 'We have, but I'm really sorry. I have to go. It's wind tunnel testing in the factory this afternoon.'

He paid up and they walked over a little bridge to the car park.

On reaching her car, he put his hand on her shoulder.

'Come with me. Calista, I want to show you something.' Without question, she followed him to the furthest corner of the car park, where his flash Audi was parked against a fence. Mario opened the passenger door and signalled for her to get in. She

130

sunk into the comfortable leather seat and before she had a chance to say a word, he got in the car, removed his glasses, put his hands either side of her face and started to kiss her. A kiss so gentle, yet so passionate. A kiss that explored every inch of her mouth. A kiss that said 'I want you.' A kiss that made the butterflies that had already been erupting in her stomach dance a passionate Tango that went from the end of her toes to her head. She gasped as he broke away.

'Calista?'

She nodded. 'Cali.'

'I will see you tomorrow, yes?' Mario's brown eyes sunk into her now shining blue ones.

'I've got to go into work briefly at one.'

'At the hotel where you work, right?'

'Yes.'

'Let me know the address and room number and be ready for me at one forty.'

'That's both presumptuous and precise.' The way Cali felt, she probably would have jumped into shark infested waters if he had asked her to.

'Like I said, I am a busy man.'

Cali smiled a coy smile and got out of the car.

Mario opened the passenger window and with his 'Until tomorrow,' being drowned out by the roar of the Audi's engine, a stunned Cali was left standing alone in the car park.

# Chapter Twenty-six

'So, are you going to go through with it?'

'Is the Pope Catholic, Annie? I'm actually outside Marks and Spencer, ready to go in and buy the sexiest red underwear I can find.'

'Do you think you better get something a bit more expensive than M&S? I mean, if he's used to undressing all those models on the Formula One circuit...'

'Thanks for that, Annie. And I don't get paid until Wednesday, so no, he can take me as I am.'

'You're right. And if he's as loaded as I should imagine an F1 engineer is, he can buy you some for next time. If there is a next time.'

'Remind me never to come to you for confidence boosting lessons.'

'I'm sorry, Cal. But he does seem a bit too good to be true. And shouldn't the second date be dinner or something?'

'Not everyone is going to be a charlatan like the vet. And he's flying out to Barcelona tonight to prepare for the next race.'

'Blimey. OK, he's a keeper. Even if it's just for an extraordinary fling.'

'I have an amazing feeling about him, Annie. I don't think he's like the others. I'm his first date. I think he's decent. We've got a huge connection and I don't feel the need to wait. Adam said to me the other day that if it feels right, then why wait? I would've shagged him in the car if he didn't have to go to work. Words aren't enough to explain the feeling between us, it was electric.'

'Well, OK, but as I've said before, be careful. You hardly know him.'

'How long did it take you to shag Rob after you met him again?'

'OK, OK, the second date.'

'And look at you two now.'

Annie sounded despondent. 'Yes, just look at us. Sex twice a month if I'm lucky and a needy toddler to look after.'

'All the more reason to have fun now then.'

'Yes. Don't listen to me, I'm just jealous.'

'How are things, though? Sorry it's all about me.'

'I'm fine.'

'Well, you don't sound fine. I've been a shit friend lately. We need a proper catch up. How about we have a late breakfast, ten at Deedee's on Monday? I haven't got to go into work until midday. I'll meet you there.'

'Sounds good. Maybe I'll swap green tea for an espresso and go crazy.'

Cali laughed. 'Love you, mate.'

'Love you too. I'd get crotchless ones if I were you. At least they may stay on for more than a minute.'

# Chapter Twenty-seven

Cali nearly jumped out of her skin when Marcus got in the lift as she was making her way up to Room 102.

'Hiya, Cali. Good of you to come in on a Sunday, dedication to the core.'

'It's not only the General Manager who cares about clients, you know,' Cali laughed nervously. 'But if I'd have known you were coming in, I might have stayed at home.'

'Err, I didn't put it on the calendar as it was a last minute decision. Christie Law spends a lot of money with us and I wanted to make sure everything was set up how she wanted it. You look great, by the way.'

'Aw, thank you.' Oh God, she could feel herself reddening. She mustn't panic, she must think, what she could say she was doing before he asked?

She also hoped her boss wouldn't wonder why on earth she was wearing killer heels, a sexy grey pencil skirt and a crisp white shirt that showed far too much cleavage for a work day. Thank God he didn't have X-ray specs to see what she had on underneath.

And then, the question she had been dreading.

'So, why are you heading up instead of going

home?'

'102 has the radiator problem again. Adam texted me and said if I was coming in to check on the plumber. Maintenance are off today.' She must remember to relay this to Adam.

'102?' Marcus said far too loudly. This was getting more and more painful: Mario would literally be at the door in fifteen minutes.

The lift pinged as it reached the first floor and before Cali had a chance to stick even one foot out, Marcus hurriedly pushed the button for it to go back to the ground.

Angels did exist!

'Bugger, bugger sorry, Cali. Chef just messaged, his second has badly burnt his finger. I'm going to have to don my whites and rekindle my old restaurant skills.'

Before she had a chance to answer, and feeling like she was now in the middle of some sort of unimaginable farce, Marcus hot-footed it towards the kitchen.

With a ding from the lift and a huge sense of relief, Cali arrived at the first floor.

Unbeknown to her, she was not quite as relieved as the pretty girl whose pained face was only just disappearing behind the closing doors of the lift next to her.

Mario shut the hotel room door quietly behind him and started undressing as quickly as his toned arms would allow him. 'Wow, just look at you, Señorita. You are hot! Now get those clothes off for me.'

Mario lay naked on the bed, watching every

136

move Cali made. Mortified at his scrutiny, she tried her best to conduct some sort of a striptease without falling from her killer heels and letting out her well held-in stomach.

He moved his head up on the pillow. 'Now, come to me.'

Cali lay as seductively as she could with her legs slightly to the side, her head in a coquettish fashion on the pillow. Her bright red lipstick matched her red balcony bra and lacy shorts, which both accentuated her best assets. It was the stance she had practised on her bed this morning, but it didn't feel as comfortable as it should.

As Mario kissed her urgently and passionately, she could feel his already hard cock pushing against her thigh. He gently stuck his fingers into her and she groaned loudly. He put his index finger against her lips with a soft shush. Then he reached for the condom Cali had pointed to on the bedside table. 'I want you so much, Cali, you are so beautiful.'

Cali panted and then almost screamed with delight as Mario pushed his hard cock deep inside her. It had always taken her at least thirty minutes to come with Jamie, but within seconds she could feel herself rising and falling into the heat of Mario's intense lovemaking. She looked at him intently, then, smacking his arse with her right hand, demanded he fuck her from behind. She loved being in control. She felt like she was on a film set as the handsome Italian pushed deeper and harder into her with every stroke. And then after all the heat and intensity, with just a very gentle sigh from him, it was over and he was facing her on the pillow.

'That, my gorgeous lady, was amazing, but I have to go. Like I said, I am off to Barcelona and will be away for a while, but I will WhatsApp you. I take it you have WhatsApp? It's a lot easier when I am away to use that and it will be free for you.'

'I bet you say that to all the girls.' Cali cringed inwardly. Why had she shown her insecurity? He had already said he wanted to keep messaging her. It wasn't just a one-off.

'Cali, I don't play games. I don't need to. I don't want to. I think you are beautiful. I can feel the attraction. Let's go with it, eh?'

Cali nodded and felt warm inside. Here was the most handsome man she had ever been with in her life, saying he liked her that much. He got dressed, stood in front of her and took her hand. 'I live in a world of glamour and falseness. When I come home, I want real. You need to be able to deal with the time when we are apart, that's all.'

'I will. I know I can,' Cali blurted. 'I must go to the bathroom, though.'

'Of course.'

Cali reappeared, still flushed.

'Hey, you.' Mario was tightening his belt. 'I must go. Goodbye, *bellissima,* and I promise I will be in touch soon. Oh, if you're not on the pill, get on it. Much easier for quickies.' Mario winked, smacked her bottom lightly, then leaned in and gave her a gentle kiss on the lips.

With a '*Ciao, ciao,*' he disappeared down the fire escape as quickly as he had been instructed to come up it.

Cali placed her hand on the back of the door and

mouthed, '*Ciao*.'

All the critics of dating app dating could eat their words.

Yes, if you wanted 'fast love' it was there. But maybe, just maybe, if you looked hard enough you could find the real thing, too.

# Chapter Twenty-eight

'Just an English breakfast tea and a peach yoghurt, please.' Both David and Annie looked questionably at Cali. 'What's wrong with you two?' Cali scratched her ear. David stood back, realising he may have got a little bit too familiar. 'I'm on a diet, OK?'

David coughed. Annie put her mac on the back of her chair. 'Blimey, this *is* serious. OK. David, can you get me a double espresso with foamy milk on the side, please. I've no idea if it has a fancy name or not. And, um, I'll have two slices of brown toast please, with marmite on one and marmalade on the other, but no butter, thanks.'

'*Dobre*. I mean, good. Thank you, ladies.'

'I'm so impressed, you never write anything down.' Cali smiled at the handsome bespectacled waiter.

'My phone has a great recording device.' David put their order in at the café counter.

'So, spill the beans, like the Italian stallion obviously did.'

'Annie Johnson, you really are vile sometimes.' Cali stirred her tea with a dreamy expression. 'I really like him.'

'So did you have a drink? Chat? Watch F1

highlights on his phone? Or just get jiggy?'

'He was naked within seconds of arriving, but oh my God, I just remembered something so awful.'

'He had a chode too?' Annie grinned then groaned with delight as she took the first sip of her sweet, frothy coffee. 'Sod my diet today.'

Cali tutted. 'No chode, and the awful bit wasn't about Mario. Marcus got in the bloody lift with me as I was going upstairs to the room!'

'Oh, shit.'

'Oh, yes. Imagine if he'd seen me open the door to the Italian in my red undies?'

'He'd have probably loved it. Anyway, details please.'

'We shagged, it was amazing. He wants to see me again. He even made sure I was on WhatsApp so I could message him from anywhere in the world.'

'Cali, I am really pleased for you, but take it slow. He's an engineer for the *leading* team in Formula One. Please don't think you're his only one.'

'He was quite bold in the fact he said he could have his choice of women but he says he doesn't like fakes. He likes me, Annie, I can tell.'

'Has he messaged you yet?'

'No. But he only flew to Barcelona last night and he works crazy hours. He explained I will need to be patient.'

'Let's have a look at his profile pic. Ah, the team and the car. Where is he in this?'

'That's his head right at the back, he said he looked down at the wrong time and the photographer was sick of trying to get all of them facing forward. I can't believe how big the team is, to be honest.'

'Well, if any of them are looking for another English rose then shout my way,' Annie laughed. 'I am genuinely pleased for you though, Cal. I hope he is as decent as you think he is.'

Just at that moment, a message pinged to Cali's phone. 'Aw, see.' She turned the phone around to Annie.

*Hi, sexy. Missing you already x*

'Better than a cock pic, I guess. How was he in that department?'

'Very good. And that's all I'm saying in case I start seeing him properly. I'd hate for you to have a conversation with him knowing what was in his trousers.'

'Ooh, I can tell you like him now. But I know what you mean.'

'Aw.' Cali looked at the message again. 'It's going to be more than just sex, I can tell already. Don't they say when you know, you know?'

'Cali, you've spent less than two hours with the man.'

'When did you know Rob was the one?'

'It took a few months. I fancied the pants off him instantly and we slept together on date two, but I didn't see me marrying him straight away.' She looked up to the ceiling and bit her lip. 'Maybe I shouldn't have slept with him then.'

Cali could see tears welling in her friend's eyes.

'Oh, Annie. What's happened?'

Annie tightened her blonde ponytail with both

hands.

'I just feel a bit down, that's all. Rob isn't checking his phone so much but I'm still being paranoid. He shows me his messages as he knows I'm having a wobble, and they're all from Brian.'

'He so wouldn't show you anything if he was guilty. Maybe you should see if Brian wants to come round for dinner?'

'That's an idea, although he's so shy he might not. It's not just that, though. I'm finding the mother lark hard. Don't get me wrong, I love Keira to pieces but if I had a choice now, I don't think I would have had a child.'

'Woah!'

'There, I've said it. I envy your life, Cali. The thought of just having to worry about myself for once.'

'I understand what you're saying, but it's lonely and I'm always worried that if I lose my job, I have no back up, financially or emotionally. Most things are easier in a partnership.'

'You have all the excitement, too.'

'Like sleeping with a variety of toads and getting a smelly fanny for the pleasure of it?'

'But now you have the handsome Italian.'

'OK, I will take that. I cannot believe my luck with Mario, he is so delicious. But Annie, however you feel now, hold on to what you have. It is a really good thing. Don't ruin it with jealousy. I'm sure that Rob has done nothing wrong. We have to think what we can do to make your life fuller. In fact, why don't you two arrange another night out soon, a weekend away somewhere? I'm happy to babysit, you know that.'

'Thank you. I'll be fine. It's just a phase. But I may take you up on that. I better get to Angie's; she was sweet enough to watch Keira while I met you.'

'That's good, too. Maybe try and get friendly with more nursery mums, then you'll have a bank of babysitters.'

'That's the plan. Did you ever hear from Will, by the way?'

'Nothing, but I really don't care.'

David brought the bill over. He went to walk back to the counter and Cali signalled him to stay. 'I've got cash, I'll pay now.' She opened her purse. 'Oh, I was sure I had two fivers in there yesterday. Sorry, we need the card machine.'

Annie hugged Cali hard outside. 'Thanks for listening. I'm genuinely pleased for you. You need some happiness and if it's in the form of a sexy, rich Italian, then bloody get in there.'

'I will keep you fully updated.' Cali started walking towards her car, then shouted back at Annie, 'Call me about babysitting, don't forget.'

Annie nodded and waved back.

Cali, picking up her dropped car key, didn't notice David at the café window, whispering *krásný* – beautiful – at the sight of her bent over bottom.

# Chapter Twenty-nine

'Blimey, you sound happy.' Marcus placed a green file on Cali's desk, causing her to stop humming her favourite Adele track. 'And can I say, looking resplendent in blue. Matches your eyes.'

'Er, thanks, Marcus. I guess I am in a good mood.'

'Happy workers equals productive workers, so it can only be a good thing.' He pointed to the file. 'I need your help on costing this one up, Louise is going to be off for a few days.'

'Oh, OK.'

'She called before you arrived.'

'What's up with her?'

'She said she has a personal problem she needs to address.'

'Ah. OK. She seemed fine yesterday. Hope she's OK.'

'So do I.' Marcus said softly and, turning back as he reached the door, he said, 'I know how busy you are so if you need a temp, just shout.'

'Will do.'

'Slut,' Adam addressed her and plonked himself down on the edge of Louise's desk.

'Lovely to see you, too.'

'You look nice today. New dress?'

'Blimey, Marcus said that too. Thank you.'

'Well, you do.'

'Must be because I'm happier. I've met a gorgeous man on Tinder. Italian, works in F1.'

'You kept that one quiet. Has he been 102'd yet?'

Cali laughed. 'Actually, yes.'

'See what happens, I have two days off and there you are doing men left, right and centre behind my back.'

'Well reminded. I snuck in on Sunday and Marcus was here, too. He got in the lift with me as I was going up to the room.'

'Woah!'

'I know! Can you imagine?'

'What did you say?'

'I just said I was here to check in on the event and you'd said to check on the plumber who was doing out of hours work in 102.'

'Cali, I will cover for you but be careful, eh? You'd be up for more than a written warning if you got caught out.'

'I'd actually be more horrified at what a decent married man like him might think of me.'

'He'd probably be jealous.'

Cali laughed. 'Maybe. My married mate Annie says she enjoys living vicariously through my antics.'

'How's the hand model?'

Adam laughed. 'Boring. Dumped.' He waved his hand over his face as if to brush him away. 'More excitingly, when are you seeing Mr F1 again?'

'I don't know yet. He's in Barcelona but

hopefully he won't be too long. He did say I needed to be patient as he will be away a lot.'

'Will you be able to cope with that?'

'Of course.'

'You say that now.'

'No. Honestly, Adam. He is so lovely. And I've been alone for so long that even if I see him twice a month that'd be amazing. Anyway, I've got to get on. I'm swamped.'

'Where's Lou?'

'Off for a few days. She's got a personal problem.'

'Oh. She seemed fine yesterday. I hope nobody's died.'

'Ever the optimist.'

'Well, if there is anything I can help with when I'm not busy on reception, just shout.'

'I will. Although Marcus said I could get a temp.'

'Blimey, he must have got a shag at the weekend too.'

They both laughed as Adam went back to his post, then ping!

*Missing you, sweetie. We won the race. Heading off to my place in St Tropez until next weekend. Be in touch X*

Missing her. House in St Tropez! Cali put her hand to her heart and accompanied another hearty hum with a little dance this time.

# Chapter Thirty

'Dirty bird, dirty bird.'

Lady P hopped from chair to table to bookshelf to windowsill while Cali, adorned in yellow rubber gloves, cleaned out her pet's cage and refreshed food and water.

Cali had put her phone on silent in the kitchen in the hope that if out of sight, out of mind, then Mario might message her. Two weeks had flown by. Initially, Mario's messages had been brief but frequent. But now, six days had passed and, despite her twice asking how he was, she hadn't heard a peep from him. In fact, his lack of response was beginning to slightly annoy her.

She wished she hadn't messaged him now, but she was not good at playing games and he had always said he'd be honest with her. Maybe she shouldn't have been so trusting again. That if she felt there was the possibility of a relationship then she should hold out. Then at least she would know they were after one thing as they backed off. It was just a bit weird that the sexy Italian had carried on messaging her after the event. He had seemed so genuine. But maybe Annie was right – he lived in a glamorous world of fast cars and beautiful women. Perhaps he had already part-exchanged her for a better model.

Sighing, she walked to the fridge, poured herself a glass of grapefruit juice and reached for her phone. Nothing from Mario, but a new Tinder message greeted her.

*Hope you got that rash of yours sorted,* followed by a smiley face with a halo on it.

Cali smiled and sat down on the sofa. The handsome officer had returned just like Annie said he would.

'Porn star, porn star, porn star.' Lady P marched around her now pristine cage.

'Don't give me ideas, Lady P.' She began to type with a big smirk on her face. If Mario wasn't interested, then why should she feel any guilt? He had made her no promises and Will *was* bloody gorgeous.

*Same to you, spotty.*

*Haha.*

*If you had asked me on that first date, I might have.*

The handsome officer replied immediately. *Really? And there was me thinking you were such a good girl.*

*Maybe I should prove to you I'm not.* Cali began to feel the same buzz of excitement she had felt before meeting Luke and Mario at the hotel.

*Maybe you should. When? Where?*

*My place, 30 minutes?*

Will had the physique you would expect an army officer to have. Broad shoulders, firm thighs, and buttocks so round and perfect you wanted to cup them and give them a squeeze. He smelt divine too, and when he began to undress and Cali could see the delicious bulge in his boxers, she knew it was time to give her first dating app blow job.

She hadn't questioned sending Will her address. She believed where he came from and had spent enough time talking to him to know he was a decent man. She had showered at the speed of light and put on a new cream lace underwear set covered by a pair of denim shorts and a white vest to show off her cleavage. When she opened the door to him, she said nothing. She just smiled, took his hand and led him to the bedroom. If Will the officer wanted just sex, then that was what Will the officer would get.

Will groaned in anticipation as Cali, now in just her underwear, pushed his glorious naked self on the bed and got on her knees on the floor in front of him.

'Now, what were you saying about dipping soldiers?' She smiled and took the full length of his erect penis into her mouth. She could hear his moans of ecstasy as she began moving her tongue deftly up and down his shaft. Conscious of herself getting wetter and feeling a huge want for this man to be inside her, she gave his cock a final suck then squirmed her way up towards him. She reached in her bedside drawer for one of the larger condoms she had got from the sex clinic and demanded that Will put it on. She then slid on top of him and gasped with pleasure as he entered her gently.

'Good girl, eh?' It was Will's turn to gasp. 'I'm not so sure now.' Cali, with no thought in her head apart from satisfying herself, moved up and down faster and faster, taking in the gorgeous mix of sweat and aftershave from her lover. She came with a shuddered 'Yes', her body shaking, then lay flat into Will's neck, breathing heavily.

'Did you come?'

'Of course I did. Cali, that was bloody amazing.'

'Water?' Cali sprung off the bed and reached for her dressing gown.

'Yes. Please. Then I best be going.'

'Sure, sure.'

Will was already dressed when Cali came back from the kitchen. He drank the water, lifted her chin, and kissed her swiftly on the lips.

'Another time, maybe?'

'If you're lucky,' Cali grinned. 'Goodbye, handsome officer.'

'Goodbye, Cali Summers.'

Cali looked out of the window and watched Will walk towards his car. What had she become? Gone was shy, single Cali. She really was becoming Calista Summers, internet dating slut. But she had no regrets about today – what had just happened was amazing.

She thought again to Mario and realised that he had obviously been a flash in the pan. It took a few seconds to send a little message, however busy you were. But he was just like all the others: had played a great game to get her into bed and then walked away. He could be put in the B for Bastard pile and jog on now.

At least Luke and Will had been upfront and confessed that fun was all they wanted. And in a way, wasn't that better? No promises, no heartache.

She watched the officer's car pull away and put her hand to her forehead in shock. No! It couldn't be. And he had a massive bunch of flowers in his hand, too. Noticing him looking up at the flats, Cali quickly darted back into the lounge. Her phone beeped the familiar WhatsApp message chime she had set up for him.

*Sweetie, what's your flat number again? I remembered the address.*

'Shit, shit, shit.' Panic flew through Cali. Her scruffy bed hair was standing on end, and her body smelt of sex and army officer.

'Dirty bird, dirty bird,' Lady P squawked.

# Chapter Thirty-one

Louise sat in her car, head in her hands. How could she have been so stupid, and on so many levels? Her dad had always told her that when the drink's in, the wit's out. And on many occasions it had been. But she didn't think she could even blame her old friend Jack Daniel on this one. She had been drunk on what she thought was love and there was not one winning solution to the decision she now had to make.

# Chapter Thirty-two

'And up, 2, 3, 4, left, 2, 3, 4, right 2, 3, 4, and now down for 6.' Cali's one, and previously unused, fitness DVD blasted out from the TV. She breathily answered the door on Mario's second knock.

'Sorry, I had to finish. Would look a bit silly to have one side more toned than the other, wouldn't it?' Her hair was dragged into the tiniest of ponytails her bob would allow, and she was wearing her little denim shorts and a cropped fitness top. Her pink lipstick was perfect and her eyelashes beautifully full of fresh mascara. 'Let me turn the bloody thing off.'

'If you'd known I was coming, you could have waited for your workout.' Handing her the flowers in one hand, he lifted her other and kissed it.

'If I'd have known you were coming I could have done a lot of things.' Will had given her an inner confidence. 'You've been ignoring me, Mario, and then pitch up on my doorstep. I'm sorry there's no red carpet.' She put the flowers down on the coffee table.

Mario took her by the shoulders.

'You look hot. And I can explain.'

'I'm going to take a shower before you do. I'll be ten minutes. Here.' She handed him the TV remote.

'Grab a drink from the fridge if you want one.'

'I could shower with you.'

Any other time, Cali thought. 'Maybe next time, eh?'

'Porn star, porn star, porn star,' Lady P squawked, causing Mario to jump then fall about laughing.

'He must have seen my CV.'

Cali made a faux open-mouthed expression.

'Mario meet Lady P, a she. Lady P meet Mario, an absentee.'

'Very funny. Now hurry up in that shower.'

Cali returned to the lounge, having thrown on her favourite pair of jeans and a pink T-shirt with a white flower motif. She had rough dried her hair and put on a bit of make-up as, after the fantastic sex with Will, she was still glowing. A big squirt of Prada d'Iris smothered her feelings of guilt.

She made them both coffee and sat down.

'It's lovely to see you,' she said coyly. The brown eyes of the Italian melted into hers. She had forgotten how sexy he was and just how much she liked him. But not contacting her for nearly a week had made her put a block up for fear of getting hurt, and she was sick of being treated badly.

'Good to see you too, sweetie, but I lost my bloody phone. I've been itching to contact you. Well, I say I lost it. I ran across a very busy road in Spain and it fell out of my pocket. I heard it bang on the road but by the time I got to it, it had been completely run over. Thankfully, and remarkably, I found the SIM card and it was untouched.'

'Nightmare. But, yes, amazingly lucky to find the SIM.' Cali bit her lip and was suddenly awash with guilt for her earlier actions.

'I know! And I was so bloody busy working and then sorting stuff at my place in France that I just used my work phone, which isn't compatible with my personal SIM. I don't have your number written down and of course I wouldn't go on Tinder on my work phone.'

'OK, OK, slow down. I forgive you.'

'I've missed you, Cali. You're a shining light.'

'What a lovely thing to say.'

'So how about you let me turn you on right now?'

'Ha. I'll let that dreadful pun go for English being your second language.'

'Oi. My English is not so bad.'

Cali laughed. She loved that some of the words Mario did say in English sounded almost Cockney.

'Say that again.'

'What?'

'Oi.'

'Oi, what?'

Cali laughed. 'Oh, it doesn't matter. I just adore your accent.'

'You have a nice place here. You own it you said, didn't you?'

'Yes, my dad made me buy it as an investment a few years ago. Glad I did as there's a good bit of equity in it now.'

'Nice. I deal in property when I get the chance. You must have at least fifty profit in this.'

'More than that now, I reckon. Having a school

nearby always helps.'

'Well, that's good. At least getting divorced hasn't left you at a loss financially.'

'I don't want to talk about my divorce, if you don't mind, Mario, but I'm fine.'

'Of course, *bellissima*, of course.' Mario cupped his hands around her face and kissed her softly on the lips. 'Let's not talk at all.'

Cali had never had sex with two men in one day.

In fact, including Luke, the vet and the handsome officer, her grand total was still only seven.

Until today, that was.

# Chapter Thirty-three

'I am officially no longer Cali Summers, spinster of the parish, but Cali Summers, complete and utter dating slut.'

'OK. I do have to say you are raising my Aphrodite on acid mantle and going all in for Marie Antoinette status.' Annie slurped on her ginger tea and grimaced.

'What's wrong?'

'Just the tea. I thought this might be a bit better than green but, I've got to admit it, I just love caffeine. And I have been good with my walking this week.'

Cali summoned David over, who smiled his wide infectious smile.

'*Ano.* I'm sorry, I mean, yes?'

'David, can you please put my friend out of her misery and bring her your finest pot of English Breakfast Tea?' David smiled. 'And a full bowl of sugar.'

'Of course. And for you?'

'I'm fine with my coffee, thanks. But menus too, please. I feel so bad now, Annie. Mario is sincere. He'd just lost his bloody phone. What if he ever found out about Will? Should I tell him?'

'Of course not. It wasn't like you were being

unfaithful. It's the very early days of a relationship. And I'm not being funny, if Mario had wanted to get another phone abroad and contact you then he could have. I mean, he knows where you work too.'

'He was busy.'

'OK. But just forget it. So … after a second sexual encounter are you saying you now have a …' Annie made inverted comma signs with her fingers, 'boyfriend?'

David put the tea and menus down in front of them and lingered slightly too long.

'Thank you.' Cali smiled at the waiter. 'That's it for now.'

'OK, just say when you're ready to order.'

Turning back to her friend, Cali said, 'I don't know, but we have already planned a third date. Mario says he has come off Tinder, so I guess that's one positive, but I'm gonna try and play it cool and see what happens. Maybe it's all too soon after Jamie, I don't know.'

'I can't actually believe you just said that when your arse of a husband was already having an affair when you were on honeymoon.'

'Ouch.'

'Shit, sorry, Cali, that was harsh. I'm down on men today. Still struggling with Rob. I want everything to be all right and it's not.'

'Oh, darling.'

'I think half of it is me still doubting him. I just need to get a new mindset.'

'Has he given you any other reason to doubt him?'

'Not really. He hasn't stayed out later after

164

football since that one night, but he sometimes goes straight to football from work, which is odd. I asked him about it the other day and he mumbled that he sometimes goes for a drink with Brian first.'

'That's not odd, Annie. I think you're looking into it too much. And you did say Brian was having some issues, so the drink is completely understandable. We have to give men some sort of free rein. Although, saying that, I gave mine a free weight and look what happened!'

'Aw. Bless you. That's the thing – how do you know you can trust a man?'

'You don't, but if you don't then what sort of relationship will you ever have? Trust is the foundation of any relationship, be it man, friend or family.'

'I realise that. My jealousy is like an animal inside sometimes. I think it's because I've been cheated on before. OK. Onwards. From now on it's positive Annie all the way.'

'Good girl! Jealousy and guilt are wasted emotions. I hate to say it, but if someone is going to cheat on you then they will. There is always going to be somebody younger, thinner and prettier than either of us for evermore. You just have to believe in love and trust.'

'Err, yes, thanks for that, Cal.'

'Look at Brad Pitt leaving Jennifer Aniston for Angelina Jolie.'

'That was years ago, and to be fair, even I would leave Rob for Angelina.'

Cali laughed. 'OK, bad example. Anyway, back to reality. Thinking on it, do you mind if we don't have lunch? The house is a complete and utter mess and I need to go food shopping.'

'Of course not. I might go for a wander round the shops while Rob has Keira, cheer myself up a bit.'

'Good plan. Can't believe I'm being so anal and organised, but work is just so bloody busy at the moment that it makes sense to get some meals in the fridge so I don't have to shop after work.'

'Did you not get a temp in?'

'No, Louise came back after three days. She's been really quiet. Which doesn't help when it's silly wedding season and there are lots of panicking brides and mother-of-brides to meet and appease.'

'Ah right. If I were to do it again, I would *so* not want the fuss. Just throw me on a beach with a bunch of close mates, a table of canapés and a bouncy castle.'

'You're mad, and you're not going to have to do it again. Everything is going to be just fine.'

'I bloody hope so. Let's pay up. I can already smell those new shoes.'

Cali laid her head back on the sofa and blew out a large breath. She hated cleaning, but once it was finished she always felt a great sense of satisfaction and karma. She had done her food shopping so had the rest of Saturday and Sunday to relax. Mario had messaged earlier to say that he was working all weekend but would love to see her on Monday evening. He said it would be a real turn on to meet her in the hotel again and she should be ready and waiting, wearing something to surprise. This had thrown her into a double panic. Firstly, whether

Room 102 would be free and secondly, what should she wear? This new dating lark took some effort. With Jamie, a pair of joggers and her cat face fluffy slippers was her usual uniform. But maybe that's why he went off with Dumb Bell, with her small, firm butt and big, soft tits adorned in Lycra. Bitch.

Ping! A new message.

*30 minutes?*

Cali laughed. It really was sod's law. Mario was the full package and looking for a girlfriend. Will was equally as hot and looking for fun. But she had to do right by Mario. He had come off Tinder so she felt that if he was that serious about being exclusive, then she should be too.

*As much as I'd like to be a bad girl for you, handsome officer, I'm sort of seeing someone.*

She wished she hadn't given Will her telephone number and was just messaging through the app. What if he'd sent a rude message when she was with Mario and he'd seen it?

*What a shame and you don't mess about, do you! Well, if things don't work out you have my number ... take good care XX*

Cali shook her head. Men were unbelievable. But she couldn't deny that she was flattered by the attention and when Annie had been Aphrodite on acid she always swore by having one on stage, one in the wings, and one in rehearsals. Thinking about that made her laugh at the memory of the dreadful amateur dramatics rehearsals they'd been to. It was a shame it hadn't worked out in a way as Gerald English was hysterical. Maybe when wedding season calmed down she could go to their pantomime auditions; after fully researching all parts, of course.

Putting a steaming cup of tea down on the coffee table, Cali picked up her phone. OK, time to delete the app, again! It wouldn't hurt to have a little look through first though, would it? Saturday afternoon was always a busy time for suitors trying to secure a date or an encounter of the sexual kind. She altered her preferred age range to 25-50 within a five mile radius. She might as well peruse the whole of her local area, young and old, just in case she had missed out on somebody on her doorstep.

She smiled as she saw David, the waiter from Deedee's, on there. He was on a beach wearing cool swimming trunks and his glasses. Great abs! She had thought he was mid-twenties but he was actually thirty-two. She would love to say something to him when she saw him, but she felt that there should be an unspoken dating code. Imagine if he outed *her* as a Tinder user in the middle of the café! No wonder he seemed to look at her funny, he'd obviously seen her on it too.

She kept flicking through. She knew that nobody would compare to Mario, but it was quite fun having a final look. She faked a retch as she saw Nigel the vet still on there. What a vile man. She laughed at Lewis, struggling with a tiger in his fake Tom Ford shades, and baulked at Roger, with his bushy beard and stomach to match. She took a sip of tea and started swiping again. Then suddenly, with eyes wide, she shouted 'No!'

The photo wasn't recent or face on, but the age was right, as was the small scar above his left eye.

Cali stood up and began pacing around the lounge. Lady P began darting around her cage.

'Cali big tits, Cali big tits.'

'Oh, shut up, Lady P! I need some time to think.'

But Cali's mind was void of thought, just complete disbelief at suddenly coming face to virtual face with her best friend's husband, a.k.a. Brian, 42, Accountant.

# Chapter Thirty-four

Monday morning in the events office at The Bridge Hotel and Louise was looking a distinct green colour.

'Are you OK, Lou?'

'Just feel a bit sick, that's all.' With that, the young brunette jumped up with her hand over her mouth and rushed for the toilet.

Adam pranced in.

'She's hungover again. Marcus thinks I'm bad, but at least I'm a Trojan when it comes to working after a night on the tiles.'

'I don't know what to do. I don't want to get her in trouble but she's not pulling her weight at the moment.'

'Marcus is not stupid. He knows she took time off before and how much work you have to get through.'

'He seems to be very lenient about it all. Maybe I'll have a word with him later.'

'Any fantastic dating news to share with me? Like if the Italian stallion is back in town?'

Just the word 'dating' made Cali feel sick as she thought of the impending moral dilemma with Rob. She didn't feel she could share this with Adam. In fact, she didn't know *who* she could discuss it with.

It was almost like if she did, it was an even bigger betrayal to Annie. But how could she tell her? How could she be the one to rock her world so badly when she was already feeling so down on herself? She hadn't slept properly last night, just tossed and turned with every scenario going through her head. What would she want her best friend to do? If it had been Annie finding out about Jamie and Dumb Bell, would she want her to tell her? Of course she would. Cali had wanted to know every single gory detail when Jamie had said he was leaving her.

Annie had been right in her assumptions, bless her, and how bold of Rob. He knew his wife's best friend was on Tinder, so there was every chance she would see his photo. She tried to rack her brains at every conversation they'd had about her being on the app and in the small hours vaguely remembered him asking what age range she was looking at; she replied saying she would never look over thirty-five. If he'd had any sense he would have blocked her profile so she wouldn't see him. It made it even more distressing that he was being so bloody blatant in his act of betrayal. And using the name of his work colleague, what was that about?

'The excitement to report is that I have come off the app and it is third date night with Mr F1. In fact, shit, he wants to come to 102 tonight, please tell me it's still out of action.'

'No, of course it's not. It's all sorted now. But we are quiet tonight, let me see what there is. Are you sure, though? This is so risky. You'll have to make sure the room is completely spotless when you leave.'

'When did you become so bloody self-righteous, Adam Radcliffe?'

'The day you became an internet dating slut, I think. I feel protective of you and your job and strangely, mine too. I love working here, Cal.'

'So do I, but just one more night of naughtiness won't hurt. And if the shit ever did hit the fan, I would cover for you. Shh now … Oh, Lou, are you OK, honey?'

Louise sat down at her desk nursing a pint of water.

'I feel a bit better now. And I'm not hungover, honest.'

Adam winked at Cali and headed back to reception.

'OK. I'm worried about you, Lou.' Cali got up and pushed the door shut. 'You haven't been yourself lately. I realise you've got some problems at home and it's difficult not to bring them to work. Actually, shut up Cali, what I'm trying to say is … putting work and the fact I'm your manager aside, if you ever need to chat about anything, I'm always here.'

Louise gave a watery smile.

'Thank you. But I'm going to be fine. I realise I've been letting you down a bit and it's not fair.'

'Are you OK to work today or do you need to go home?'

'No, no I'm fine. Why don't I go and get you a coffee, and we'll sit down and go through everything that needs covering this week?'

'A peppermint tea, please, but that sounds like an excellent plan.'

With Louise firing on more cylinders than she had been of late, Cali was pleased at the productive day they'd had. She was also relieved that Room 102 was free. It was so much easier for Mario to hop up the fire escape than walk through the hotel entrance. She was just shutting down her computer when Marcus appeared at the door, looking terrible.

'Don't tell me you're sick too? Louise was rough for most of the day.'

'Not again?'

'Yes, just this morning but by lunchtime she had perked up and managed to stay the day.'

Marcus's face looked even more pained. 'Cali, have you got a minute?'

She checked her watch. She needed to go home and come back again before meeting Mario. 'I've got twenty if that helps.'

He smiled. 'Come to my office, it's more private there.'

All sorts flew through Cali's head as she followed her boss on the short walk to his office. Had she done something wrong? Was he leaving? Was he about to fire Adam and ask her advice? Or worse, had he found out about Room 102?

He ushered her through the heavy mahogany door and shut it behind them.

'How are you, Cali?'

'Fine, thanks. It's been really busy, but I managed to cope without a temp and we caught up on a lot of wedding proposals today.'

'I meant how are you personally after splitting with Jamie? I can't tell you how sad I was when it happened. You seemed such a great couple.'

'Err, I'm doing well now. I mean, I can't lie, it hasn't been easy, but I've been on a few dates and I'm putting myself out there now.'

'Oh, yes, the inevitable dating app for singles of the world.' He managed a slight smile. 'I wanted to say I'm sorry if I've been a bit snappy lately.'

Cali knew she had to help him out. Remembering back to something presenter and DJ Chris Evans had said in one of his books, she asked the ten million dollar question that everyone should ask when someone is floundering. 'Marcus, what's really the matter?'

He put his right hand through his fringe. 'You're a clever girl, Cali, and that's why I'm giving you a pay rise, effective from June. I'm trying to push for two grand.'

'Thanks, Marcus. That is … well … that's amazing. I really appreciate it.'

'No. I appreciate you. You're a joy to work with and, most importantly, I trust you.'

Cali quickly glanced at her watch, then back at him. He was usually so upright, so smart, so good-looking, but tonight he looked slightly broken and his face seemed to have more lines.

'It's Patricia. She's not well.'

'Oh God, nothing serious I hope.' Cali knew how much Marcus adored his wife.

'I'd like to say no, but she's got postnatal depression, quite bad postnatal depression, actually, and it's been a very hard couple of months.'

'I don't know a lot about it.'

'I could actually teach on it given the amount of

research I've done. She feels unhappy most of the time, her libido is non-existent, and she has trouble sleeping. With an eight-month- and a two-year-old you can imagine the stress at home.'

'Poor you. And her, for that matter. Have you got any help for her?'

'Yes, we're doing everything we can, the au pair is … well, she's just amazing, really, and her mum is a Godsend. Cali, I've done the most terrible, terrible thing but I feel I can tell you. Probably because my friends and family would be absolutely horrified and I know you won't judge. Or at least I hope you won't.'

'Go on.' Cali took Marcus's hands over the desk.

'Have you ever seen *Love Actually*?'

'About ten times,' Cali smiled.

'Of course you have. Great film. Anyway, you know the character Alan Rickman plays? His wife is Emma Thompson?'

'Marcus, just spit it out and put both of us out of our misery.'

'He gets involved with someone, but only because she is a complete vixen, and he doesn't really want to because he does love his wife and mother of his children very much. And … I love sex, and going without it for a few months has been hard and it meant absolutely nothing …'

'Marcus, slow down.'

'And she's young and doesn't understand that it was what it was. And now I'm absolutely terrified she will go to Patricia. If she does, the way her self-esteem is at the moment, it will kill her. I love her so much, Cali, and I really don't know what to do.'

'Who else knows about this?'

'Just you and the girl in question.'

'OK, so keep it that way.' Marcus nodded as Cali continued. 'Are you still in touch with the girl?'

He put his head in both hands. 'Every day.'

'Oh, Marcus. Please don't say what I think you're going to say.'

# Chapter Thirty-five

'What are you, Jamie, a man or a bloody mouse? I bet she bloody loves having this control over you.'

'She's not like that, Belle. I know she'll sign and send off the papers as soon as she receives them.'

'Yeah, right. Tell her to hurry up. The sooner we move in together, the sooner we can think about our wedding plans. Plus, I'm getting sick of living with my mother.'

Jamie gulped. 'Wedding plans?'

'Yes, wedding plans, Jamie. Maybe I should check out The Bridge for that reason, that'll shake her up.'

'Don't you dare.'

'And don't you dare stick up for her! You're with me now.'

'Just because I'm with you doesn't mean I don't care about Cali. We were together a long time.'

'Whatever. I'm off to the gym, I'm teaching until ten. By the time I'm home I want some sort of answer concerning a moving in date. *Byeeeeeee*.'

Jamie put his hand to his head and sighed deeply.

# Chapter Thirty-six

Cali had left the hotel door card poking under the door so that when Mario arrived she didn't have to move from her posed if-I-lay-like-this-my-stomach-and-legs-look-thin position on the bed. Her chat with Marcus had gone on a lot longer than she had hoped, so she had literally rushed home, fed Lady P, grabbed a sandwich and turned herself around in less than an hour.

She was aware that the last time they'd been here, Mario had suggested she go on the pill, but after her fanny-humming scare she didn't want to. Safe sex was key and she didn't want to go through the embarrassment of the clinic again. Once they were 'properly' dating they could have the conversation again.

She just wouldn't mention it – she would address it if it came up.

'Wow!' Mario started pulling off his top as he rushed over to the bed and leapt on top of Cali. 'Stockings become you, Señorita Summers.'

'Isn't "Señorita" Spanish?'

Mario laughed. 'I am going to make love to you in a thousand languages.'

'I'm sorry again for being so stroppy last week. I just missed you, that's all.'

'Don't be silly, you weren't to know I'd lost my phone, and you certainly made up for it.' He undid her bra clasp. 'Well, hello. I've missed you two.' He started to lick and tease her already erect nipples.

Cali gasped in pleasure as Mario stroked, caressed, teased and brought her to heights she had never reached with Jamie.

They lay back on the bed, silent apart from their gentle panting. Cali reached for Mario's hand.

'I know you're busy, but maybe next time we can go out for dinner and follow up with dessert at mine?'

'Let's see what my schedule is like first.'

'I'm not being moany, but it would be good to go out and do some other stuff as well as … well, … this.'

'Sure, sure, like I say during the racing season, it is quite mad. However, what I'm going to ask you now might make you happy.'

'Ooh, what?' Cali propped herself up on her elbow and kissed the sexy Italian's nose.

'This may seem a little forward, but I do have a summer break in August and I go to my house in the South of France. I was wondering if maybe you'd like to pop over and see me? A weekend, a week, you choose the dates and I'll work my friends and family around you.'

'Are you being serious?' Cali couldn't control her beaming smile.

'Cali, what did I say about me not playing games? I told you, I think you're beautiful, you're real. Have a think, just let me know. You'll need to fly into Nice if you want to check flight times. If you don't mind getting that, everything else will be on me.'

'I don't need to think. I'm there. I just need to check dates with work. And I just got a decent pay rise so flight costs are no problem.'

Mario kissed her firmly on the lips. 'Yeah! My sweetie is coming to my house. You will love it. It's got a pool, is right on the beach and I have my favourite car in the garage.'

Cali was open-mouthed. 'I'm so excited. Do you mean a Ferrari?'

'Maybe. Maybe not.' Mario laughed as he got off the bed and started getting dressed.

'You've got to go now?' Cali's face dropped.

'I'm sorry. We are packing at the factory for Monaco tonight. I'm going to be away for a week, but I will see you as soon as I'm back. I'll message, I promise.'

'It's OK. I understand and I have so much to look forward to with you.'

'Exactly. I'm so glad I met you, Cali.'

'And me you.' Cali hopped off the bed and pulled her dress on.

After giving Mario a lingering kiss at the door she lay back on the bed and, with thoughts of the perfect holiday flying through her mind, began to grin like a Cheshire Cat.

# Chapter Thirty-seven

'And boom! He shoots and scores again. Quite hot actually. Pretty dumb on the dating scene, by the sound of it. Very trusting and about to get divorced.' Lighting a cigarette, Mario put his feet up on the sofa and took a slurp of his cider.

'How old is she?' Mario's mate grabbed a cigarette from the stray pack on the floor.

'My age.'

'Really? What have I told you about the young ones, don't you go falling for 'er, will ya? Or worse, get her pregnant.'

'Course I bloody won't. Good tits and a great fuck. But it's fine; she's a brunette for a start, and too prissy. She's playing the divorce card, that's why I'm carrying it on. And to be honest, I'm sick of banging mooses.'

'But the mooses are what make us the money.' Mario's friend attempted a smoke ring. 'What car does she drive?'

'Just a Mini, but it's only a year old. She's got a good job, just got a pay rise, deffo reckon she's naïve enough. I turned up the St Tropez card too, so she's hooked.'

'What about yours?'

'She's proper rich, and pig ugly. Fifteen years up

on me too, already divorced, with a grown up son who lives abroad, so perfect. She couldn't believe her luck when I pulled up. Not sure if I'll ever be able to get a hard on, though. Coffee and innuendo over a chocolate muffin was my limit today.'

Mario laughed. 'What name are you using this time? I've gone with Mario Milli. It rolls off the tongue.'

'Ha, like it. Luigi Rossi for me. She loved it.'

'Well, we haven't got long until we have to hand over the cash for the Amsterdam job, so you best get some Viagra down you, mate.'

Billy tutted. 'Grabbing a few grand each shouldn't be hard, I reckon. She may be a fat bitch, but she's well rich. Got a pool and everything. If I give her one in the jacuzzi how she told me she likes it, I reckon we will be able to borrow her Audi when we need it too, so no car hiring required.'

'Billy Flynn, you're a genius. That'll save us a good few quid. Actually, another result is that the hot one works in a hotel. Can shag her there. She always has her handbag handy for pocket money, too.'

'Cameras?'

'She'd already checked 'em. It's in her interest not to get caught! It's easy, mate.'

'Gonna be a breeze this time, then. You should have seen the rock the moose had on her finger today. Must've been at least three carat.'

'Good, well, when you're rolling around in her jacuzzi, just think of England and the stack of cash we're gonna be taking away with us to Barbados very soon.'

'Jacko Wilson, you're a dirty Cockney wanker.'

'Always, my friend, always. Now throw me another fag; it's been a good week's work and it's time for me to do a bit of research.'

Billy interjected. 'Me too. Just in case any of 'em happen to be fans of Formula One, or worse, are starting to learn Italian.'

# Chapter Thirty-eight

Jamie pulled up in the car park outside Cali's flat, turned his engine off and sighed deeply. He didn't realise that having a girlfriend in her twenties would be such hard work. When he had first met Belle he had been sucked in by her beauty. Spending so much time with her at the gym allowed him to get to know her and he was turned on by her ability to motivate him. She had always been so positive, so happy. Lately, however, she had become a bit of a nag, putting the pressure on about moving in with him. Dropping the M word earlier had also thrown him. He wasn't even divorced yet and she already wanted a ring on her finger. If he was totally honest, he didn't feel ready. In fact, if he was *really* honest, he had been missing Cali a lot lately.

Beautiful, gentle, loyal Cali who had loved and trusted him with all her heart. He had been walking around in the night recently, feeling a bit sick at how he had treated her. She wasn't demanding or pushy, her only ask was to start a family with him when they got married. Not an unreasonable request at thirty. It wasn't as if they hadn't had loads of fun already in their relationship. What was wrong with him? What was he frightened of? Belle had given him the buzz and excitement of a new relationship, the bit that lasts for six months if you're lucky.

His dad had talked to him seriously when he had announced the split. His speech had fallen on deaf ears at the time but, thinking on it, he was right.

Wise Sam Summers had told him how great a girl Cali was and that he loved her, but it was Jamie's life and his decision. His killer question for him to consider was 'When you are old and grey and your looks have faded, which one could you see yourself having a laugh with over breakfast every single day?' At this moment, it was Cali.

He looked around the car park. Cali's car wasn't in its space.

Where was she on this summer's night? He used to know her every move, and he suddenly realised that he didn't know what on earth was going on in her life now.

He would text her and if she was going to be back shortly, he would wait. He glanced to the brown envelope on the passenger seat. Inside was a thin piece of white paper that would finally end their deep and colourful connection. He sniffed and coughed, not quite knowing how to cope with the emotion he was feeling. Just as he was about to start a text to Cali, she pulled up beside him in her blue Mini and made a face.

Getting out of her car she pressed the key fob, causing the alarm to go off.

'Bugger! Not sure why but it keeps doing that.'

'Do you want me to take a look?'

'No, no, I'll sort it myself, thanks.' Oh, how Cali had frequently yearned for someone to take away a few of the pressures of everyday life, but she had

Mario now, so soon she would. 'Anyway, what on earth are you doing here? And J, a bit of warning would be nice. I mean, imagine if I had a man with me.'

'I guess you're imagining that at the moment.' Jamie paused. 'Aren't you?'

She suddenly thought to what she had been doing forty minutes ago and couldn't help but smirk.

'So you are seeing someone? You kept that quiet.'

'Maybe. Actually yes, and I really do like him. Why on earth would I come rushing to tell you, anyway?'

'Good, good. That's good, really good.' Jamie felt like his throat was about to close over. He coughed again. 'Name, age, what does he do?'

'Mario, my age, and get this, he's an engineer for Formula One. I'm going on holiday with him. Well, I say holiday, it's to his place in St Tropez.'

'Yeah, right.'

'I am. It's funny, isn't it? Well, maybe you haven't ever felt like it, but I thought I'd never get over you and now ... it's like my life has started again.'

'How long have you known this, err, Mario? He surely isn't English with a poncy name like that.'

'He's a sexy Italian, thank you very much. Do I detect an incy wincy bit of jealousy, Jamie Summers?'

Her flustered ex took a deep breath. Incy wincy? If he stayed any longer he feared a green dragon might actually jump out of his throat and eat his head.

'Of course not. I'm really happy for you, Cal.' He handed the envelope to her. 'I'm actually here to get the final papers signed. The same as these. Wanted to check you'd got them.'

'They hadn't come when I left this morning, but come up if you like. You can take them with you and drop them off at the solicitor's on your way home, if that helps.'

'No, no it's late, Cal, don't worry. I've got an early start tomorrow.'

'It'll take two minutes.'

'No. It's fine. I'm sorry I keep rushing you.'

'Well, if you're sure. I am pretty tired.' She smirked. 'Latin men certainly know how to keep a girl on her toes.' Her new-found inner strength continued. 'Oh, and next time you're passing, don't forget that little table and the glasses from Marcus.'

'Cali big tits, Cali big tits.' Lady P greeted her owner with glee.

'Hello, Lady P. Sorry I've been out so long.' She went to the fridge and fetched her noisy bird an apple piece. 'Here.'

'Big boy J, big boy J.' Cali was sure her wayward bird missed her 'daddy' a little bit, too. Surely she hadn't heard his voice outside? But she had left the top window open a crack, so she might have done.

She made herself a cup of tea and sat on the sofa. Damn, she had forgotten to check her post tray to see if the divorce papers were there. It was strange how time was a healer. Seeing Jamie tonight hadn't phased her. She would have a look tomorrow.

She checked her phone. Mario had messaged something rude and flirty which made her smile. There was also a message from Annie.

*You OK, my lovely? Haven't heard from you for ages.*

'Shit.' Cali took a slurp of tea. Annie hadn't heard from her because she couldn't look her in the eye. How could she possibly tell her best friend that her husband was messing about on a dating site? If her head hadn't been so full of her lovemaking antics with Mario and her want to make Jamie jealous, she could have got her head around it earlier.

In fact, why *hadn't* she talked to Jamie? She talked to him about everything – well, she used to. She felt now that as they were on an equal footing and both seeing someone else it would be OK. It was nearly eleven, too late to phone. In fact, what was she thinking? She and Jamie were over. They couldn't possibly be friends. So sad that for years they had been best friends. How cruel the end of an affair was, not only stripping you of love, but of friendship as well.

Annie and Rob had such a good thing going. She still found it hard to believe that he was cheating on her. But, maybe like her and Jamie, it was the least likely couples who split. A cruel irony.

OK, a plan. She would text Annie now, sleep on it, and then decide the best course of action. If it was her in the same situation, of course she would want to know. It wasn't even worth tackling Rob alone, as what line of defence could he possibly take? She had caught him red-handed.

*All OK. Busy at work and I've just 102'd Mario!*
*Bed now ... to sleep ☺ Promise to catch up properly*
*tom. Hope you're alrite xx*

*Lucky bitch! Let's walk after you finish work, if*
*you can?*

*I fancy that. Love you, mate XX*

Lady P started darting around her cage. 'Shit,
shit, shit, shit.'

'Shit indeed, Lady P, shit indeed.'

# Chapter Thirty-nine

Cali arrived at work with mixed emotions.

She had a spring in her step because of her amazing encounter with Mario the night before, but a heavy heart at having to tell her best friend such terrible news.

Adam bounded into her office and plonked himself down at Louise's desk. 'I hope you put that bedroom back as the chambermaids had left it, you dirty slut.'

'Shh. Of course I did, I'm a pro.'

'Quite clearly.'

'I'll have you know, I am now officially dating. And guess what else?'

'He wrapped you up in spaghetti and started singing Pavarotti?'

Cali couldn't help but laugh. 'OK, maybe I'll ask him that next time. But no, he's only got a bloody place in the South of France and wants me to go and visit him in the summer. All I've got to pay for is the flight.'

'You lucky cow.'

'I know.'

'But isn't it a bit soon? I mean, he hasn't even spent a whole night with you yet? When he finds out you snore like a pig with a mask on he may change his mind.'

'You are so wrong. I don't know, it just feels right for both of us. He's really keen.'

'Well, you seem happy and that's a good thing. I'm pleased for you, Cal, and it's nice to see you smile for a change.'

'How are you, anyway?'

'I'm fine. No romance to mention but the weekend is a-coming. And I haven't been in trouble with Marcus for ages. But he doesn't seem himself lately, so that's probably why.'

'Oh. I hadn't noticed.' Cali realised her loyalties lay in so many directions, but one of her best qualities was loyalty and she didn't intend to change that any day soon.

'He's not in for an hour, so I'll get a coffee and we'll have a proper chat. Miguel can man reception on his own now the morning rush is over. Where's sick tits?'

'If you mean Lou, she's doing a show round until ten. And I'm busy,' she shouted to deaf ears.

Adam reappeared with two steaming coffees, shut the door, and sat down at Lou's desk. His eyes were more full of mischief than usual.

'You'll never guess what.'

'You're going to tell me, whatever it is.'

'Lou's pregnant!'

Cali nearly dropped her coffee.

Adam's eyes widened. 'I know! She told me last night. Of course she said not to tell anyone, but I had to tell you. Possibly the best bit of gossip that has graced the corridors of The Bridge Hotel; well, since you started shagging in 102, anyway.'

Cali raised her eyebrows in mock horror. 'I didn't realise she was seeing anyone?'

'That's the thing, she's not. I know that she casually sees the barman from The Swan, but she didn't cite him as the father.'

'Does she want to keep the baby?'

'I don't know. She was telling me with a large glass of Pinot Grigio in her hand, so she can't be that bothered.'

'How far gone is she? She's such a skinny little thing.'

'All these questions, Cali. I'm a gay bloke, just the fact she's pregnant was enough for me. I didn't want any more of the gory details.'

'OK. Well, thanks for telling me. At least I can be sympathetic when she's sick again. And Adam?'

'Yep.'

'Promise me with all your heart you'll never mention me using 102.' How she wished she hadn't confided in him now. But if it came to the crunch, Marcus didn't really have a moral leg to stand on, and she was sure no guests had seen her. So it was just her reputation at stake.

'As if. It'd be my job on the line, too.' He jumped up. 'Right, best get back to my perch before Miguel throws a hissy fit.' He stopped at the door. 'You couldn't lend us a tenner until tomorrow, could you? I've left my wallet at home and can't do a day without my cigs at this place.'

'Course I can.' Cali smiled, opening her purse.

'Oh.'

'What's up?'

'Sure I had fifteen quid in here last night. Take

the fiver anyway; I don't need the cash today.'

'Thanks, Cal. You're all right, you are.' Adam flicked her hair with his finger.

Cali tutted at him, then started to go through her emails just as Lou arrived back at her desk.

'How did it go?'

'Green Room too big, Red Room too small. Now she thinks she wants something more contemporary than olde worlde.'

'Bloody brides.' Cali smiled.

'I know. Give me a corporate event any day.'

'How're you doing, Lou, feeling better?'

'What do you mean?' Lou looked sheepish as she sat down at her computer.

'Just you had that time off and you were feeling sick last week.'

'I'm fine. But if it's OK with you, I need to leave at four – I have an appointment. I did come in at eight to compensate.'

'Of course.'

'Sorry it's such short notice. I'm really trying to be better with my time.'

'Lou, it's fine, just go. We've got a big team meeting with the Operations Department first thing, so just make sure you're in bright and breezy for that.'

'Oh. I'd forgotten.'

'It's fine. I'll work on what events we've got coming up this afternoon and give you a copy to make sure you're up to speed on everything.'

'Cali, you are officially the perfect manager.'

'I don't know about that.' Cali felt warm at the comment, but she also felt genuine concern for her colleague. Bless the poor girl. She must be in a terrible state, but wasn't showing it. It all made sense now – Marcus had said that whoever it was, he saw them every day. How on earth would he cope if the baby was his? Should she tell him anything? Or just stay out of it? Imagine if Patricia found out that she knew and came storming into the hotel, it would be like something out of a film.

But Marcus couldn't know Louise was pregnant or he would have surely told her when they'd had their heart to heart? And he hadn't actually said it was Louise he had slept with, she had just assumed. Had put two and two together and made five. But he had seemed over-attentive to her lately, the painkiller incident being a prime example.

Who else could it be? Who did Marcus see every day that fitted the criteria? Rosie in Accounts was in her early twenties and pretty, but was just back from maternity leave and was clearly besotted with 'her Aaron'. There were a lot of pretty young waitresses who worked the functions, but most of them were agency staff, and it was common knowledge that Penny in Housekeeping was a lesbian. It had to be Louise. But she would wait and see if Louise said anything. If she was going to have this baby then eventually it would become obvious, unless she decided not to have it, then nobody would ever know.

Whatever the situation, it was a bloody mess and the best thing she could do was keep her mouth shut and support them both when it came to the crunch.

'That was a big sigh.' Marcus poked his head

around the door and smiled. Then, 'You on your own?'

'Yes, Louise had an appointment at four.'

'Ah, right. Do you know where?'

'She didn't say.'

'So, all set for the Ops meeting tomorrow?'

With his obvious change of subject, Cali decided not to push it. Her stressed boss obviously didn't want to talk about his indiscretion. And it certainly wasn't down to her to reveal that he may become a father for the third time!

'Hmm. Dreading the meeting, to be honest. Think I'm all set. I've prepared this.' She waved a ten page, stapled A4 document.

'Do you want me to have a quick look? Sir Ops is on the warpath that we are not giving him correct numbers and there is too much waste, hence loss of profit.'

'If you could, that would be amazing. I'm not ready for a stand-off in the boardroom.'

'Why, what's up?'

'Oh, it's nothing I can easily discuss.'

'Go on, Cali, it's not as if I haven't bared my soul to you this week, is it?' Marcus put his hand on her arm. 'Sit back down, come on. Patricia's mum is at home so I haven't got to rush off tonight.'

'OK, I am going to talk to you hypothetically.'

'OK. I'm ready.' Marcus cocked his head to the side and looked at Cali intently.

She took a deep breath and started. 'Say a good girlfriend of yours was happily married.'

'OK.' Marcus nodded and grimaced.

'Sorry. Can I go on?'

'Of course, you said to me to spit it out, so come on.'

'Well, what if you saw their husband on a dating app? Would you tell the friend and blow her life as she knew it apart? Or would you keep quiet, and hope and pray she never found out that you'd seen it and let the marriage carry on, knowing that she'd already confided in you that she feared that something was wrong?'

'Bloody hell.'

'I know.' Cali ran her hands through her hair.

Marcus looked pained. 'I know what I've done is very, very bad and I just hope and pray I don't get found out. But I also know it was a one-off and will never ever happen again. The guilt would kill me. And if Patricia found out, it would kill us. We have too good a thing going to let one moment of middle-aged stupidity ruin it.'

'Amazingly, I do agree you are best to keep quiet. Us women are unforgiving creatures. After what Jamie did to me, I don't think I'll ever fully trust another man again.' Marcus tapped his fingers on her desk as Cali continued. 'But I can't keep this from her, it's too big and it would kill her if she found out I knew and hadn't told her.'

Marcus tapped again, looked to the ceiling, then in an eureka-type moment, leapt of his seat. 'Honey trap. You honey trap him.'

'And how exactly do you propose I do that?'

# Chapter Forty

Cali's mind was whirring with everything she had discussed with Marcus. It did seem to make sense doing some kind of set-up to see just how far in Rob was with his Tinder treachery. Get all the facts on the table then go to Annie with them in a sensible fashion.

She really had wanted to put off seeing her for another night, but Annie was insistent they meet and she didn't want her to suspect that she had been avoiding her on purpose.

She pulled up at the park gates and turned her engine off. It was a beautiful sunny June evening, perfect for a walk. She checked her phone and laughed.

*30 minutes?*

Men were unbelievable. She had made a point of telling Will she was off the market, but he was still trying to see her. He would be quite frustrated by now, as the message had come in two hours ago and she had been so engrossed with talking to Marcus that she hadn't even seen it. Saying that, he had probably already moved on to Plan B.

*Sorry, just seen this, hope all good with you.*

*Would be better if I was there.*

*I'm just going in the park where we met,*

*actually.*

*Well, have fun and let me know when you want some more...*

Cali replied with a winky face. There was nothing wrong with an innocent bit of flirting and she would never see it through. She messaged Mario a quick *Hello, how are you?*

She was used to his periods of not texting now and knew not to bombard him, and had quickly realised what he had meant when he said his profession was more like a marriage than a career. Because of the stress of it, lots of relationships didn't make the whole racing season.

However, just the excitement of St Tropez looming was enough for her. She knew she had his commitment and when she saw him it was even more special. Thinking of that, she really must look at flights this week and let him know when she was coming, so he could arrange his friends and family around her. She must also try and shift a few more pounds and buy some new outfits. It looked bloody fancy in St Tropez and if she was going to be getting in and out of a Ferrari, she needed to look the part. It all seemed like a wonderful dream and sometimes she had to pinch herself. But no, she had bagged herself a rich, handsome Italian who made her happy. If she was honest, she was a little bit besotted with him. He was the first person she thought of when waking and the last when she went to sleep.

Her daydream was interrupted by Annie tapping on her car window. She was wearing denim shorts and a baggy pink T-shirt.

'Ready, my elusive friend?'

'Born ready. Look at you, with your legs out and everything.'

'It's still warm and they are so bloody white a glare comes off them at the moment.'

Cali got out of the car and breathed out noisily.

'What's wrong with you?' Annie started stretching her calf.

'Knackered, that's all.'

'We don't have to do this if you don't want to.'

Cali gave a little smirk. 'Pub?'

Annie nodded and laughed. 'I thought you'd never ask. Mind you, look at the state of me.'

'You're fine. I don't know why you worry about your weight, your legs look great.'

'Really?'

'Yes, really. Now what shall we do, car-wise?'

'Let's both drive so at least our cars are in one place if we decide to have a drink.'

'Annie Johnson, did you just say *if*?'

The garden of The Feathers was heaving with after-work drinkers.

'I'm not getting as drunk as I did last time we were here.' Annie took a sip of her chilled white wine.

'Nor me. I've got an Ops meeting tomorrow morning and have got to be on the ball.'

'How is work?' Cali was so relieved that Annie had not mentioned her and Rob yet, and she certainly wasn't going to ask. Plan Honey Trap was going to commence tomorrow night and she wanted to keep her head clear from any further judgement before she made the initial contact.

'It's not quite as busy as Louise has started pulling her weight again, but bombshell news of the day is that she's bloody pregnant.'

'No!' Annie nearly spilt her wine. 'She's only a baby herself.'

'She's twenty, and I'm not sure I can tell you the next bit…'

'Cali, I wish you wouldn't do that, you know we have secrets to the grave. If you say "Don't tell" then I don't, never have.'

Cali's guilt nearly came up as a bit of sick in her mouth. Annie was right; she could trust her with her life. But she had to have all the facts concerning Rob, she just had to. It was too big a deal to just blurt out something that would break her best friend's heart in two.

'I'm sorry, get ready 'cos it's a biggy. I reckon it might be Marcus's.'

'Shit the bed!'

'Tell me about it.' Cali took a slurp of wine. 'Anyway, I don't want to talk about it tonight. It's too much to deal with, especially as Marcus confided in me that he had slept with someone and didn't say who. Just said that it was someone he saw every day. It has to be Lou.'

'Oh, Cal, what a nightmare. Bloody men, eh? Rob's been great lately, actually, I got flowers tonight. Keira is at Angie's as it's football practice, but he went off at the normal time and promised that he wouldn't be late.'

Cali breathed an internal sigh of relief.

'Actually, if we have another then I'm sure he'll

pick us up.'

'Sod it, let's get a bottle then.'

'Cal, what about your important meeting?'

'Oh, it's fine. I'm prepared and I'll make Marcus do the talking. I haven't seen you for ages. I've got so much to tell you.'

The wine flowed and just as Annie was taking in the recent antics of Room 102, she suddenly ducked.

'Oh God.'

'What?'

'Only half the bloody Bramley Am Dram Society coming outside with Gerald "I've still got popper indents in my arse" English at the helm.'

Cali laughed. 'I'm ready for them after a few wines. But don't worry, they won't see us in this corner. Anyway, we didn't do anything wrong.'

'Ooh, the handsome ginger is there.' Annie threw her arm out dramatically. 'Handsome ginger, handsome ginger, wherefore art thou, handsome ginger?'

Cali laughed. They hadn't been this drunk on a school night since the am dram debacle.

On taking another large gulp of wine, Annie's mood suddenly changed. She bit her lip and reached for Cali's hand.

'We haven't had sex for three weeks, you know.'

'That's not so bad when you're married and have a toddler, is it?'

'Cali, it is. It had gone down to twice a month but this is ridiculous. I feel like he doesn't fancy me any more. I feel ugly. Why doesn't he want me?' She began to cry.

'Oh, Annie.' And then suddenly without warning or compassion, the Pinot Grigio took over Cali's mouth. 'Maybe I should tell you.'

'Tell me what?'

Cali put both her hands over her face as if it would make the pain for Annie less to bear. She fired out the words at great speed. 'I saw Rob on Tinder.'

If there had been a back to her bench, Annie would have slumped into it.

'You what?'

'I wanted to wait and see if it was a horrible mistake, find out more before I told you, but I can't keep something so huge from you.'

'Let me see.' She grabbed Cali's phone then immediately sent it flying back towards her. 'I don't know how to work it. Show me, show me now.'

At that moment, Gerald 'I've still got popper marks in my arse' English sauntered across. 'I thought that was young Juliet sitting there, how are you, ladies? Can't tempt you along to be extras? We need some more trees,' he guffawed.

'Err, no. I couldn't deal with all that fame and publicity.' Cali noticed that Annie was about to internally combust opposite her.

'Lovely evening though, eh?'

'Yes, super,' Cali smiled, assuming his posh accent.

'Do come and join us if you fancy, we don't bite, unless you ask.' He guffawed again. 'It's Jilly's birthday, so we're filling the old girl up with pink fizz and innuendo. Be rude not to.'

'Maybe in a bit,' Cali said politely as he went

back to the group.

Annie was bright red and agitated. 'For fuck's sake, Cal, get the app open and show me, please.'

'Are you sure?'

'Of course I'm bloody sure.' Cali had taken a photo of the profile in case she couldn't find it again. On seeing Brian, 42, Accountant, Annie exploded. 'I'm ringing the bastard now!'

'No, no, Annie. I know you're angry but let's be clever about this. If you ring him then he has the chance to hang up and think of a good story before you actually see him. You're drunk too, oh God; I wish I hadn't told you now.'

Annie poured herself another large glass of wine and downed it.

'Message him. Message him from the app.'

'No, listen to me, it doesn't work like that. We need think carefully about this. We need to set up a dummy profile and then message him. Try and lure him that way, see exactly what his game is.'

'Blimey, you weren't wrong about the Calista Summers Detective Agency.'

'Jamie was telling me that some of his mates who have girlfriends go on there just to sext. It may be totally innocent.'

'Great, that makes it all right then.' A funny little noise came from Annie's throat as she tried to gain her composure. 'OK. OK, but I don't think I will be able to contain my anger tonight.'

Cali looked at her friend. The memory of Jamie confessing about Miss Dumb Bell suddenly came rushing back. 'I feel your pain, Annie, I really do, but this is what's going to happen. You are going to ring Angie and ask her the massive favour of having Kiera sleep at hers for the night. You can tell her what she needs to take back with her and Keira will be fine. We'll think of a good excuse, like you have to take Rob to A&E as he's got to have an X-ray after falling at football.'

'OK, OK.' Annie nodded. 'And that's not such a lie because he could well be in A&E after I finish with him.'

'I'll text Rob and say you have crashed out and are in no fit state to look after Keira, and you don't want to wait until late to get her settled with him.'

Annie blew her nose. 'You are right. Revenge is a dish best served cold and all that.'

'We don't even know what he's done yet, if anything.'

'Cali, just being on there is enough for me to want to kill him.'

At that moment, rotund Jilly bounced from her table to theirs with a bottle of bubbly in her hand. 'Come on, girls, join the party.'

'No, no, I really don't think so, thanks.' Cali felt like she was in some sort of bizarre farce.

'I do.' Annie stood up and staggered slightly.

'Annie, come on, we need to get home.'

But it was too late: her scorned friend was on a mission. She plonked herself down at the am dram table and looked to the handsome ginger. He smiled sweetly. 'Hello.'

'Hello, handsome ginger.'

Cali cringed. 'She's really drunk, sorry.'

'It's fine. I'm George.' He held out his hand.

'Hiya.'

'And I'm Annie, George.'

'Are you OK?'

Her eyes were red from crying.

'Terrible bloody hay fever.'

'Ah. Poor you. Glass of fizz?'

'Why not?'

She raised her glass to Jilly and started singing 'Happy Birthday' really loudly.

George and Cali's eyes met and they both made a face.

'Annie, one glass and we are going.'

'How boring are you?' Cali had forgotten how belligerent Annie got after too much wine. When they were younger they always used to laugh that she had a limit before the White Wine Witch came out. It was as if a completely new character took over her body. Sober, she would just about manage to comment on another man, but now, here she was, on the verge of trying to seduce one!

'It's back to Jilly's for a pool party in a minute, anyway.'

'Pool party?' Cali asked George quietly.

'Yes, she lives up Bramwell Hill. Massive house, loaded.'

'Nice. OK, could you just keep an eye on Annie for me, please? I need to go to the loo.'

In taking control and looking out for Annie, Cali had sobered up considerably. By the time she arrived back at the table, Cali had called Angie to sort babysitting duties and texted Rob with a blatant lie.

'Come on, Annie, we've got to go. I've got to be clear headed for my meeting tomorrow.'

'Fuck your meeting.'

'Yes, darling girl, don't be so churlish, fuck your meeting.' Jilly stood up, staggered slightly and shouted at the top of her voice, 'We've a party to go to.'

Annie started dancing on the bench. 'Party, party, we're going to a party.'

Gerald English was now fully involved. 'Yes! Tell your husbands you are busy, ladies, we are going to get wet.' He let out a resounding burp. 'If you have husbands, that is?'

Annie discreetly slipped her wedding ring into her handbag.

'Err, I have a boyfriend,' Cali announced, short of holding her head in her hands.

'Yeah, and he's hot. Italian and works in Formula One,' Annie announced.

'Snap, and how bizarre!' Jilly shouted. 'I've bagged myself the same combination of marvellousness, too.'

# Chapter Forty-one

Cali woke to a pounding headache, her 'Like a Virgin' alarm (thanks, Annie!) five minutes in and her doorbell ringing incessantly.

'Wakey, wakey, wakey.' Lady P began hurtling around her cage.

Needle-eyed and hair everywhere, Cali struggled out of bed and pressed the intercom button.

It was a frantic Annie who greeted her in the doorway. 'Oh my God, Cal. Oh my God. I woke up next to him. Fuck, fuck.'

'Fuckety, fuck, fuck, fuck.'

'Shut up, Lady P,' they shouted together.

'Who, who did you wake up next to?'

'Well, it wouldn't be Gerald fucking English, would it?'

'Annie, you were so drunk nothing would surprise me this morning.'

'George. I woke up next to Ginger George. Why the hell didn't you bring me home with you?'

'Annie I tried, but I've never seen you so drunk or belligerent. George and I even tried carrying you to the taxi, but you struggled so hard we gave up in the end. He promised me he would look after you and I trusted him to.'

Annie put her hand over her mouth and rushed to

the toilet. She came back looking green and desperate. 'What's the time? I need to go get Keira.'

'Just gone seven. Have you spoken to Rob yet? Here.' Cali handed her distressed friend a pint of water. 'And you really shouldn't be driving.'

'No. He's been texting already. I don't know what we said to him. It made sense to get my car from the pub before coming here; I can give you a lift to yours, then.'

'It's fine. I sorted everything last night, but ring Angie now, then we can work out what you say to Rob.'

'What if I had sex with him, Cal? It makes me just as bad as him, worse, as we don't know what he's done yet.'

'Did you have knickers on when you woke up?'

'Yes.'

'And, did it ... err ... feel like you'd had sex or did you spot a condom anywhere?'

'I don't know, I rushed out so fast. Left everyone sleeping. Oh, Cali. I can't bear it.' Annie started to cry. 'And what if we did do it and didn't use a condom! I've been off the pill since April as it wasn't helping with my weight.'

Cali squeezed her friend's hand. 'You would know, I'm sure. This all feels like the end of the world now, but as my dad says, there is a solution to everything except death.'

'If you hadn't seen Rob on Tinder, none of this would have bloody happened.'

'I know. I regret telling you last night.'

'No, it's good that you did. I would do the same for you. But what a bloody mess. I'm as bad as him

214

now, but I still want to start the honey trap proceedings on the bastard.'

'Are you sure, Annie? You need a bloody early night by the look of you.'

'I'm certain. He's going to the driving range with his dad tonight – well, he says he is anyway – so you must come over.'

'OK, OK. Let's get the practicalities sorted first. We can worry about everything else later.'

Ping! A WhatsApp message appeared on Cali's phone. Mario.

'Typical.' Cali shook her head.

'What is it?'

'Mario. He's got some free time at lunch and wants to meet, and I've got that bloody Ops meeting all morning.'

'You're so lucky, Cali. Decent man on the horizon, great holiday to look forward to. Get him to sneak into 102 during work hours, how hot would that be?'

Just the thought made Cali bite her lip.

'Don't give me ideas like that. Sort out Keira and tell Rob all is OK. I'll hop in the shower and if you can get me to my car by eight-fifteen that would be so helpful.'

'Porn star, porn star, porn star,' Lady P piped up as Annie went to the kitchen and downed another pint of cold water.

# Chapter Forty-two

'How rough do you look? Good night, was it?'

Cali just put her hand up to Adam as she walked past him on reception, only to be greeted by Louise being sick into the bin under her desk.

The girl stood up, tears running down her face. Cali realised that despite her early sobering up last night, she was still pretty hungover and had to stop herself gagging. Without another word, she handed Louise a tissue from the box on her desk, opened the window and dropped the bin outside.

'Go get yourself sorted out, then put that into the big wheelie bin in the refuse area.'

Louise nodded. 'I'm so sorry, Cal, I couldn't hold it.'

'Go, go. I've got to get ready for this meeting and I'm not feeling too great myself.'

Adam appeared in the doorway.

'Jesus, what's that stench? It smells like sick.'

'It is sick, Adam.'

'Ha! You could have cleaned your teeth before you came in.'

'Really not in the mood today, Adam,'

'Ooh, hark at you. What's wrong? Pav dumped you?'

'Quite the contrary. Is 102 free today?'

'Tonight, you mean?'

'No, lunchtime?'

'Cali, you are a fox and I love you.'

She laughed. 'Sorry I'm so moody. I'm hungover and had a very late night with Annie.'

'It's fine, you miserable bitch. Let me go and check if your sex hole is free, even if just for you to cheer the fuck up.'

Marcus rushed past Cali's office then doubled back and popped his head in.

'All set?'

Cali nodded. 'As ready as I'll ever be, but I'd love it if you could talk through the figures bit if that's OK.'

'Of course it is. Where's Lou going? I was going to see if she could bring some cakes up from the kitchen.'

'Err, in the loo, I think.'

'All OK with her?'

'Um, she's feeling a bit sick.'

'Again?'

Wanting too much information, Cali thought. He must surely be getting the hint by now that she was up the duff.

'All OK with *you*, Marcus?'

'Yes, yes. I've decided to remove the cause, so to speak.'

'What?'

'I've got to run, chat to you later.'

Shit, surely he wasn't going to fire Louise? Selfishly, she *so* wasn't ready to train anyone up and if the poor girl was going to have this baby alone, she would need every penny she could get.

Still deep in thought, she got her paperwork for the meeting together. Hopefully he would have the decency to chat it through with her before he did anything.

Adam came in, fresh from having a cigarette.

'You smell like an ashtray.'

'Thanks. Beats the sick, I guess. Anyway, 102 is being cleaned as we speak so you can go at it with Pav anytime you please. Here.' He handed her the room key and headed back to his post. 'I've yet to see him in the flesh, by the way. I might have to redivert the CCTV.'

Smiling, Cali quickly ran up to 102, left the room key poking out enough for Mario to reach it, and then headed for the boardroom.

# Chapter Forty-three

Thankful that the meeting had gone quicker than expected and without too many incidents, Cali sped back to her office. Wanting to look and smell fresh for her Italian lover, she grabbed her wet wipes and make-up bag from the top drawer of her desk. If she was quick, she'd have time to get ready in the room and be lying on the bed waiting for his arrival, rather than the other way around as planned. It seemed an age since she had seen him and she was starting to feel turned on at just the thought; especially as it would be that extra bit dangerous during work hours.

Just as Cali was heading out, Louise was heading in with a huge cheese baguette in one hand and a glass of milk in the other.

'Milk?' Cali made a face.

'Yes, I seem to be craving it lately. Actually, Cali, do you have a minute?'

'I ... err ...' Cali checked her watch. Mario would literally be arriving in five, and had said he had just forty minutes to see her. 'I'm meeting someone for lunch, can it wait until afterwards?'

Cali saw the young girl's pained expression. She shut the office door and sat back at her desk.

'Come on then, quickly.'

'I'm pregnant, Cali, and I don't know what to do.' Louise burst into tears.

Ping! *Here, hard and horny, now's where my English rose? You know I haven't got all day.*

'I have to say, I was beginning to wonder. You did seem to be sick rather a lot in the mornings.'

'That's why I wanted to tell you, Cali. Woman to woman. I knew you'd understand.' Louise sniffed loudly.

Cali was desperate to ask outright if Marcus was the father, but she would wait for the girl to offer up more information.

'My mum and dad don't know. They would go mad. I've told a few friends. I haven't even told the father.'

'Are you going to?'

'This is why I wanted to talk to you.'

Bingo! Confirmation it had to be Marcus's – why would she have said that?

Ping! *Shall I start without you? Xx*

'Lou, I'm so, so sorry but that was my friend again. I really must go, they haven't got a long lunch break. I promise we can talk from two.'

'OK, that's fine.'

'Have you been to your doctor?'

'Yes, of course. They gave me the details for the abortion clinic.'

'Oh, Lou.'

Cali squeezed her colleague on the shoulder. 'Promise to talk more when I'm done. I'd normally stay as this is so important, but...'

'Go, Cali, go, it's fine. I'm actually off this afternoon, remember? Just going to stuff food down

222

then I'm going to stay with a friend for the weekend.'

'OK, as long as you're sure.'

'I'm sure. Nothing will have changed on Monday, well, apart from me releasing some of my burden by sharing it with you.'

Mario lay back on the bed, gently stroking his ever hardening cock. He was getting quite agitated that Cali was late; especially as today there was work to be done. He was also, however, quite aroused at the fact that she wasn't towing the line like she had done in the past. In the real world, he preferred blondes, but he also loved a feisty woman.

She poked her head around the door and smiled.

'Woah, that's what I call a greeting.'

Mario pulled her towards him and put his hand up her skirt. He felt for her stocking tops. 'Nice work, Señorita Summers.' He squeezed her right buttock tightly, causing her to gasp.

'Oi, you.'

'No time for talking. Guess you did as you were told and got yourself on the pill.'

'No, sorry. I, err …'

'Tut, tut, you are a naughty girl.' Mario span Cali around and pushed her face down on the bed. He pulled a condom from his pocket, roughly pulled her skirt up to her hips, and without an ounce of foreplay, inserted into her and started to fuck her hard and fast. She put her head in the pillow so as not to scream out loud. She actually found this mixture of rough sex and naughty talk a real turn on. Mario came in his usual quiet fashion.

'I missed my little English cupcake.'

'What are you like?'

Mario got up. 'Need to quickly shower, if that's OK. I've got to go to work this afternoon.'

'Sure, sure. I best take a cold one too, my face is so red!'

Once dressed, Mario sat on the stool facing out from the dressing table. He checked his watch.

'The most important thing was not to make love to you today, it was to see if you have found some flights to run by me for St Tropez. Makes sense to get them booked early.'

'I've got as far as booking the first week of August off work, but haven't checked prices yet, sorry. Lots going on.'

'Aw, sweetie, no need to be sorry. It's good in a way. Was going to say that we have such a fantastic relationship with the airline we use for the team that I can get you a much better deal.'

'You're just too good, Mario Milli, too good.'

'I know, the perfect boyfriend,' he grinned.

Cali felt even warmer at the word. It had been a long time coming to get over Jamie and be in the arms of somebody so gorgeous and it felt good, so very good.

'So, is the first week of August OK with you?'

'Si, si, that's perfect. My brothers are coming out the last two weeks, so I can spend some quality time with them too, *cara mia*.'

'*Cara mia*?'

'Ah, sorry, sorry, it means my darling.'

'I feel like I'm dreaming.'

'You haven't seen anything yet. Wait until I have

224

time to spoil you properly. Now all I need to get these flights sorted are your credit card details.'

Cali reached for her purse and wrote down the details on hotel notepaper. 'Don't book first class; I only have a six thousand pound credit limit left on this one.'

Mario laughed. 'Six grand, you say. I will be getting my first class *chica* first class seats for economy prices. Trust me.'

# Chapter Forty-four

It has been a lot easier than Cali had thought to set up the honey trap mission. Marcus had lent her a spare work phone and had a SIM card he said he didn't use any more. Sandra, an old friend of Annie's who was an ex-beauty queen and now lived up north, was in on the plan. She had kindly agreed that they could use her photo as long as they deleted it immediately once they had snared him.

Cali had immediately swiped her liking of Rob and now here they were, both sat at Annie's kitchen table, barely able to breathe as they waited for the recognisable ping of a message coming in.

After literally two minutes, there was a ping.

'Oh my God, oh my God, what's he saying, Cal? I feel too sick to look.'

Cali took a deep breath. 'Oh.'

'You can't just say "oh".' Annie was frantic. '"Oh" what?'

'It's not him, it's a text from someone called Ivana. "If you don't bloody reply then I'm coming to the hotel Saturday. I know you will be there."'

'That's odd. This was an old SIM in Marcus's drawer. The phone must have belonged to someone who worked there. Mind you, that's a bit sinister. Do you think I should reply?'

'No, no, you haven't got time. Whoever it is will get the message that the number is not in use and it's nothing to do with us.'

'I've just thought of something else, though, Annie – if Rob *is* on the driving range then he may not reply for hours.'

Annie got up to fill the kettle and sighed. Before she had even turned on the tap, another ping.

Cali put her hand on her forehead and grimaced. 'Oh, Annie, I feel for you.'

'What's the bastard saying?'

Cali groaned. 'I don't want to tell you.'

'For fuck's sake, Cali, just say it.'

'That he can't believe he is so lucky to have matched with such a beautiful woman.'

Cali started typing.

'What are you saying back?' Annie began pacing around the kitchen.

'I just put, "Aw, how sweet. Let's hope I live up to your expectations".'

'Oh, God. I can't bear this. I feel like outing him right now, but no, ask him how long he has been on the app.'

'OK.' Cali dutifully did as her friend asked, then grimaced again at the reply.

'What? What? Tell me what the bastard is saying.'

'He just said a couple of months, but he's been waiting for someone just like me/her. Agh, this is so confusing.'

'A couple of bloody months. I think I'm going to be sick, but I guess it all makes sense now.'

Another ping!

Annie grabbed the phone off Cali. She was shaking with anger. 'Right, I've had enough of this mucking about. Let's see where he has been conducting his dirty little secret meetings, shall we?' Annie read the immediate reply with a pained expression.

'Tell me,' Cali said softly.

'He certainly doesn't waste any time. He's already suggesting The Malsters Arms in Moulton tomorrow night at eight. I can't believe it.'

'What do you mean you can't believe it?'

'Football practice night and exact time?' Annie bit her lip and began to cry. 'The Malsters, that's where you met that Luke, isn't it?'

Cali nodded. 'I'm sorry, Annie, I really am.'

'Can you babysit?'

'No, of course I can't, I'm coming with you.'

'Yes, of course, I won't be able to concentrate enough to drive.' Annie pulled off some kitchen roll and blew her nose. 'Goodness knows how I'm going to keep it in until then.'

'You don't have to put yourself through this, Annie, you could just speak to him when he gets in.'

'No, just to see the look of horror on his face when he sees us. I want him to suffer, and suffer badly. I mean, where is he tonight? His dad did come in and see Keira before they left and has driven him, maybe he's in on it too, some sort of father/son set up.'

'Annie, don't go crazy on me.'

'Crazy! My husband, whom I thought I could trust with my life is being unfaithful with God knows how many women and you say to not go crazy?!'

Cali put her arm on her friend's. 'OK, I'm sorry. That was a stupid thing to say. Do you want to come to mine tonight? You can sleep in the spare room.'

'No, no, I can't disturb the little one again, bless her. It's fine. I'll be asleep when he gets in and pretend to be when he leaves. I want to see exactly what he takes with him when he goes off with his football bag. God! I can't get my head around it, Cal. It's too much to bear.'

'I know, darling. But we'll get through this, and I'll be here for you like you were for me when it all kicked off with Jamie. I love you, mate.'

'Love you too.' Annie wiped her eyes with the back of her hand. 'OK, I've got a bottle to warm and a little one to get to sleep. You go, Cal. I want to make sure I'm in bed early and asleep.'

'Are you sure?'

Annie nodded.

'What time does he usually leave for football?'

'I'll call you as soon as he does.'

'OK.' Cali gave her friend a massive hug, and as memories of Jamie's infidelity came flooding back, she shut the front door behind her and got into her car with a heavy heart.

# Chapter Forty-five

The brown envelope that had dropped onto the door mat first thing that morning had cemented Jamie's decision that he would work from home today. Bella was training most of the day so he would get some peace from her, too. She had taken it on herself to stay a couple of days a week as she was getting sick of living at home. He knew she wouldn't be able to stick to staying there permanently until the divorce was finalised.

Not being bothered to actually read all of the small print, he opened his laptop and searched for the words 'Decree Nisi'. He took a swig of coffee and read slowly down the screen.

*When the court gives you your decree nisi you have to wait six weeks and one day before you can make your divorce final. This is to allow time for anyone who objects to the divorce to tell the court why they object.*

*After six weeks and one day you can apply for the decree absolute.*

*This means your divorce is completed and you are no longer married to your partner.*

As a lump began to form in his throat, he rattled

around in his desk drawer for the memory stick he had kept with the wedding photos on. Tears began to prick his eyes. Six weeks, that was nothing. Then it would be final.

As he scrolled through them, he realised he hadn't even noticed how naturally beautiful his new wife had looked that day. How the dress she had agonised for hours choosing accentuated her perfect curves and made her look like the woman she was. So engrossed in what he was doing, he hadn't noticed that Bella had been standing quietly behind him for five minutes and had watched his every move and heard his every sniff.

She softly walked down the stairs, shouting back up when she reached half way.

'Hey, I forgot my weights. You OK?'

'Yeah, yeah. Decided to work from home.' He quickly snapped his laptop shut.

'Fab, fab. I'll see you around five then.' Bella noticed the little side table from the spare room and a box of glasses next to the front door and shouted up the stairs again. 'What are you doing with this stuff by the front door?'

'Er, Cali wanted them back. I said I'd drop them in at some point. Will give me a chance to check she's signed the papers.'

Bella's face fell. 'OK, darling. Good plan. See you later.'

Her words fell on deaf ears as Jamie reopened his laptop and photo file.

# Chapter Forty-six

Jack Wilson lit a cigarette and opened his laptop. Billy would be back from seeing Jacuzzi Jilly in a minute and soon it would be time to buy what they needed to with the acquired credit card numbers and get out of the area.

Dedcot sure was full of rich pickings so it was a shame they couldn't stay a bit longer, but such was the nature of their work. Find 'em, fuck 'em, fuck 'em over, then fuck off.

But then Cali had come along.

Jack heard the key in the door. Billy ran in and grabbed a cigarette from the pack on the table. He was sweating profusely. 'Jacko, mate. Her son only came back from Spain to visit a day early. I literally had to jump the fucking huge back fence and run all way to the train station. The air con wasn't even working on the train, so I'm fucking roasting.'

'You made sure you left nothing in the house or car?'

'Of course I did. It's fine; it was just a bit of a close call, that's all. Right, come on, let's buy these watches and get 'em sold. Big Al is expecting the drug money by next Friday so he can do the deal. We can book our flights with the cash I nicked last week. Then we just need to get rid of the laptop and phones and be long gone. Did you get any cash off the hotel one?'

Jack coughed. 'You're right; it's a scorcher today, ain't it?' He didn't dare tell his mate that he was finding it hard to con Cali. He had slipped the money he had stolen from her back in her handbag the last time he had seen her.

'Jacko, it's not me you wanna be worried about, it's Big Al. He'll kick the living shit out of us if we don't deliver. You've got her card details, right?'

'Yeah, yeah, course I 'ave.'

'OK, come on then, let's do this thing.' Billy started dancing around the scruffy living room singing, 'Oh, we're going to Barbados.'

# Chapter Forty-seven

Cali was rushing in to work when she heard a message ping on her phone in her handbag. After all the trauma with Annie the night before, she had had trouble going to sleep and, when she did finally drop off, she had dreamt of Jamie marrying Dumb Bell at the very hotel she was walking into.

She quickly glanced at her phone. There were two messages. A *30 minutes?* from Will from last night which she had missed. She had to smile. The other text was from Mario, which was just a big *X*. She was wondering if he had booked her flights yet, when she saw Adam leaning out of her office door screaming for her to come quickly.

He pulled her in and just started pointing wildly at the floor while shouting 'Louise, Louise, bleeding.' And with that, like a drunk giraffe, he crashed to the floor and was immediately out for the count.

Cali dialled 999 and rushed to Lou, who was on the floor behind her chair. 'It's OK, Lou, I'm here.' She grabbed the young girl's hand tightly and wiped the fringe from her clammy forehead.

'It hurts, Cali. I'm frightened I might die.'

'Ssh, ssh, you are not going to die, darling.' Cali, conscious of how much blood Lou was losing, rang

999 again. 'How long to The Bridge Hotel?'

Louise's eyes started to roll back. Cali took a massive breath and tried not to panic. At that moment, Marcus came in, looked at both Adam and Lou on the floor, and began gabbling with shock.

'Oh my God. What the …? I can't stay with her like that. And what's happened to him?' Adam was still out for the count.

'Are you a man or a mouse? It might be your baby she's bloody losing!' Cali shouted. 'Go get me some towels from housekeeping.'

'It's Marcus's baby?' Adam suddenly sat up, looking at the wall so as not to face any more blood.

'Well, it was an immaculate conception if it was,' Marcus replied before running to do as he was told.

Before he had a chance to come back, the air ambulance had arrived and a doctor quickly started looking after Louise.

Cali walked to the side of the stretcher as they carried Louise outside. 'It's not his,' she said weakly to Cali, then started to cry. 'I mean, it wasn't.'

Cali began to well up too. 'Shall I call your mum?'

Louise nodded.

# Chapter Forty-eight

Annie wanted to look amazing when she met with her philandering husband in The Malsters, make him realise exactly what he would be missing from here on in. The plan was that she would be at least five minutes late and would just breeze into the pub with Cali and act really surprised that he was there. She would tell him that they had decided to go out as her mum had surprised her with a visit that day and said she would babysit.

He would obviously go into panic mode; thinking that ex-beauty queen Sandra was about to arrive, and that he would have to deal with his feisty mother-in-law once he had been busted.

At exactly five past eight, Cali and Annie arrived at the pub. Cali parked in a dark corner and turned off the engine. Her mind suddenly turned to the last time she had been here.

How far she had come since that first sexual encounter with Luke. Her run of internet dating had only had two sharks in it, and it was always going to be a gamble to meet Mr Right, using a dating app or not. She hadn't regretted her dalliances with Luke or Will and Mario … well, Mario was just a dreamboat.

'I feel sick.' Annie put her hand to her mouth.

'Here.' Cali handed her friend a water bottle from the back seat. 'You don't have to put yourself though this.'

Annie sighed. 'I do. Let's just do it. Can you see his car anywhere?'

'No, but there is an overflow car park around the back.'

'OK. I'm just doing this. Do you want to wait here?'

'No, I'll be right behind you. I want to see his face, too.'

'Look at the app again. Where did he say he was sitting?'

'Table fifteen, adjacent to the bar. Here. Take the pay as you go phone in case you can't find him. I'll be right behind you.'

Annie went to push the pub door, then stopped. She knew her life was about to change dramatically, but she had to do this. She had to know why her husband had taken this road, why she had made him this unhappy to choose other women over her.

She took a deep breath and went in. There was a quiz going on and the pub was heaving. Without looking around, she headed straight to the bar and ordered a glass of wine.

'Who shot JR?' The voice of the quizmaster boomed from his microphone.

With a shaky hand and wishing she was carrying a gun, Annie drained her glass, then asked the bartender where table fifteen was. In a complete daze, she made her way through the crowd and towards her fate.

'Brian? What are you doing here?'

'Err … Annie? I haven't you seen you for ages. How are you?'

'I've been better.' She laughed nervously. 'Just out for a drink with a friend of mine. You on your own?'

'Err … yes.'

'Rob at the bar, is he?'

'Um … no, he's at football practice I think. I'm … waiting for a friend.'

Brian was far geekier than Annie remembered, and she could see he had broken out in a sweat.

'So what time is your friend coming, Brian?' Annie tried to keep her voice level. Maybe they were double dating. Cali pitched up beside her.

'Cali, this is Brian, Rob's friend from work. He's waiting for somebody.'

'Oh, hi, Brian. Who you waiting for – Rob?'

Brian stood up. 'No. Like I said to Annie, I'm waiting for a friend. A lady friend.'

'Ah, right.' Cali was as bemused as Annie. 'We were just going to the loo, have fun.'

'Were we?' Annie screwed up her face at Cali.

'Yes.'

Cali dragged her friend and positioned themselves behind a pillar. 'Give me the phone. Trust me.' She started typing.

*I'm so sorry Brian, but I met somebody last night I actually quite like and I forgot to tell you so tonight is off.*

They watched Brian check his phone and saw his face drop. He started typing.

Then ping!

*Never mind, Sandra. I wish you good luck.*

And with that he finished his drink and walked despondently out of the pub.

As he reached his car, Cali shouted out to him.

'Brian, wait a minute.' He tried to scramble in but Cali stood in front of him. She put the profile photo of Rob in his face. 'Does Rob know about this?'

'I have to go.' He managed to sit in his car and started the engine. Seeing the torn look on Annie's face, he wound down his window.

'I'm so sorry, Annie. Rob knows I'm on Tinder but he doesn't know I've used his picture. He's far better-looking than me, so I figured I had half a chance of getting some girls to meet me at least, then they could get to know me for me. It hasn't worked. They don't seem to like the fact I use a fake picture.'

'That surprises me.' Annie's sarcastic tone cut through him.

'Rob has been amazing, telling me what to say to get the dates. He'll kill me when he knows I've used his photo. I'm rubbish with women, rubbish. I look at you and Rob and see how happy you are and that's what I want. He loves you so much. He worships you and that little girl, you know. You are his world. He would never hurt you.'

Annie put her hand on Brian's arm. 'I propose a deal but you have to promise to stick to it.'

Cali had no idea what was going to come out of her friend's mouth.

'Go on.' Brian looked nervous.

'You change your profile immediately. Be yourself. From what I know of you, you are a lovely man. You look great now, your hair is much better shorter and you scrub up well in those new clothes.'

'Really?'

'Yes. Now have some confidence in yourself. To think any woman would want to carry on seeing you after putting up a fake profile is madness. Shows you are not honest from the start.'

'I guess. I'm confused about this deal, Annie.'

'It's quite simple. You take down the photo and be yourself and I won't mention a thing to him.'

'And my part of the deal?'

'You never mention that you saw me or Cali here tonight.'

'That's it?'

'That's it, Brian. I'll have a think about any women who would be a good date for you.'

'You'd do that for me, after all this?'

'Everyone deserves happiness, Brian. Go and have a nice evening.'


Cali and Annie got in the car, looked at each other, and started laughing.

'Don't you dare think I'd be a good match for Brian.'

'What, you mean you don't like nose hair?'

They laughed again.

'I'm a silly neurotic cow, aren't I?'

'Of course you're not. But thinking on it, if you had just spoken to Rob in the first place, you could have saved yourself a lot of heartache.'

'I disagree. He doesn't need to know that I doubted him in the first place and have bad feelings towards his mate, who is fundamentally a good guy.'

'Do you trust Brian not to say anything?'

'Yes, I do. From now on, trust is the word, my lovely friend. Thanks for helping me out of another scrape.'

'Always here for you, you know that.'

'And me, you.' Annie gave Cali a kiss on the cheek as she started the engine.

'Not quite Cagney and Lacey tonight, though.'

Annie laughed. 'We'd have given Laurel and Hardy a run for their money, though.'

# Chapter Forty-nine

David smiled his best smile at the two attractive twenty-year-olds who took a window seat in Deedee's.

'Can I get you some drinks, ladies?'

'Um. A mango smoothie for me, please.' Bella checked her phone quickly before sitting down. Her skin-tight pink leggings caused more than one glance from customers.

'And for you?' The handsome waiter addressed her smartly-dressed brunette friend with a slight cock of his head.

'Coffee, please.' She turned to her companion. 'Are we eating?'

'You know eating's cheating.'

Bella's friend laughed. 'Just the drinks, please.' David made his way back to the counter. 'Why the urgency to meet me, Bell?'

'I caught him bloody snivelling over wedding photos of his poisonous wife, that's why.'

'What!'

'I know. He got the decree nisi through this morning.'

'What does that mean?'

'Basically, in six weeks and a day, if there is no objection then the divorce is final and you can apply

243

for a decree absolute, which means the marriage is officially over.'

'No one is going to object, surely?'

'No, but he can still change his mind.'

'Don't be silly. He loves you, Bell. Why on earth would he have given up on her if he didn't? He was with her for years. And from what you tell me, she is not exactly a catch. Look at you, you are so fit.'

'Then why was he crying?'

'Maybe it was hay fever or he was just having a final reminisce. I mean, divorce is massive.'

'I really think he's getting cold feet. I've told him I'm not moving in properly until the divorce is finalised. Maybe I need to get in there straight away so I can get wind of what's happening.'

'No, you mustn't. This gives him more reason to stall if you were pushing him to do it for that reason.'

'Oh yeah. I didn't think of that.'

David put their drinks down in front of them without a word of thank yous and with a sly smile. Bella's friend carried on. 'I know exactly what to do.'

'Go on.' Bella sucked through her straw.

'Tell him you're pregnant.'

'But I don't want a baby for years, and I think that's half the attraction. He wasn't ready for a family with her, which caused him to have the wobble.'

'It doesn't matter. He seems a decent bloke. He will do the right thing. And then in six weeks and one day you will be on the way to being Mrs Bella … what's his surname?'

'Summers.'

'Mrs Bella Summers. What a lovely name.'

'I'm not sure. I want to make the most of spending his money as a couple without a little rugrag in tow.'

'Bella, you won't really be pregnant.'

'Ha, oh yeah.'

'Once you have the ring on your finger – which you will as you can say you don't want to be a fat bride – then you're laughing.'

'And when he finds out I'm not pregnant?'

'Pretend you've lost the baby.'

'That's cruel.'

'It's life, Bell, it happens. Do you want to marry him or not?'

'Yes. I do think I love him. I'm twenty-four and haven't felt like this about anyone before, and he does treat me like a princess.'

'Well, you know what you have to do.'

Bella finished her drink and got David's attention for the bill.

'He's cute,' Bella whispered to her friend.

'You can't say that when you are a married woman.'

'I can look, can't I? OK, I'd better get home. I've got lies to tell and a wedding to plan.'

# Chapter Fifty

'Wow.' Rob lay back on the pillow and grabbed Annie round the waist. 'Where did that come from, you delectable wife of mine.'

'I just love you.'

'And me, you.' Rob stretched both his arms behind him. 'You look great, by the way. Not that I wouldn't love you if you were a whale in a wig.'

'Really?'

'OK, maybe it would have to be a blonde wig.'

Annie laughed and pretended to hit him. 'Bless Keira staying asleep too, she knew we needed some *lurrrving*.'

'Talking of loving, poor Brian, he got stood up last night.'

'Oh no.'

'Yep, he's been on the same app as Cali, not been having much luck. I feel I can tell you as I did say she'd had a few nightmares. Thought it might make him feel a bit better.'

'Oh right.' Annie bit her lip, loving her husband just a little bit more.

'Yeah, you know when we had that weekend away, he was literally sending me messages women were sending him and asking what I should reply. It got ridiculous. I can see why you got annoyed. I had sworn to secrecy that I wouldn't tell you because he was embarrassed. You know how bloody loyal I am, I felt I had to honour my word. I should have just told you when I knew it was beginning to annoy you. But there you go. I'm a man and I don't always get what women think.'

'What sort of things were they saying?'

'I can't remember now, but one had a foot fetish and one wanted to bring her friend along.'

'Surprised you weren't tempted to join.' Annie slid off the bed and headed to the toilet.

'Annie Johnson, you come back here.'

'What?'

He pulled her back on the bed and held her tightly. Looking at her, he kissed her lightly on the lips. 'I love you. I love everything about you. Your kind heart, your beautiful face, the way you bite your lip when you're unsure of something, the way you rub your nose when you have an itch. I even quite like your wonky little toe. And not forgetting what a brilliant mother you are to our little girl. I will never, ever hurt you, Annie. I mean that.'

'You, husband, have been reading too many Mills & Boon novels.' She kissed him on the forehead and pulled away. A shower was needed to wash away her guilt.

Perish the thought if he ever found out about her spending the night in a bed with another man. One she didn't know if she had slept with or not!

# Chapter Fifty-one

'All right, you bitch, feel like we haven't had a chat for ages.' Adam pranced into Cali's office and sat on Lou's desk, his bright red hair in a Mohican style.

'Did your hairdresser die on the job?'

'Cheeky mare. This is all the rage, I'll have you know.'

'So has it attracted the man of your dreams?'

'No, but this bloody scar on my face from when I fell has. Evidently, I look more butch than camp. I had a headache for days after that.'

'Bless you, Ads, what a day and what a fall. On a serious note, are you all right?'

'Apart from being emotionally scarred at seeing a woman have a period like Niagara Falls, then yes.'

'You're so wrong.'

'I know, but that's why you love me. Anyway, poor Lou. And what was that about it being Marcus's baby? I mean, really?'

The door of the office flew open.

'Really what?'

'Nothing, Marcus. Adam and I were just discussing Saturday's wedding. We're both happy to work it.'

'Yep.' Adam stood up. 'Even I get out of bed for

double time and the chance to see hot boys in tails.'

'Good, good, even paying you double will still save on agency staff fees.'

'What the hell am I doing not working for an agency, then?'

'The staff get less than you, Adam. The agency as a company gets a big cut. I don't actually know why I'm explaining this to you as you're not going anywhere.'

'Was that a backhanded compliment?'

Marcus winked at the lad and smiled.

'Any news on Lou, Cali?'

'Actually, her mum messaged me this morning. She's still in the London hospital. The poor love had to have a blood transfusion and now has some sort of infection. Will be in for another week at least.'

'Bless her, that's dreadful. Send my good wishes and make sure she gets full sick pay.'

'I will, might pop and see her when I can. She thanked us all for the flowers, by the way.'

'I can't believe I missed an air ambulance crew.' Adam checked his hair in the reflection of his phone. 'Why not a normal ambulance, anyway?'

'They were in the area and deemed it serious enough to get her to hospital quickly. She had lost a lot of blood.'

'Ew. Vile.' Adam stuck his tongue out and made a face.

'Can you manage without her?' Marcus put his arm on Cali's shoulder.

'Yes, I'm fine. Rosie from Accounts is helping out at times with the contracts when I need her.'

'Good, good. And Adam?'

'Yes, boss.'

'Get that bloody thing cut off your head. This is The Bridge Hotel, not a hostel for wannabe punk rockers.' With that, Marcus disappeared as quickly as he arrived.

'Before I go back to my perch, do you need me to book you and Pav into 102 soon?' Adam smirked.

'Am I still seeing him, you mean?'

'Well, you aren't grizzling and haven't got a face like a smacked arse so I guess you still are.'

Cali laughed. 'Very much so. He took my card details to book my flights for St Tropez.'

'You gave your card details to a stranger? Cali, wise up.'

'He's not a stranger, he's my boyfriend. He gets cheap flights through work. I've got a calendar in the kitchen counting down the days until I go.'

'Well, that's all very sweet, but be careful, eh?'

'Shut up, Adam, it's fine. Right, I must get on. This event is in two days and I need to make sure Operations have got everything they need.'

Once alone, Cali looked to her email, then to her phone. Mario hadn't replied to the text she had sent yesterday afternoon, not even with a kiss. And when she tried to call him, the phone had gone straight to voicemail. She wasn't sure where he was in the world; he had said leading up to his holiday period he was mad busy and to be patient with him. She suddenly realised that she didn't have any photos of him to fawn over. Well, apart from the grainy one he had originally put on Tinder that she had saved in her photo library. When she had gone to take a photo of him he had always laughed, saying it wasn't his best side. She must get him to send her a new one of him, and of his place in St Tropez.

Ping! A text. *Amazing sex with Rob last night, back on track. Love him. I was a silly bitch but do need to talk to you. PS. We've set up a double date, the Johnsons plus you and Brian.*

Cali shook her head then smiled when the next one came in. *Just joking about Brian! But I do need to talk to you.*

# Chapter Fifty-two

'Callerina, Callerina, Callerina, bitch.'

'Evening, Lady P. I know I haven't been here much lately but that's not a very nice greeting.'

'Porn star, porn star, porn star.'

'If only at the moment,' Cali said, checking her phone to see if she had any messages from Mario – still nothing.

She got some fish fingers out of the freezer and put the kettle on. She thickly buttered white bread and dolloped on some ketchup. She had been so busy lately, it was lovely to have an evening in. She had it all planned; easy dinner, a long bath, a naughty piece of cheesecake from the local deli and back to back episodes of *Sex and the City*. Complete bliss.

She scoffed down her sandwich without an ounce of guilt. Healthy eating could start again tomorrow and, anyway, she had a good few weeks before her trip to France.

Just as she was pouring her favourite bubble bath under a steaming stream of hot water, a text pinged in.

*Hey, Cal. Thought I'd text first so I didn't get told off for taking your parking space. Got that table and glasses for you. J xx*

Hold the kisses, was what she wanted to say. Instead she chose, *Oh thanks, J. I'm chilling after a hard week, so would rather if it could wait.*

*Out with lover boy, are you?* Cali ignored as her now seemingly persistent ex continued. *When can I come, then?*

*I really don't know.*

*Look, Cal, I really need to speak to you.*

Cali shook her head. Why was it that when she had wanted him to be banging her door down, he never did? He probably only wanted to nag her about the divorce papers, which were sat on the side ready for her to sign and get posted.

In six weeks and one day she would be a single woman. In six weeks and two days, she would be on her way to St Tropez with the sexiest man she had ever met in her life. It couldn't have been timed better.

She sighed. In the past, when Jamie said he really needed to speak to her about something, he did. He was outspoken, but he definitely wasn't a drama queen. Maybe something serious had happened to his parents or he'd lost his job. But then, he could surely speak to the Dumb Bell about that.

She suddenly felt weird that she was still thinking about his life like this. But they had been an item for so long it was nigh on impossible not to break the chain. But that was what she had to do. If there was any way she could move forward with her new relationship with Mario, she had to be strong. Once the divorce papers were signed then there was no reason they needed to see each other again. She shut her eyes and imagined that scenario. Opening them again very quickly, she texted back.

*OK, come now, but I literally have half an hour.*
*On way xx*

'Big boy J, Big boy J.'

For the first time ever, the errant bird didn't raise a smile from Jamie as he walked through the door.

'Hey.' Cali pulled her sumptuous new purple dressing gown around her tightly. 'Thanks for bringing these. She put the box of glasses and table in the kitchen, out of the way. 'Drink?'

'Do you have any whisky?'

Shit, Cali knew this was serious. 'No, but I have the dregs of some ouzo if that'll help?'

Jamie nodded. Worse than serious! Just picking up the ouzo bottle caused a memory of Nigel and his disgusting chode to come flooding back and Cali felt quite sick.

She looked to her husband, as if taking in his good looks would erase the memory of that awful night.

It felt weird thinking that despite everything, he *was* still her husband. For the next six weeks and one day, at least. The husband whom, despite making the biggest mistake of 'their' lives, was still deep down a kind, loving, considerate, generous and fun human being.

Jamie drained his glass then sat next to Cali on the sofa. He looked intently at her. Ready for her bath and stripped bare of any cosmetics, she looked so pretty, so innocent. Unlike Bella, who couldn't even walk to the corner shop to get a pint of milk without putting on a full face.

'Love you, Callerina.' Lady P cocked her head and put it through the bars of her cage. Jamie coughed, sniffed, then stood up to stroke their pet, his back to her.

'Do you want me to take her?' His voice was strained.

'Actually, I've grown to love her. She's good company.'

Jamie turned back around to face her. He managed a smile. 'Like someone else I used to know.'

Closing her eyes and taking a deep breath, Cali forced herself to think of Mario's handsome face and the way she felt when she was with him. Her future was not in this room with her. It had left the day she was made to feel worse than second best.

She got up off the sofa and walked through to the kitchen to put the kettle on. 'So why the sudden urgency to come round? What's up?'

He followed her and propped himself against the kitchen worktop.

'There's no easy way to tell you this, Cal.'

'You can't shock me any more. Jamie, you did that months ago. And if you're telling me you are getting married, then so be it. I hope you'll both be very happy.'

'We're not getting married, Cali.' Jamie looked to the ceiling, his expression pained. 'Bella's pregnant. I ... err ... I didn't want you to hear it from anybody else.'

Lady P spoke for her, 'Bella, Bella, Bella, Bella, BITCH!'

Cali remained mute.

'I'm sorry, Cali, but I had to tell you.'

'Well, you've told me now.'

'I wanted you to know, it was in no way planned. It's a shock for me, too.'

Cali got a mug out of the cupboard and slammed it down on the table.

'Do you know what, Jamie? I don't care. I don't care about you, your stupid little bimbo of a girlfriend or the fake little family unit you're about to create. Just go.'

Jamie's voice cracked. 'I know how much you wanted a baby, Cali, I'm so sorry.'

'Sorry!' Cali's face suddenly contorted in anger. 'Sorry! Sorry is a word. A futile five letter word as insignificant as the way I feel about you now. Leave.'

Jamie turned around as he reached the doorway. 'I miss you, Cali. I miss you more than I ever thought a human being could possibly miss someone else.'

'You should have thought about that before you decided to stick your dick in a fake tan with tits.'

'I've made a massive mistake.'

'Yes, you have. And now you're going to have to live with the consequences for the rest of your life.'

'I still love you, Cali.'

Cali's bottom lip started to wobble.

'Go, just go. Now.'

'But…'

Cali didn't realise she had the capacity to scream quite so loudly. She grabbed the TV remote from the coffee table and launched it at him. 'GO!'

Lady P flew around her cage, not knowing quite what to do. When she eventually settled, she chitter-chattered as if trying to comfort her inconsolable owner.

Cali sat with her head back on the sofa and her eyes closed. She actually could even have coped with the marriage bit. But a baby? A baby meant the blonde one would be in his life for ever and ever.

She was surprised at the extent of her own emotions. 'The heart never lies', her mum used to say to her as a teenager. But she didn't want him back. She wanted Mario. Where was he, though? Still no answer to her messages.

'Tits and arse, tits and arse,' Lady P piped up.

Cali got up to retrieve the TV remote from the floor and in doing so, noticed that Jamie hadn't shut the door behind him properly. As she was about to shut it, she noticed a glint of something behind the door.

She peered out to the hallway and leaning against the communal banister was a mirror.

But not just any old mirror. It was an exact replica of the one she had bought with Jamie at Portobello Market.

# Chapter Fifty-three

Cali managed a weak smile as she walked towards Annie, who was waiting for her at the main park gate.

The beautiful summer's evening had encouraged joggers, cyclists and families to make the most of the summer's last rays.

'Busy here tonight, but *so* glad to be getting some me time. Keira has done nothing but screech all day at the delights of the paddling pool.' Annie took in Cali's strained expression. 'You look bloody awful, Cal, are you all right?'

'Start walking and I'll start talking.'

'That sounds serious. I'm actually demented, too. But you first.'

'Bella's pregnant.'

'Shit.'

'I know that I'm with Mario now.' Cali let out a huge sigh. 'Even though I haven't heard from him for bloody ages. But honestly, I can't believe how I reacted. It's floored me.'

'I'm not surprised. What a complete bastard. Of course you're going to be gutted. You're still technically married and the reason he got cold feet was because he didn't want a baby. I'm so sorry.'

'I was so angry I threw the TV remote at him.'

'I think I would have thrown the television. What are you going to do?'

'What can I do? I think I'll get the divorce papers sent and forget I ever knew him. Saying that, I looked for them this morning and can't find them. I was sure I'd left them on the table by the front door.'

'I don't know what to say to you to make you feel better.'

They walked in silence for a few minutes, Cali biting her lip, Annie clasping her friend's hand lightly.

Cali broke the silence. 'It's just so sad.'

'Yes, it is, but at least you have the holiday to look forward to.'

'I guess. If the elusive Mr Milli bothers to return my calls.'

'He will. He's just busy. Rob was trying to explain the schedule to me the other day. Loads of travelling, so I'm sure he is telling the truth.'

'Yeah. I know. It's just frustrating. And him being away gives me time to think too much. Maybe I wasn't completely over Jamie, so in a way her being pregnant is a positive. There's no going back now. The divorce would have been an end to a chapter, but this signifies the end of the story and maybe I needed that.'

The friends sat down against a big oak tree and put their faces to the sun.

'Anyway, sorry, Annie, enough about me. Tell me why you are demented.'

'I'm not sure I can tell you.'

'Don't be silly. It can't be as bad as my news.'

Annie's voice cracked. 'It is. I'm pregnant.'

'Shit the bed, Sherlock. Really?'

'Really.'

'I bet Rob is delighted.'

'I haven't told him yet.'

'Oh Annie, you are going to have the baby, aren't you? I know motherhood isn't your favourite thing, but...'

'Cali, you're not thinking ... what if it's bloody George's?' Annie's voice raised an octave.

'God, I'd forgotten about that. It won't be, it can't be.'

'I really don't think you slept with him,' Cali soothed.

'I could have slept with Gerald English; I was so pissed. I've got to meet up with George and just ask him. It's the only way.'

'And what if he says yes?'

'Then I don't know.'

'I thought you were so adamant you didn't want another baby that you were taking two pills at a time?'

'Ha! No, I came off it as I thought it was making me fat.'

'Annie, how many times, you are not fat!'

'The thing is, I don't have George's number.'

'You're lucky because I do. I took it as I was so worried about leaving you that night.'

'Well done. This is going to be so embarrassing.'

'Yes, but for your own peace of mind you have to do it. Or I deliver the baby with you at home with black hair dye on hand in case a little ginger bubba pops out!'

They both laughed.

'Fuck me, Annie. At least our lives aren't boring.'

'I am craving boring. But if it doesn't kill you and all that. Now, give me that number.'

# Chapter Fifty-four

Cali popped her head around Marcus's office door. 'You look nice.'

'Thanks, Marcus, I brush up all right when I need to.'

'I really appreciate you helping out today, but it does makes sense for you to oversee a wedding you've arranged from start to finish.'

'I agree. And gay weddings are usually such fun, so it was a no brainer. There's a drag act tonight. If we can keep Adam under control it will be a laugh.'

'Ooh. I may have to stay until the end. The wife always said I'd look good in a full face of make-up.'

'On a serious note, how are things at home? How's Patricia doing?'

'Much better, actually. She said she might pop her head in later and see how things are going.'

'That's nice.' Cali rooted around in her handbag. 'Actually, while I remember, here's your phone.' She noticed the random message was still on the screen. 'Oh yes. I meant to tell you a weird message came through from someone called Ivana. Guessed it was someone who used to work here.'

She could see the colour drain from Marcus's face. 'Read it to me.'

'"If you don't bloody reply to me then I'm

coming to the hotel Saturday. I know you will be there.'"

'When was this?'

'Last Thursday.'

'Fuck!'

'What is it?'

'I guess I'd better tell you. You know I told you I'd done something wrong and that it was close to home?'

Cali pushed the door shut with her foot. 'Yes. So who is this Ivana?'

'Our au pair. Well, our ex-au pair. I also told you I was going to sort the situation, didn't I?' Cali nodded. It all made sense now. Close to home, literally. 'I thought I had by paying her off. I hoped she would go back to Poland with the money and just keep quiet. But obviously not. This was the phone we used to communicate with when … you know.'

'Oh Marcus.'

'I know. I know. I told Patricia I had caught her stealing and had fired her. She was fine with it.'

'So what do we do if she shows up?'

'Well, she can't bump into Patricia. Money obviously wasn't her motive. I think the silly girl thinks she loves me. Why on earth was I so stupid?'

'We all mistakes, Marcus. Not always big whoppers like this. But don't worry, there's always a solution. This is what we are going to do.'

Marcus ran his hand through his hair. His expression was pained. 'Go on.'

'Well, we'll talk to Security Bill, he's on CCTV today. I take it you have a photo of her?'

'On her CV, which I think I kept in my office drawer. After I paid her off I realised she had been working here illegally. I should have checked but my cock had already taken over my sanity.' He frantically started going through a messy array of papers in his desk.

'OK.' Cali was assertive. 'Tell Bill he can walkie talkie one of us if he sees her so we can be ready. Just tell him that the people having the wedding on no account want this woman present. He doesn't have to know why.'

'Good idea.'

'If she does get spotted, we can deal with the consequences when they arise.'

The wedding day flew by in a blur of 'Hello, darling's', beautiful outfits, pink champagne and much laughter. Adam was in his element, charming a lot of the younger male guests and older ladies alike.

As the band warmed up for the evening's entertainment, Marcus eventually caught up with Cali.

'Great event, Cali. Everyone seems more than happy. And it must have been an idle threat from …' Before he had a chance to finish his sentence, Bill's strong Northern accent resounded through Marcus's walkie talkie. 'Boss, just seen that girl pull up in a taxi at the front. What should I do?'

Cali grimaced as Marcus responded. 'Shit, OK, thanks, Bill. If she asks for me say I'm not here, and on no account let her in.' At that moment his mobile rang. 'Oh, hi, love.' His face was pained as he mouthed to Cali, 'Patricia.'

'Fuck,' Cali said quietly.

'No, darling, that's fine. Can you give me thirty, just sorting the evening entertainment … You're going to be here in fifteen minutes … OK. Yes. Great, really great that your mum could babysit. I must go, see you soon. Come round the back by the fire escape entrance, it will be easier to get in.'

Adam suddenly appeared. Marcus put his arm on the lad's shoulder. 'Hurrah for you being somewhere when I need you for once. Now, where are the drag artists getting ready?'

'In the back toilets by the Red Room, why?'

'OK, good. Take me there. Cali, go to the front. Are you sure you can handle it?'

'Of course I can, now run!'

# Chapter Fifty-five

George had said that he would briefly meet Annie in the pub after this week's am dram rehearsal. He smiled sweetly as he saw her approach him at the bar. She was relieved that Jilly, Gerald English and a couple of the other thespians were sitting in the corner of the garden and would not need to hear what she had to say.

'Drink?'

Annie laughed. 'Never again.'

'You weren't that bad, Annie … Actually, I take that back, you were.' It was George's turn to laugh. 'Cute with it, though.'

'You don't have to sugar-coat it. I behaved appallingly.'

George looked to her wedding ring. 'I see congratulations are in order. That was quick.'

'Shit.' Annie put her hand to her head. 'What on earth must you think of me? I promise it was so out of character. I'd just had some bad news, that's all.'

'Hey, it's fine. I saw you slip your wedding ring into your bag.'

Annie cringed. 'This is so embarrassing, but the reason I'm here is to say sorry for my behaviour. And also … well, did we …?'

'Have sex?'

Annie screwed her face up in horror. Her 'Yes' came out in a squeaky fashion.

'Firstly, I don't tend to make a habit of sleeping with married women and, secondly, I'm not really into necrophilia.'

'Oh God.' Annie was filled with both relief and remorse.

'I'm a gentleman, Annie, you were out for the count. I had said to Cali I would look after you and that's what I did. There were no other beds free, so I got you some water, turned my back when you stripped off, put you on your side in case you were sick and then I kept to my side of the bed. All I can say is you were lucky you didn't pick Gerald as your target.'

'He's gay though, isn't he?'

'Gay? Gerald? Ha, no. But he is the campest straight man I've ever met in my life.'

'Such a relief.'

'Hey, I'm not that bad.' Annie dug him in the ribs.

'I'm joking. I'd better go. I can't face the others. Thankfully I can put this behind me now and carry on a settled life with my hubby.'

'It's all good. Nobody even knew you stayed, they were all so trashed, so don't worry. This can be our little secret.'

Annie kissed George on the cheek.

'Thanks for being such a gent.'

At that moment, Jilly chose to come to the bar. She was red-eyed and sniffing.

'A treble gin, barman, with one squirt of tonic.' Her posh voice boomed across the pub dramatically.

268

'What on earth is the matter, Jilly?' George put a reassuring arm on her chubby one.

Not wanting to miss the reveal, Annie bent down to tie an imaginary shoelace.

'It's the Formula One Italian, he's fleeced me. Said he was taking me to St Tropez, but my credit card limit has been maxed and now he's disappeared without a trace.' She began to sob loudly, causing everyone at the bar to stare. 'If my son catches up with him he said he'll kill him, as will I.'

Annie's heart began to pound. She stood up. 'I think you should show us a photo of him, so that we can all be alert and help you find him.'

'You are so right, dear.' Not even remembering who Annie was, Jilly scrolled through her photos.

Snapping the grainy photo with her own phone, Annie said a quick goodbye and exited stage left.

# Chapter Fifty-six

Patricia fell about laughing when she saw her husband appear at the back entrance of the hotel in a blue sequinned dress, six inch stilettos, blonde wig and full make-up.

'Now that really is job commitment. Hilarious. I told you you'd look hot as a woman.'

Marcus laughed. 'The guys in the act were so taken with me they said I could keep the outfit in case we have a similar theme. Anyway, my darling, sorry this is short and sweet but I've booked a cab. We are going back home for me to change, then we are going out for dinner.'

He whisked his wife out to the waiting cab that Adam had organised. On noticing Cali in deep conversation with Ivana at the main entrance, he grabbed his wife and, making sure he completely covered her face with his red feather boa, threw her backwards and kissed her passionately.

# Chapter Fifty-seven

'Oh hi, Marcus. Or should we be calling you Maria now?' Adam shook his head. 'Please somebody shoot me if I ever have to resort to some misplaced fantasy like that.' The lad had clearly missed the point.

Cali laughed. 'I have to say, blue really is your colour.'

'OK, that's enough, everybody.' Marcus winked at Cali. 'Have you got a minute to catch up on figures in my office?'

Cali dutifully followed her boss.

'I'm so sorry I left you to deal with my mess like that, but there was no way Patricia could have seen her.'

'All in the day of a hectic Events Manager, it's fine.'

'So, what happened?'

'It was easier than I thought. All I had to say was that you had found reason to believe that she was working here illegally and that my dad worked for immigration. If she went quietly and never made contact with the Clarke family ever again, no more would ever be said about the matter.'

'Genius.'

'I know, I'm brilliant,' Cali grinned.

'It's a big lesson for me. I feel so guilty now Patricia is back to her old self. I don't know what got into me. It will never happen again.'

'Make sure it doesn't. You've got a lovely family, and imagine if Patricia had found out. One moment of madness could have ruined your life and everybody else's.'

'I know, I know. I've been a complete fool. Every time I wake up I feel such guilt. Sometimes I think I should just confess.'

'I'm all for honesty but in this instance I see no point. The trust would be gone; your relationship would be destroyed, just for you to feel better about what you'd done.'

'I'm going to arrange a family holiday at a villa in Portugal. Get us all back on track.'

'Now that's a great idea.'

As Cali stood to leave, a text pinged in. She reached for her phone. Seeing it was Mario made her smile, then on reading the words *I'm so sorry*, her smile immediately turned upside down.

'You OK?'

'I'm not sure.' Cali felt slightly dazed. 'It's fine. Catch up later, Marcus.'

'Actually, Cal, I was going to say to take the rest of the day off. I owe you, and the weather is beautiful. We can catch up on everything tomorrow.'

'Are you sure?'

'Of course. You said you were thinking of popping to see Louise after work, you can do it now.'

Cali walked outside into the bright sunshine and

immediately called Mario. It didn't even go to his usual voicemail, just cut off after one ring. She tried again and got the same. When she checked to see if he was on WhatsApp, the screen was blank.

What was 'I'm so sorry' supposed to mean? If it was his way of dumping her after being so close and with a holiday planned, then that was unthinkable.

Annie was working and not answering either so to keep herself from going mad, Cali hopped on the train to London.

The sun was shining when she arrived at the hospital where Louise was staying. She picked up a colourful mixed bouquet from a street flower seller outside, then went to Reception to enquire where Ward Eight was.

Enjoying the feeling of freedom that a mid-week day off brought, she sauntered along the corridor to find her recovering colleague.

All of a sudden there was a commotion as hospital staff and paramedics pushed a stretcher at speed towards her. One of them caught her bag as they sped by, causing the contents to fly all over the sterile corridor.

Shocked, she steadied herself, then looked ahead to catch a glimpse of the poor man on the stretcher.

Despite struggling to breathe with an oxygen mask and looking like he had gone ten rounds with Mike Tyson, she was sure that under all that blood and bruising, it was none other than the very handsome, very elusive Mario Milli.

# Chapter Fifty-eight

Rob was fully engrossed in a film when Annie got home, Keira sleeping soundly on his lap. She smiled at the people she loved most in the whole world, leaned over the back of the sofa and kissed her husband on the forehead.

'Hey, sexy.'

'Hey. You all right? I see missy is OK.'

'Yep, all good. I was going to put her up to bed but she seemed so comfy.'

'Cali all right?' She felt bad that she had lied to him but he must never know about her drunken indiscretion. The easiest thing to tell him was that she was meeting her friend for a quick drink. And especially now she knew her only crime had been getting very drunk, he never need know anything more about the matter.

'She is at the moment.'

'What's that supposed to mean?'

'Oh, Rob. I left my card behind the bar by mistake, so Cali had left and I went back in and overheard something awful.'

'Go on.'

'Well, you know she's seeing the Italian, Formula One guy, the one she's supposed to be going on holiday with?'

277

'Yep.' With one eye on the TV screen, he gasped as somebody was shot. 'Sorry, go on.'

'I overheard this woman saying she'd been fleeced by a guy and it was exactly the same story. Italian, Formula One, St Tropez, the lot.'

'What do you mean, fleeced?'

'He used her credit card without her knowing and Cali told me that this guy Mario had taken her card details to book a flight, too. I got all nosey and involved and now have a photo of the guy. The thing is, I only saw Mario's photo once so I don't even know if it's him.'

'It's too much of a coincidence not to be, surely?'

'That's what I think.'

'You are going to tell her, right?'

'I have to. Poor Cali, she's just found out Jamie's new woman is pregnant, too.'

'Bloody hell. Bless that girl. When is she going to have some luck?'

'I know, I know.'

'All those bloody secrets and lies.' Rob placed Keira gently on the sofa next to him and turned off the TV. 'Talking of secrets and lies, have you got something you need to tell me?'

Annie went hot, then cold, then tingly, then felt sick. 'Um, what do you mean?'

'Follow me.' He got up and walked to the kitchen. 'I emptied the bin earlier and saw this in the bag.' He held up a pregnancy test box with a glint in his eye.

'So, are you? When exactly were you going to tell me?'

Annie laughed with relief. Suddenly being pregnant and not busted for spending a night with another man seemed like a magical thing.

'I was actually going to tell you tonight. I went to the doctor's earlier to get the ball rolling. And, yes, Keira is going to have a little brother or sister.'

Rob kissed his wife on the lips and swung her around. 'That, my darling, is the best news ever!'

'Isn't it.' She kissed him back.

'Are you sure you're OK? I'm not stupid, Annie, I know you find it hard sometimes, but I'll make sure I help as much as I can. We can get someone in to help. It will make us a proper family. Do you know roundabout when you're due?'

'Spring next year, so at least no cold, dark nights when I'm feeding. Quite the textbook family, eh? 2.4 kids, we just need to get a Labrador now.'

Annie suddenly felt very happy. The thought of losing Rob had made her realise just how much she liked the stability. Plus, seeing the trauma Cali had been through – and was about to go through – made her thankful for all that she had.

'That ain't so bad, is it, girl?'

'No, it's not so bad at all. In fact, I'm quite excited.'

With that, Keira started to cry.

'You go and put your feet up. I'll put her down.'

'Thank you. And Mr Johnson.'

'Yes, Mrs Johnson?'

'I love you.'

'I love you more, you crazy woman.'

# Chapter Fifty-nine

Cali stopped in her tracks, not quite believing what she had just seen.

'Bugger, bugger.'

She ignored the flowers that were strewn everywhere and very quickly scrambled around picking up the contents of her bag. By the time she began to run after the speeding stretcher, it was too late. The corridors all looked the same and she reached a dead end.

She was gasping for breath when she reached the main reception. 'Hi. My boyfriend has just come in. His name is Mario Milli and … and I really need to see him.'

The middle-aged lady on reception started to breathe in and out deeply in front of her. 'Now, do what I'm doing, dear, in and out, in and out, deeply to your tummy, it's fine. Mario Milli, you say?'

'Yes, yes, that's him. He's Italian.'

'We don't seem to have anyone of that name here.'

'You must have, it was him. I just saw him on a stretcher, he was covered in blood.'

'Are you sure you were not mistaken?'

Cali began to doubt herself. It had all happened in a split second. Maybe it was just somebody who looked like him. Checking her diary, Mario should be overseas getting ready for a race.

'OK, let me look again. I can't give you names because of patient confidentiality. We did just have an emergency case come in, but he is not of Italian origin.'

Cali sat down in the waiting area. Maybe she had imagined it. Maybe after receiving the text, her longing to see Mario was so great that she had thought the guy on the stretcher was him.

She walked back to reception.

'Can I go up to where the emergencies come in and see if it is him?'

The receptionist, now obviously frustrated, looked at Cali as if she was mad and repeated, 'There is definitely nobody here of that name.'

Cali ignored the no use of mobiles sign and called Mario again immediately. Something was very wrong, whether it was him she had seen or not.

It rang about ten times, Cali feeling that amazing sense of relief when someone you want to pick up the phone eventually does, and she spouted at top speed. 'Oh, Mario, I don't even care I haven't spoken to you for ages or what you need to say to me, I'm just so relieved you're all right. I'm going so crazy I just thought I'd seen you in a hospital.'

A rough Cockney accent greeted her. 'Sorry, love, I think you must've got the wrong number. I um … I bought this phone off a bloke in the pub last night.'

Laying her head back on the train seat, Cali gasped and put her hand to her forehead. In all of the kerfuffle and confusion she had totally forgotten Louise. Maybe she *was* going mad. But if she was being honest, she couldn't face being bright and cheery. There was just too much else to deal with at the moment.

As the train chugged back to Dedcot, Cali tried to put the horror of seeing Mario, or whom she thought was Mario, to the back of her mind. But even that was overshadowed by questioning why on earth he would sell his phone and not give her his new number. What did his text really mean?

# Chapter Sixty

Billy Flynn looked agitated as he made his way through border control. He had warned his mate many times that if they didn't deliver the money on time, Big Al would get his boys onto them. And true to his word, that was exactly what had happened.

Jacko didn't usually let his feelings get in the way. All he'd had to do was get the money off her and they'd be home and dry. How on earth did that stupid Cali bitch know he was in hospital, anyway?

On a positive note at least he now knew Jacko wasn't dead.

*Passengers for flight AFG 123 to Amsterdam, please make your way to the departure lounge.*

Shrouded in guilt, Billy picked up his small holdall from the floor and slowly began walking towards the gate. His only comfort being that as soon as Jack was better, he could contact him using the dummy email they had set up.

# Chapter Sixty-one

'Cali big tits, Cali big tits.'

'I haven't heard that one for a while, Lady P.'

Ignoring Annie's two texts to call her as soon as she had a minute, Cali put her bag on the table and poured herself an orange juice. She couldn't just let what had happened lie. She had to find out if she really had imagined Mario and why on earth someone else had his phone. She realised now how little she knew about Mario. He had never really mentioned any family or friends. There was literally nobody she knew to call to find out if he was OK. Because she saw him so infrequently, they hadn't really done the usual finding out about each other thing. It had been more quick references to work, having sex, and their pending trip. She realised she didn't even know his address. He had said he stayed somewhere now and then and was always on the move, so I guess it hadn't made sense for her to go to his house.

If she was honest with herself, thinking back, it had all been a bit shallow. But in the honeymoon period, maybe that's what it was supposed to be like. It was so long ago since she'd experienced one she had forgotten. But shallow or not, she couldn't help the way she felt about him and if it *was* him lying hurt in a hospital bed, she had to find out. She looked at her WhatsApp. The photo of the Formula One car was now just a blank space, but then it would be if the new owner didn't use the app.

Thinking of that photo, she suddenly realised what she could do.

Mario had always said that there was high security around his work and it would be better if she didn't contact him there, but this was an emergency.

The head office reception phone of his team was answered in two rings by a very efficient-sounding young woman.

Cali cleared her throat. 'Oh, hello there. It's Worldwide Flowers here, I wonder if you can help me. I have been asked to send some flowers to an employee of yours in hospital. A lady has scribbled a name and hospital for us to put on the card but her writing is not clear – maybe you can confirm it?'

'Of course. Firstly, who are they for as our guys are all over the place during race season?'

'The gentleman concerned works in aerodynamics and it says Mario. I think the surname is Milli.'

'Mario Milli? Hmm. I don't recognise that name. Let me just check the telephone list in case he's new.'

'OK, thank you.' Cali could feel her hand shake and her heart drop.

'We don't have anyone by the name of Mario working for us. Are you sure that's correct?'

'That really is very odd.' Cali tried to keep her voice level as the receptionist continued.

'We are a tight-knit bunch here; I believe we would know if someone was in hospital and I hadn't been informed.'

'OK, I'll clarify everything with the customer. Thanks for your help.'

Cali sat back on the sofa with a thud. Why on earth would somebody lie to her about where he worked? To show off? Or worse – maybe he was having an affair. That would definitely make sense with all their snatched time together. But then why on earth would he have invited her on holiday? Her instinct was telling her something was very wrong. No contact for two weeks, seeing whom she thought was Mario in hospital but being told no one of that name had come in, and not working where he said he did! He was just telling lies.

She quickly phoned the hospital again to check in case his details had been registered as he had been brought in as an emergency, but no, there was still no one going by the name of Mario Milli there.

'Love you, Callerina.' Lady P started careering around her cage.

'That you might, my darling feathered friend, but I need to find out who exactly I have been sleeping with for the past few weeks.'

She texted Annie. *Emergency meeting required as soon as you can?*

Annie replied immediately. *I've been trying to instigate one all day! Deedee's in an hour?*

# Chapter Sixty-two

On seeing Cali come into Deedee's, David smiled widely and asked how she was. He pointed to where Annie was sitting and said he would be over shortly.

Cali kissed her friend on the cheek and sat down.

'Blimey, Cal, you look awful. What's up?'

'I don't think Mario is who he says he is.'

Annie went cold. Maybe she was too late in warning her.

'Why do you say that?'

Annie listened intently as Cali relayed her tale about the hospital and phone and workplace happenings.

'I hate to be the bearer of bad news, but I think he is a charlatan.' Annie bit her lip. 'Do you remember Jilly from am dram saying she was seeing someone who worked in Formula One?'

'The fat, posh one – is that Jilly?'

'Yes. Well, I went in to see George. Who, by the way, I didn't sleep with. In fact, he didn't even touch me. Anyway, that's by the by. Well, Jilly had a dramatic outburst saying she'd been fleeced by the boyfriend. She also said she was supposed to be going to St Tropez with him. I hate to tell you but I think it's the same man.'

Cali went white. 'I don't believe you.'

'Hang on a sec.' Annie scrolled through her photos. 'I asked to see a photo and snapped this. I assume it is him?'

With a shaky hand, Cali took the phone and with a sigh of relief, said, 'It's not him, that is definitely not him, but this is too weird. What do you mean he fleeced her?'

'She said he used her credit card to its maximum limit.'

'Oh, God.' Cali felt sick. 'He took my card details to book the flight, but no, it has to be a massive coincidence. Mario wouldn't do that to me. That isn't even a photo of him, no, no.'

'Phone your credit card company now, quickly.'

'But Annie, I checked my online statement only yesterday and everything was in order.'

'Do it now.'

'Your balance is £549, Mrs Summers, and to confirm, your last transaction was £25.00 at Denbury garage, the polite advisor offered.

'Block your credit card,' Annie whispered.

Cali shook her head furiously.

'See, no money has come off the card.'

'Yet! But that does mean he hasn't booked the flights like he said he would, either. Mario wouldn't do this to me. It *must* have been him I saw earlier and that's the reason he hasn't been in contact. Maybe he had an accident a week ago and his symptoms got worse and they've moved him to a different hospital.'

'Cali, be realistic. It all sounds too fishy.'

'Will you come with me to the hospital? I have

to find him and see what's going on.'

'But they were adamant it wasn't him.'

'They were adamant it wasn't Mario Milli, but after his work said he didn't exist, and now you are putting so much doubt in my mind, maybe that isn't his name.'

'So you want to go all the way to London?'

Cali and Annie entered the hospital reception donned in big sun hats and large, dark glasses. Cali was relieved to see a different receptionist at the main desk. Annie said she would do the talking just in case anyone recognised her.

She put on a foreign accent. 'Oh 'ello, my boyfriend is here. He came in earlier. Accidentey. I do not know what ward he be on.'

Despite the seriousness of the situation, Cali had to stifle a giggle at her friend's dreadful accent.

'What's his name?'

'See, zis is the thing. I only see him for one month and he give me his nickname, Mazza. That is the trouble when a man is new.'

The receptionist smiled.

'Modern love, eh?'

She looked down the list of emergency patients. 'There isn't anyone called Mazza, or anything like it.'

'I have a photo, this is him.' Annie showed the receptionist the grainy picture of Mario that Cali had sent earlier. A porter peering over her shoulder spoke up.

'Yes, he's here. Ward 12. I'll show you the way.'

In trepidation, Cali and Annie followed the

young porter. Cali didn't know if she was more scared of seeing how bad a state Mario was in or finding out for sure he wasn't who he said he was.

'I'll leave you 'ere, ladies, end of the corridor, turn left. I'm sorry about your bloke.'

There was a staff nurse at the door to the ward as they went in.

Annie started talking. 'My English bad, my boyfriend here.' She held up her phone with the photo of Mario.

'Oh, yes, Jack.'

Cali grasped Annie's arm as the nurse continued. 'You'll find him in the end room on the right. He's heavily sedated so don't expect much from him.'

'We should just phone the police,' Annie whispered.

'No way. He has done nothing wrong to me … well, apart from lie,' Cali whispered back. 'I just need to see him with my own eyes and ask him what the hell he is playing at.'

Annie followed Cali to the end of the corridor. The door to the room was shut. Cali took a deep breath and pushed it open.

There, instead of being greeted by her handsome lover, they were greeted by another nurse stripping the bed.

'If you were coming to see Jack, he's not here.'

'Oh.' Cali's face dropped.

'Are you a relative?'

'Not exactly; I'm his girlfriend.'

'Well, the silly man has discharged himself. He's high on painkillers. So make sure when you see him he gets proper rest and, if he has any sense, he'll come back in to get his wounds properly dressed. He had to have a lot of stitches.'

'When did he go?' Cali was close to tears.

'Around an hour ago. He was very edgy. I tried to dissuade him but he was having none of it. He's a feisty one, your boy.' The nurse managed a slight smile.

'That he is,' Cali agreed, realising again how little she knew about this man.

Annie and Cali swiftly made their way to the train station.

'At least we know his name now.'

'There are a lot of Jacks in this world, Annie. What should I do? I want to find him.'

'I don't think you should do anything. He's obviously up to no good. Maybe you've just been lucky. Definitely block your credit card though, mate.'

Tears welled in Cali's eyes. 'I want to see him. I want to know why he lied to me. In my eyes, he's innocent until proven guilty.'

'I should think he's long gone, Cal. I mean, he hasn't exactly been banging your door down to see you.'

'He's been busy.'

'Cali, don't be deluded. If Jilly hadn't had such a similar story then I'd give him the benefit of the doubt, but I think it may have just been a matter of time before he fleeced you, too. In fact, maybe he already has. It would explain the apology text.'

'I, somehow, don't think a conman would apologise in advance, do you? I really don't know what to do,' Cali wailed.

'I think you should go to the police. If he is a charlatan then you need to do it for other women he might target.'

'Don't say that. I can't bear the thought of it.'

'What if he's dangerous? You know nothing about him.'

'Of course he's not dangerous. He was so nice.'

'Don't let love blind you. If he knows you have blown his cover, goodness knows what he will do. I think you have to give him a wide berth and just put it down to experience.'

'I can't get my head around it, Annie. I have to know the truth or it will drive me mad.'

'Oh, Cal. Come on, let's get on this train. A good night's sleep will make everything clearer and we'll talk in the morning.'

# Chapter Sixty-three

Shattered, Cali let herself into her flat and turned the light on.

'Cali big tits, Cali big tits.'

'Not now, Lady P, sleep time.' She put the cover over her noisy bird's cage and started getting ready for bed. Just as she was removing her last bit of make-up, the door buzzer went. Cali froze.

With her heart beating faster than a frightened bird, she threw on her dressing gown and pressed the intercom.

A shaky voice greeted her. 'Cali, it's me. I need to talk to you.'

Cali's face fell. 'Jamie? It's late, what do you want?'

'I know and I'm sorry, but please, give me ten minutes.'

Cali sighed. 'Come up, but you'll have to be quick. I'm really tired and I've got work tomorrow.'

She opened the door to a broken-looking Jamie. He came in and handed her a brown envelope. She screwed up her face.

'What's this?'

'Your divorce papers, I took them when I left the other day. I can't bear that we may never see each other again.'

'Oh, Jamie.'

'I know I've caused all this, but now Bella is pregnant and I realise you don't want anything to do with me, I can't cope.'

Cali, full of her own turmoil, couldn't be angry with him. She replied calmly, 'It was your decision to leave me, J. It takes two to tango – boy shags girl, girl gets pregnant. You obviously knew she wasn't taking precautions.'

'I didn't, actually. She told me she was on the pill and had a stomach upset, and that was when she must have got pregnant. You having a boyfriend now has made me realise we are meant to be together. I lie in bed at night thinking you're with him and it kills me.'

'And how do you think I felt when I found out my husband, yes, *husband*, was sleeping with our – and I repeat – *our* personal trainer of however many years my junior?'

'I know, I know. I've been a fool.'

'You're just scared of the bed you've made for yourself.'

'No, I've realised that without you, I'm rubbish.'

'Oh, shut up, Jamie! You just can't bear that I've found happiness without you. Give me one good reason why I should want you now.'

'I told you, I still bloody love you. Isn't that good enough?'

'Big boy J, big boy J.' Lady P wasn't used to Jamie raising his voice.

'Shut up, Lady P,' they said in unison.

'I object, I object.'

'See, you've been saying you object to the

divorce.'

'I object to a lot of things, Jamie, and somehow I don't think a judge would listen to an African Grey.'

'I've realised that if it had been you telling me you were pregnant then I would be the happiest man alive.'

'It's too late for back tracking.'

'So, is it serious with this new man?'

Cali shuffled from foot to foot. 'Yes, actually, it is.'

'And what if I said I wanted you back?'

'I would say that you were a fool to think I'd be so stupid to entertain it.'

Cali could see the tears well in Jamie's eyes and suddenly felt like she wanted to fall into his arms and feel safe again. Meeting someone new was a minefield and now she was in this predicament with Mario, or whoever he was, she wished she'd never started internet dating.

'I know you. You will have to stand by her and the child. So don't come at me with "I love you" and "sorry". Anyway, my heart is closed for business.'

'Except for the Italian lover boy?'

'I think you'd better go. Bella will be wondering where you are.'

'But, Cali.'

'No buts. Go and sort your life out at home. Our boat sailed the minute you left me.' She opened the front door. 'Thanks for the mirror, by the way. That was a kind gesture, even though you smashed it into the same pieces as you did my heart.'

Jamie's heartfelt 'I'll never give up on you,' was wasted on Cali as she shut the front door.

Noticing him looking up to her window from the car park, she quickly pulled the curtains shut.

Cali's mind was whirring at a hundred miles an hour as she got into bed. She closed her eyes and images of a bloodied Mario and a heartbroken Jamie flashed through her mind. Just a few months ago she was the newlywed Mrs Summers with a bright future ahead of her, and now what? Her heart was a whirlpool. She took three very deep breaths down to her stomach to calm herself. Then, just as she was dropping off, she heard the buzz of the intercom.

'Oh God, Jamie,' she said out loud, looking at her phone. With her kind nature overriding her urge to ignore it, she sleepily walked to the door and pressed the button.

'Can it wait until tomorrow?'

'Cali, it's me, Mario. Let me in.'

# Chapter Sixty-four

On hearing Mario's Italian accent, Cali melted. Annie was being paranoid. He had come to her, and that's what mattered. Once she had allowed him to explain, all would be clear and they could carry on as they were.

'I'm a complete mess, but come up.' Cali pulled the belt on her dressing gown tight.

Mario knocked quietly, then quickly shut the door behind him. Despite it being nearly midnight, he was wearing his dark glasses with a baseball cap pulled low over his face.

'*Ciao*.' He kissed her on the cheek and all the feelings came flooding back. He took off his cap and she gasped. His left eye was swollen shut and his jawline had several stitches. His bottom lip had an open cut on it.

Cali broke the silence. 'And there was me thinking I looked a mess.'

'You always look beautiful, Cali.'

Mario made his way to the sofa, wincing as he went, and sat down. He tapped the seat next to him.

She put her hand on his. 'What on earth happened?'

With a strong Cockney accent he began to tell her. 'Please don't be afraid when I tell ya what I'm

301

going to tell ya. My name's not Mario Milli.'

Cali shook her head. It was as if a total stranger was sitting opposite her. 'I know who you are, Jack.'

'How….?'

'By complete fluke, I saw you in the hospital.'

'Really?'

'Yes, really, but never mind that.' Cali stood up and walked to the other side of the lounge.

'I'm a bad man. I've lied to you in a big way, Cali.'

Cali bit her lip and tried not to cry. Finally, knowing the truth meant all the big dreams she had with this man would be over.

'I don't work in Formula One. I don't own an Audi. There is no house in St Tropez. I stole money from your purse and I took your card details to steal more money from you, too. But please, please don't be afraid, because there is one thing in this whole sordid mess that isn't a lie and is the reason I'm here now.'

'I don't know if I care to hear any more.' Cali reached for her phone.

He jumped up to stop her.

'I don't blame you for wanting to call the police, but please hear me out. I've fallen in love with you, Cali.'

Cali shook her head as Jack carried on. 'From the minute I saw you. Your cute face and curvy body, your feisty nature, your ability to make me feel like there was no other man on the planet.' He ran his hand through his hair. 'You're one in a million and for all the money I could have made, I don't want it.

302

I want you, just you.'

Cali looked to the ceiling. 'But I don't even know who *you* are.'

'I am me, even behind the Italian façade. I'm Jack, a Cockney lad from a poor family but fundamentally my personality is still the same. I put on an accent and tell lies. But I liked you so much I couldn't go through with the scam me and my mate had planned.'

Suddenly everything began to fall into place.

'Oh my God, so it was your mate that was seeing Jilly?'

'You know her?' Jack's eyes were like saucers. 'I thought you lived miles apart.'

'This is a small town, Jack. Maybe it's time you upped your game.'

'I wanted you to know that I took nothing from you, Cali.'

'Apart from my heart and hopes and dreams, that is.' Cali welled up.

'Please don't cry. I put the money I stole from your purse down the side of your bag the other day. I just couldn't go through with it. Couldn't bear to hurt you.'

'So when did you plan to contact me again?'

'I was on my way to you,' he pointed to his face, 'when this happened. In order to make money, I had to pay some people. Some very bad, dangerous people. Because I couldn't take the money from you I didn't have enough for my part of the deal, and this is my punishment.'

'What exactly were you on your way to say?'

'I would have said exactly the same as I am now.

That I'm falling in love with you and, despite this fact, I have to go away for a while. Keep a low profile.'

'Abroad?'

Jack nodded. 'You're too good for me, Cali, and I know now I've told you this, you will run a mile. But I didn't want to leave you thinking that it was your fault, or with unanswered questions about what you could have done to make it better. You couldn't have done anything better. I'm a conman. But you are the only woman who has ever stopped me in my tracks. In fact, stopped me in my tracks long enough to realise that it isn't worth it. Money is great but happiness is greater.'

'When do you go?' Cali felt her stomach lurch.

'I have to find the five grand I owe first. This was just a warning. If I don't pay up, then who knows what they'll do when they find me.'

'Can you find it?'

'In time, but I don't have any.' Jack looked straight into Cali's eyes. 'I love you. I really do.'

Cali covered her face with her hands. 'How much do you really need?'

'I'm desperate, but I'd never ask you to do that. Not after what happened.'

'Answer me!' Even Cali was shocked by her elevated tone.

'Give me six weeks, Cali, and I promise with all my heart that I will pay you back every single penny. I need five grand. Well, six would be better.'

'By when?'

'Midnight tomorrow. But I need cash.'

# Chapter Sixty-five

'Bet you wish your boyfriend was hot like me.' Adam bounced into the events office expecting to see Cali, and he was surprised to see a fresh-faced Lou.

'Not even funny, Adam. And after the couple of weeks I've had, I don't care if I ever see another dick again.'

'You say that now … Anyway, it's good to see you, Lou. We've all missed you. Well, a little bit. How you feeling?'

'Good, actually. I'd have been all right if I hadn't got an infection in my –'

Adam put his hand up to halt her. 'Enough. See this?' He pointed to the scar on his forehead. 'That's where I fell when I fainted due to the bloodbath you created.'

'Enough from you, Adam.' Marcus appeared in the office and spoke over the Geordie. 'I'm sure Lou doesn't want to be reminded of that awful day.' Marcus put his hand gently on Louise's shoulder. 'Good to see you. I wasn't expecting you back yet, don't rush into work if you don't have to.'

'I'm fine. It's good to be back. I got released from hospital, had a day at home, and felt bored. Where's Cali? She's usually here by now.'

'Hmm.' Marcus scratched his head. 'Have you heard from her, Adam? She hasn't contacted me.' He checked his phone, then his watch. 'Ten o'clock, that is late for her.'

'Let me try her now, it's not like her not to ring in.' Adam reached to his pocket for his phone.

'Fine, fine, let me know when you get hold of her.' Marcus went back to his office.

Adam got Cali's answerphone twice. The second time he decided to leave her a message. 'I guess you're either sick or shagging. Good news is that Lou is back so we are all one big happy family. Call me. Laters.'

# Chapter Sixty-six

Cali breathed in the fresh air and tranquillity as she started to jog and then run at full pelt. It was so nice to be in the park with hardly anyone around. After twenty minutes spent and, with hands on hips, she tipped her head back to refill her lungs.

If she had made a video of her life over the past few months, it would be like some sad, mad rom-com that women would either be jealous of because it was so action-packed, or happy that they had life on an even keel with no stress, worries or angst.

She sat against an oak tree and sighed deeply. If someone had asked her to explain how she was feeling, it would be somewhere between wanting to be anywhere and nowhere.

She reached for her mobile and turned it on. Then, purposely not looking at any messages, she quickly texted Marcus to say she was sick and would let him know when she would be in next, then turned it off again.

Space.

She had woken up that morning to an empty bed, yet feeling so hemmed in she might burst.

Shutting her eyes, images hit her in the face like a dirty cloth. The wedding, Jamie wanting the Dumb Bell, moving into her little flat, hating Lady

P, hating men, Jon's piles, lovely Luke, thirty minute Will, Nigel's chode ... and wife. Marcus's indiscretion, Lou's miscarriage. Dumb Bell being pregnant. Jamie wanting her back. Mario/Jack confessing his undying love for her and needing money to prevent him being beaten again, or killed.

If she had a stressometre, she would have exploded off the scale.

Even knowing that Mario still loved her and the way he had gently made love to her last night was not enough to pacify her. How could she have let herself become so embroiled with someone who had so easily hoodwinked her? But whatever her head was telling her – that he was a bad man and she should run a mile – her beating heart stopped the flow of truth and her caring nature wanted to help him. He loved her, had taken the chance of his life to be with her. His sincerity last night couldn't have been be faked. She had to help him. She knew he would pay her back. In fact, he even said he was happy to sign something. And if he wasn't being genuine there was no way he would have told her literally everything. She could easily go the police. Maybe when he had sorted everything and gone straight they could be together properly and create the family she had always desired. Surely some leopards could change their spots?

She pulled her little rucksack off her back and put it in front of her. Not deterred by it being just eleven-thirty, she downed a whole tin of gin and tonic and, despite not having had a puff of a cigarette since university, pulled out a pink lighter and clumsily lit a Marlboro Menthol from a pack she had just bought from the corner shop. Her world was in turmoil and she needed to escape from reality, even if just for a moment.

After two puffs and coughing like a docker, she realised that taking up smoking probably wasn't going to help her pilgrimage to peace and extinguished the offending object.

An egg mayonnaise sandwich and ready salted crisps suddenly seemed like a much healthier remedy. Just as she was pulling open the cellophane of her supermarket snack she noticed another jogger about to cast a shadow on the nearing midday sun.

The jogger began to slow and, in a vain hope to deem herself invisible, she shallowed her breathing and looked down to the shadowy roots she was sitting within.

'Cali? Cali? Is that you?' Cali opened another tin of gin and tonic. 'You look different in running clothes.'

Cali managed a weak smile. 'Hello, officer.'

Will crouched down to her level and continued. 'Look. Sorry. I'll go, I understand. I often need peace. After a mad week of training those army boys this is my escape, too.'

He looked even more handsome with strings of sweaty blond fringe sticking to his forehead.

'No. Join me, it's fine.' The relief of seeing a face without hope or agenda was suddenly really quite pleasing. 'What brings you over this way?'

'After we came for a walk here, I thought it so beautiful. So now, if ever I get the time, I come here for a long run. And, of course, there was always the chance I might bump into you.'

Cali managed a weak smile. 'Charmer. I'm surprised I didn't get a "five minute" request, then.'

'No, I eventually realised you must be serious about your new fella. And, to be honest, I am never anyone's second best.'

Will sat down next to her and put his legs out straight. 'So, madam. What brings you to be drinking gin and tonic at this unearthly hour, and please don't tell me you're smoking, too?'

Already feeling drunk after one double measure on an empty stomach, Cali hiccupped.

'It's a long story. I don't want to bore you.'

'Tell you what. Share your sarnie and crisps with me and I'll happily listen. Deal?'

Cali handed him a sandwich. 'Deal.'

With the gin loosening her tongue, she began to relay her tales. It was almost as if there was a Tinder code, whereby it didn't seem strange to discuss the experiences you'd had on there, even if it was to one of the people you'd slept with already!

Will seemed to be able to coax information out of her without judgement and she was soon telling him all. The handsome officer listened intently, only butting in when he wanted to reconfirm exactly what she was saying.

'So, your cheating, soon to be ex-husband now wants you back and you've been dating a conman who is now evidently in love with you?'

'He *is* in love with me, Will. Do you really have to make it all sound so simple? I'm tearing my hair out here.'

Will took a long drink from his water bottle.

'Do you know what I think?'

'Tell me.' Cali took the water bottle from him and took three big gulps.

'I think you are too good for both of them. I also think you need a bit of time on your own.'

Cali bit her lip, then burst into tears. 'It's been so bloody stressful.'

Will pulled her towards him. Her memory senses sighed as she took in his warmth and lovely smell. Hugging him felt so good.

'I'm sorry.' She went to pull away and he pulled her closer.

'What are you sorry for?'

'You don't really know me and look at me. I'm a bloody mess.'

'A bloody brave mess. You felt the fear and came out here on your own anyway.'

'Yeah right, drinking and smoking and skipping work. And not facing up to the fact I've made some pretty bad mistakes; really brave.'

'Cali, you didn't create either situation, you are not to blame. There are just some men who aren't decent and that's a fact. And because you are so kind and forgiving, they take advantage of that.'

'I was so in love with Jamie.'

'I'm sure he loved you too, but shit happens, Cali, some men are weak and now he can see that he is losing you, his ego has bumped up to the top again. And as for Mario ...' Cali had been careful not to tell Will his real name. Will let Cali go and they both leaned back against the tree. 'Has he really treated you like a man who loves you? Think about it.'

'Well maybe not at the start, but he realises

now.'

'Show me a photo of him if it will help me understand how you're feeling.' Cali turned on her phone and found the grainy photo. 'Yeah, he's good looking. But aside from that, are you going to lend him the money? I think you're mad if you do.'

Cali stood up and brushed herself down. The gin had not only made her drunk but a bit bolshie. She assumed a childlike voice. 'I think you're mad if you do.'

Will stood up calmly. 'It's your life, Cali, but think carefully. What would your dad say?'

'He would say don't be so bloody stupid. But I'm thirty-one, only I know how I feel about him, and it's my decision.'

Will nodded. 'So midnight tonight?'

Cali staggered slightly. 'Midnight in the alleyway next to Deedee's. I think it's rather romantic.'

'So romantic. I take it you don't have a car here. Can I give you a lift home?'

The fresh air from being in Will's convertible had sobered Cali up slightly by the time they reached her flat.

'Cup of tea?' she offered.

Will shook his head. 'You've got my number still, haven't you?'

Cali did a funny little dance as she got out of the car. 'Thank you, handsome officer, and yes, I have.'

'Don't drive later, will you?'

'Oh, I'll be fine by midnight. I'm going to have a nap and drink plenty of coffee.'

Will looked directly at her. 'Take care, Cali. You're a special lady.'

'Gee, thanks.' Cali walked backwards, blowing him a kiss.

With a face of concern, Will parked up round the corner, picked up his phone and quickly thumbed through his contacts.

'Mate, I need to talk to you. Are you around later?'

# Chapter Sixty-seven

Jamie was driving home from work when Bella called.

'Hi, darling. Client was slightly late so I'll be back around seven. The food shopping is being delivered between then and half past. I should be there to unpack it as usual but if not, leave it, I'll do it when I get in.'

'OK. I don't mind helpi –'

'No. Just leave it,' Bella cut in abruptly. 'You've had a hard day. See you soon.'

Jamie pushed open the front door, put a couple of letters on the side and went to the fridge. Just as he was opening a beer, the doorbell rang. It was the shopping already.

He put the bags on the kitchen table and took a slurp of beer. Noticing freezer stuff in one of the bags, he began unpacking it. Maybe Bella had picked up on how unhappy he had been this week and that was why she was being so thoughtful for once.

In robotic fashion, he began unpacking the bags. His mind wandered to Cali. He was sure there was still love for him in her eyes. But she had obviously moved on. If only Bella wasn't bloody pregnant. He would have left her, and, whether it took five or

315

fifteen years, he would fight for Cali. Prove to her that he had made the biggest mistake of his life and would rectify everything. How could he have been so stupid?

He was just unpacking the last bag when he heard Bella's key in the door. She literally ran into the kitchen and snatched the bag from him, causing it to split. You couldn't have put a wager on whose face was more shocked. Lying on the grey stone tiles, plain to see, was a box of tampons and a pack of panty liners.

'Err ... thought I'd stock up for after the baby. Great offers on at the moment.'

If she hadn't been so adamant about him not unpacking the shopping, he might have let it go.

'Liar.'

'What?' She ran over to squeeze him.

'There's not one sign of a bump.'

'I told you, because I'm so fit it probably won't show until at least month four.'

'You haven't even mentioned a scan date.'

'I'm waiting for it to come through.'

Jamie felt a rage wash over him. He roughly pulled down Bella's joggers.

'Jamie, stop!'

He carried on and pulled down her knickers. He put his fingers to her crotch and felt the obvious string of a tampon between her legs.

With her joggers around her knees, she went to run up the stairs but ended up falling forward on her knees.

'Why?' Jamie shouted. 'Why?'

Not used to her usually placid boyfriend being so

316

aggressive, Bella began to cry.

'I saw you looking at photos of Cali. I didn't want you to leave me.' She hurriedly pulled up her trousers.

Jamie leant his head against the hall wall. His voice softened. 'I'm so sorry for doing that.'

'Whatever.' Bella was flushed. 'You still love her, don't you, J? I'm not stupid.'

'I'm not going to lie, I still have feelings for her. I was with her a long time.'

'Answer me!' It was Bella's turn to scream. 'Do you still love her?'

Jamie put his hand over his mouth and nodded.

'I fucking knew it. Well, have her. Have your boring, plain woman back. I'm not sure I'm ready for all this domestication anyway.'

'No, but…'

'Jamie, it's fine. Thank God I didn't move in properly.' She flounced up the stairs, shouting as she went. 'I've only got a couple of cases to pack. I'll go tonight.'

Jamie walked back to the kitchen and downed his beer in one. Cali or no Cali, he'd made a terrible mistake with Bella. The sense of immediate relief that washed over him confirmed that.

# Chapter Sixty-eight

After two cups of coffee and an hour's nap, Cali had sobered up. She felt slightly mortified that not only had she been in such a state in Will's company, but how she had spilled her heart out to him. Her memory of their conversation was slightly fuzzy, but she was sure the only major details she had given him were that Jamie still loved her and Jack hadn't conned her.

A text came in from an unknown number. *Hi, DON'T reply to me on here. Last night was so special. Love you and see you at midnight.*

'Aw,' Cali said as she turned on her laptop. With money transferred into her current account ready to pick up from the bank, she shut down the lid.

'Love you, Callerina.' Lady P inputted as she shut down the lid.

'Love you too, Lady P.'

Her phone rang. It was Annie. 'Afternoon. You all right?'

'I'm OK.'

'I take it you didn't hear from him?'

'Err, no. I haven't gone to work today. Just need to get my head around it.'

Cali grimaced at lying to her friend. She had never lied to Annie in their whole friendship.

'Aw, bless you. Sleeping on it, I think you should really try and forget about him. He would never have been good for you. I know you feel like you love him but I think you were in love with the idea of him. It all seems wrong and dark to me, Cal.'

'Maybe.' The image of making love to Jack last night came into her mind. Once he was back on the straight and narrow she would be able to introduce him to everyone properly, but for now to anyone who loved her, it had to be, as Jack had said, 'their little secret'.

'Well, as long as you are OK. I thought you would have been playing Detective Summers again.'

'No. No. I mean, where would I start?'

'Exactly, it's going to be hard but let him go.'

'Right. I need to quickly go to the bank, then I'm coming back to watch crap TV and chill.'

'Good. You chill. I'm always here, you know that.'

'I know. I do have something to tell you, though. Jamie came round last night.'

'Again?'

'Yep, declared his undying love for me, *again*.'

'Oh, God. How do you feel?'

'To be honest, Annie, I'm flattered, but she's pregnant. I don't know what he's playing at.'

'I want to know everything he said.'

'Look, sorry to rush but I don't even want to talk about it now. I'm knackered and need to walk to the bank.'

'OK, I understand. How about Deedee's for a

quick cuppa before you start work tomorrow? Keira will be with me but she'll be fine.'

'Sounds like a plan.'

'Cali?'

'Yep?'

'I only say what I do because I care about you, you know that.'

'Everyone needs an Annie Johnson in their lives,' Cali laughed.

'Don't, I'm crying at everything at the moment. See you tomorrow.'

'See ya.'

# Chapter Sixty-nine

Cali put on her favourite blue summer dress and summer sandals. Despite it being late, it had been such a hot day that there was still a warm breeze. She reapplied her red lipstick, Mario/Jack's favourite, and grabbed her car keys from the side.

She checked her phone quickly. No more messages. She made sure the cash was securely sealed in an envelope, grabbed her keys and headed for the door.

She was no more than fifty metres down the road from the car park when she saw the blue lights of a police car behind her. She pulled over to let them pass then realised they were signalling her to pull over.

Suddenly remembering Will's words of warning about driving, she panicked. But surely she wouldn't be over the limit? Especially as she had eaten, slept, and at least ten hours had passed. She quickly put the envelope filled with cash in the glove compartment and opened her window.

'Madam.'

'Evening.' Cali looked to her clock. Only fifteen minutes to get to Jack.

'We noticed one of your back lights is out.'

Cali exhaled with relief. 'Oh, no. OK. I shall

make sure that I get it fixed tomorrow. Which one is it?'

'Nearside.'

'That's my side, isn't it? I always get confused.' Cali laughed with nerves as the policemen seemed to lean far too near her.

'That's correct. Is this your car, madam?'

'Yes.' She shuffled about in her bag to find her driving licence. 'This is me, I don't have any other paperwork.'

He looked at it closely. 'Ah, Cali Summers. You're lucky it matches with our data. Now, just one more question.'

She looked at the policeman. He must have been around her age, and was bald, tall and broad, with full lips that reminded her of Jack's. Another older-looking PC was standing behind her car.

'Have you been drinking tonight?'

'No, not tonight.'

'So you have earlier?'

'This makes me sound bad, but yes, I had a small gin and tonic before lunch.' Cali glanced at the clock again. 'Look, I don't want to be rude but I'm meeting a friend and I'm going to be late.'

'I'm sorry but now you've told me you've had alcohol I'll need to breathalyse you.'

'Really?'

'Really. Problem is, our roadside breathalyser has faced a malfunction so I need you to come to the station.'

'Can I meet my friend quickly first?'

'No, sorry. But you can give them a quick call.'

Cali remembered Jack saying she mustn't use the

number he called her on.

'It's fine, don't worry.'

She tipped her head back. He would be so upset with her. She couldn't bear the thought of him waiting, but if he wanted to call or text her then he could. Ah. Although there was no way the police could see his number. She suddenly felt like a criminal herself.

With a heavy heart and praying she would not be over the limit, she was escorted into the police station. Just as she was being asked to fill in some forms there was a commotion at the front desk.

Her heart did a somersault as she recognised Jack's distinct London twang. 'Get off me, will ya? I've done nothing wrong. I was waiting for this bird I'm seeing.'

She could see the horror on his face when he saw her. When he could tell nobody was looking directly at him, he mouthed, 'You grassing bitch.'

Tears pricked Cali's eyes as she shook her head and mouthed back, 'No.'

As Jack was taken down to a room for questioning, he shouted back down the corridor.

'Let the bird know it would have been the last time anyway, will ya?'

It was two a.m. by the time Cali got home. Crying her eyes out, she plonked herself down on the sofa. Thankfully, she had not been over the limit. She was devastated that Jack had been arrested and, worse still, that he thought it was her fault. She had pretended she knew nothing of him and hoped she wouldn't get pulled up for questioning. What a wanker. She felt sick that he could have taken her money. How could she have been so stupid? Annie and Will had been right. She had been so blinded by his clever ways, lies and fake love that she could have been fleeced for a lot of money. She felt abused. Thank God she had used condoms with him as goodness knows how many other women he could have been scamming along the way. But surely it wasn't all lies. He wouldn't have got beaten up so badly if he didn't love her? He would surely have taken the money in the first place. And he had put the cash back he had stolen. Or maybe this was just all part of his game to finally get the money off her? She guessed she would never know.

'Will, mate, it's Joel. Sorry it's so late but you said to call.'

'Is she OK?'

'Yep, all sorted, she blew clean.'

'Good. And did you get him?'

'Result, thanks. He had a knife on him, too. The Met have been looking for him for weeks. Nasty piece of work.'

'I'll sleep properly now. Thanks. Night.'

'Night. And Will?'

'Yeah?'

'She's hot!'

# Chapter Seventy

David greeted Cali and Annie with a big smile and showed them to their usual table.

'You look rough.'

'Thank you. I didn't go to sleep until around three.'

'Oh, darling. Was Marcus all right about you having another sicky?'

'I actually came clean and said I would take today and tomorrow as holiday as I have a few things at home to sort out. He was fine. We have a good understanding and we are not so busy this week, anyway.'

'All good, then. Keira's in nursery now so we can have some peace.'

'How're you feeling?'

'A bit sick but not like I was with the little lady. I'm rather hoping it's a boy.'

'Look at you creating the perfect family you never wanted.'

Annie laughed. 'I know. Thinking I might lose Rob and, not being rude, but seeing what you've been through, I'm quite happy with my lot. If I want to go out or even on a girlie weekend Rob said he'd babysit, so life ain't half bad. Now, it's not about me. Tell me everything.'

David brought over their drinks.

'Mario, Jack, whoever he is, *is* a conman.'

'Ah, so his name is Jack then?'

'Yes, Jack Wilson.' Cali exhaled deeply. 'Look Annie, I'm sorry, but I lied to you last night. He did come to me. Declared his undying love and tried to get six grand cash out of me.'

Annie was open-mouthed. She put her hand on Cali's as she continued. 'It was as if the angels were looking after me; I got pulled over for suspected drink driving. And, weirdly, that saved me from him and losing the money.'

'Oh, shit. Please tell me you weren't over the limit.'

'Thankfully, no. It was so scary. Anyway, the worst bit was that I had arranged to meet Jack in the alleyway next to here, but, for whatever reason, he was brought into the police station.'

'Oh my God!' Annie took a slurp of her smoothie.

'Tell me! He thought I had grassed him up. But then he said something horrible, so I knew it was true that he was bad through and through.' Cali's voice cracked. She looked up to the ceiling to suppress her tears.

'What did he say, darling?' Seeing her friend in such distress caused Annie to well up, too.

'He shouted out to tell his "bird" that it was the last time he would have ever have seen her, anyway. 'Even so, I still feel bad that he thinks I betrayed him.'

'Cali, OK, you do need to sort your head out. He's a wrong'un. Why do you feel bad?'

'Because, despite everything, I still feel so much love for him. For the nice person that I knew.'

'Was he ever really nice, though? A quick fumble in a hotel room doesn't count as nice in my book. Did he ever buy you a gift? Take you anywhere? I'm sorry to say it but you were just part of his sordid little plan.'

'But when he came to me he said he was going straight and the reason he'd got beaten up was for me, because he realised he loved me and didn't want to stay in the world he was living in.'

'And you believed him?'

'We made proper love, too.' Cali blew her nose. David, on his way to see if they wanted food, noticed her distress and went quietly on to the next table.

Annie handed her friend a tissue. 'It's OK, Cal. It'll be all right.'

Cali exhaled. 'I know, I know it will, I just feel so raw and such a bloody fool. And so angry now. How could I have been so stupid? I see myself as an intelligent woman.'

'Men like him are very clever, Cal. They have no real emotions. They take what they can get from empathetic women like you. Did the police question you about him?'

'No. I didn't say anything when I saw him. I don't want to talk to them.'

'But if this man has done this to you it's your right to tell the police so they can stop him.'

'It looks like they've stopped him already.'

'Hmm. He's wily though, Cal, probably clever enough to have covered all his tracks. And the police aren't stupid, they may even check CCTV footage and recognise your face.'

'I really can't face that today. I have Jamie to deal with.'

'Shit, yes, what did he say this time?'

'He loves me. If Bella wasn't on the scene he would be with me in a heartbeat. He took the divorce papers from my place home with him so I couldn't sign them.'

'Shit.'

'I know.' David came over. 'No food, thanks David, but I would love another large coffee. Annie?'

'Orange juice, please.'

Cali yawned. 'I'm bloody exhausted with it all.'

'How do you feel about Jamie now?'

'Kind of numb, I guess. I was in the park yesterday thinking would I go back to him if things didn't work out with Jack. They obviously haven't, but now I'm not sure if I could. Trust is so important to me.'

'It's important to everyone, Cal. But you had a massive bond with Jamie, basically soulmates.'

'*Had* being the main word in that sentence. If Rob had been cheating on you could you have him back, knowing that he'd done it once? Why wouldn't he do it again?'

'I don't know. Maybe I would have tried.'

Cali quickly stood up. 'Annie, we've gotta go.'

'What, what is it?'

'Fuck. Bella's walking in with some girl.'

'Where?'

'David is walking them this way.'

'Sit down, your back is to everyone. Just keep quiet. I'll ask for the bill and we can quietly leave.'

'I don't want to even look at that woman.'

'I know, I know; it's fine.'

Cali went under the table to pretend to fetch something from her bag as Bella sat down. They were back to back.

Annie summoned David for the bill as Bella's friend started talking.

'Are you saying he actually put his hand in your crotch?'

If a train had come along at that moment it could have fitted in both Cali and Annie's open mouths.

Putting her fingers to her lips, Annie mouthed, 'Ssh.'

'Yeah. Stupidly forgot I had ordered tampons, totally busted, though I tried to get out of it. It was bloody early or he wouldn't have even thought of unpacking.'

'What did he say?'

'He was furious, but that's it now, we're done. He confessed that he still loves the bloody poison dwarf wife.'

'Oh, Bell. That's terrible.'

'No, it's not. I was getting bored, anyway. The age gap isn't massive but I was beginning to feel it. And, if I'm honest with myself, I'm not ready to settle down yet.'

'A lesson learned then, but pretty shit that you broke up a marriage along the way.'

'Thanks for that, but he was the one who played for me.'

'What if he goes back to her? How will you

feel?'

'I don't care. He's a good man but not for me. Glad I realised. His money would have been nice but you still have to wake up next to someone every day. And if that someone loves someone else, not even I'm prepared to hold out. I don't think he'd have gone through with the wedding. He's not even bloody divorced yet.'

Annie and Cali got up without scraping their chairs and made it to the car park undetected.

'Cal, I've gotta rush, Keira's just about to finish. Are you OK? I feel bad leaving you with all that.'

'It's fine, you go. She is an evil witch, obviously. I have a lot of thinking to do. Call you later.'

Cal waved Annie off and got into her Mini. Just as she was winding down her window she could see David walking towards her. He leant down to her level.

'Ahoy.'

'Hey. Did I leave something in there?'

'No, no I just … err … want to see if you are OK?'

'I'm fine.'

'I saw you on Tinder. Was too scared to swipe as I thought, why on earth would someone as beautiful as you want to date a mere waiter like me?'

'That's very sweet. But if a man has a good heart that is worth a million of anything.'

'Pretty and real, too, what a combination.'

'I've been mixed up in another situation so haven't even been on the app for ages.'

'Show me the man who made you cry.'

'That's very direct.'

'Us Czech boys are like that.'

For some reason she felt it OK to open up her photos and show him.

'His eyes are not kind.'

'Nothing about him is kind.'

'Well … if you ever fancy a drink to cheer you up, here's my number. My speaking English is good, my written is not, so much easier to talk and understand than message you.'

'If only everyone thought like that. This modern world is the scourge of human relationships.'

'Scourge?'

'Sorry. Not even sure I know what it means. I just like human contact.'

'OK. So if you want human contact, call me.' He winked at her. 'But if you don't, I still give you best seat and coffee in the house.'

'You've made me smile, at least.'

'Five quid, please.' He held out his hand as if waiting for a tip.

Cali laughed. 'Have a good day.'

'You too. No more tears, eh, no man is worthy of them.'

# Chapter Seventy-one

Cali had only been home a few minutes when there was a tap on the door.

'Cali big tits, Cali big tits.' Lady P darted around her cage.

Cali raised her eyes as her elderly neighbour handed her the most beautiful bunch of flowers, commenting, 'It's better than "porn star, porn star", I guess.'

'I'm so sorry,' Cali laughed. 'I didn't realise she was that loud.'

'It's fine; that bird of yours keeps me and my Bert amused for hours. Lucky girl, someone must love you.'

'Yes. They must.'

Cali kicked the door shut gently with her foot and opened the envelope that was tucked down the side. Inside was a letter.

*Dear Cali,*

*Bella and I have split up. She wasn't pregnant after all. I know how you feel about me at the moment and that you are seeing someone else, but I'm never giving up on you. I love you so much it hurts. Meet me at Luigi's on Saturday night at seven; we can have a nice dinner and chat, just like the old days. I know I don't deserve it but please give me the respect of an answer.*

*Yours forever,*
*Jamie XX*

Re-reading the letter, Cali sat back on the sofa and shut her eyes. Luigi's was where he had proposed to her. It seemed like centuries ago now.

She kicked off her shoes and started to cry. If anyone asked her how she was feeling, she would say she felt like a little bird that a cat had been toying with, shaking and vulnerable, lying under a bush. If she could wrap herself in a warm blanket and stay there for a month, then she would. She had fallen for someone who wasn't even real, which would make it all the harder to get over, and now this with Jamie. It was all too much to bear.

Before Jack had come on the scene, she could have waivered any second and would not have had a second thought about meeting up with him. But after being betrayed so badly a second time, she wasn't sure if she was strong enough for anyone.

Just as she was about to text her answer, the doorbell rang.

'Mrs Summers?' Hearing the word, Mrs. Even wobbled her slightly. Her marriage had been a farce and it didn't sound right coming out of someone's mouth.

'It's PC Davies from Dedcot Valley Police. Is now a good time?'

'Not really, but you'd better come up.'

'I can come back later if more convenient. We usually call first but I was in the area.'

'No, no, come up.'

Cali quickly wiped her eyes and put on mascara and lipstick so as not to look such a fright.

It was the same policeman who had stopped her for drink driving. He was taller than she had remembered, towering over her.

'Cup of tea?'

'No gin on offer?'

Cali managed a smile. 'That was a one off.'

'Mind you, I'm not surprised you turned to drink knowing what you may have been through.'

Cali went into the kitchen to make tea.

'Big boy J, Big boy J.'

She poked her head around the door, cringing. 'Me and Lady P never knew him as Jack until days ago, OK?'

The policeman laughed. 'I want one of those. Hilarious. And how did it know my name is Joel?'

'Oh, God,' Cali thought, please don't let the policeman be flirting with her. It was hard enough thinking about what she might need to confess to him already.

She sat down next to him on the sofa.

'I just need to ask you a few questions about Jack Wilson.'

'That was his name?'

'What name did you know him by?'

'Do I have to answer all of this?'

'It will help a lot of women if you do.'

Cali suddenly realised how mad she was, thinking she should protect him. He thought nothing of her. He was a charlatan, he had hurt her badly and she had nearly lost a lot of money. She began to tell her story before any more questions were even asked.

'He said his name was Mario Milli, that he was Italian, worked in Formula One, and he drove a black Audi…'

By the time she had finished, an hour had passed. The policeman now not only knew she was nearly a drink driving offender, but also that she'd had casual sex in Room 102 on countless occasions. She was mortified but relieved to have cleared her conscience. And somehow chatting through it made her realise she hadn't been that much of a fool; it was just Jack who had been clever. Not that clever, however, as he had been arrested and, with evidence mounting, was probably looking at even going to prison for fraud.

'Can I just ask you why you picked him up that night?'

'You can ask but I can't tell you, I'm afraid.'

Cali cringed. 'It just makes me feel sick to think of all the other women he may have done this to, and at the same time as me. I am so angry with myself.'

'That's a common reaction, don't worry. You wouldn't, or couldn't, have known. Men like these are charming, they disarm you of reasonable thought and then discard you when they get what you want. Nasty creatures. At least he's off the street now.' He stood up. 'Thank you for being so candid, Cali. It will really help. Take time to heal yourself. Surround yourself with people who really love you. You'll be fine.'

Just him being so kind made her want to cry. She tipped her head back to keep the tears from flowing. 'Thank you.'

He stopped in the doorway. 'And if you think of anything else, or are worried about anything unusual, just call me. Here.' He handed her a card. 'If I'm on duty I'll pick up, if not it will divert to somebody who is fully aware of the case. Bye, Cali. Thanks for the tea.'

With the words 'surround yourself with people who love you' ringing in her ears, she texted Jamie and ran a bath.

# Chapter Seventy-two

'Bet you wish your boyfriend was hot like me,' Adam sang and shimmied into the events office. Then, perching on the end of Cali's desk, 'All right, slapper? Nice of you to show your face for once.'

Cali shook her head, trying not smile. '"Oh, hello, Cali, how lovely to see you, I've missed you", was that?'

'You know I have really. Everything OK?'

'I really don't want to go into detail, but not really. You were right to be wary of Mario. That's not even his name. He was a conman.'

'Oh, Cal. I'm sorry. My mum always used to say, if it seems too good to be true then it usually is.'

'Yes, but love is blind and all that. I can't actually believe how stupid I've been.'

'Well, when you're ready you can tell me all the gory details but, for now, let me get you a cup of coffee.'

'That would be lovely, thanks, Adam.'

Cali turned on her computer, the wedding screensaver almost burning her eyes. She navigated her way to the settings and swiftly replaced it with a lake vista where two swans peacefully glided on the surface of calm waters.

She looked to her calendar. In less than a month she would be another statistic of love gone wrong. Why was love so bloody complicated? Jamie declaring his love for her again had confused her further. After going through the dreadful experience with Mario, maybe just being comfortable with someone who knew you inside out was the way forward. After all, nobody is perfect.

Lou arrived. 'Hey, Cali, good to see you back.'

'You'd think I'd been away for months, not a few days.'

Marcus then popped his head around. 'We missed you, that's why. Your sweet disposition and smiley face make The Bridge Hotel events team what it is today.'

Adam put Cali's coffee down. 'Excuse me while I'm sick in the waste basket.' He nodded his head to Louise. 'Oh, but that's your job, isn't it?'

Louise screwed her face up. 'Enough, Adam.'

Adam went back to reception.

'That boy.' Marcus put his hand on Cali's shoulder. 'When you're settled, pop in my office for a second, can you?'

'Sure.'

Cali quietly started going through her emails. Her concentration levels were almost zero as she kept reliving over and over the time she had spent with Mario, and couldn't believe how stupid she had been. She thought back to the vile vet and her first encounter with Luke. At the time he had filled a need, but now she just felt cheap. And Mario. He must have laughed his head off at the ease she had jumped into bed with him and said she would happily hand over six grand!

Louise broke her thoughts. 'You OK, Cali? You've been staring at your screen for ten minutes.'

Cali let out a big sigh. 'Not really, Lou, but I will be. How are you feeling?'

'Great, actually, thanks. It has all been a good lesson for me. I'm not going through that again. I'm concentrating on me now. Men are a bloody inconvenience, if you ask me. I'm running every day and trying to eat healthier. I feel so much better for it.'

'Good on you. I'm really pleased. Right, I'd better go and see Marcus.'

Cali knocked on Marcus's door.

'Hey, you. Come and sit down.' Marcus looked up from his computer and smiled. 'How's things?'

'Sorry to be so flaky, I needed some time out.'

'Don't be silly. I knew it must be serious, you hardly ever take a sickie and when it comes to affairs of the heart, I for one know how complicated it can be.'

'How did you guess it was man trouble?'

Marcus tutted. 'Cali, I've worked with you for five years. I know you better than yourself sometimes.' Cali rubbed her face as Marcus continued. 'Don't take those extra days as holiday; I'll book it in as sick leave.'

'Thank you, but only if you're sure.'

'I'm sure.'

'How are you and Patricia getting on?'

'Very well, thank goodness. I think sometimes you have to shake things up to help you see what's really important. But enough of the diversion tactics; it's you we need to sort out today.'

'Oh, I'm all right,' Cali sighed. 'Just made a stupid mistake trusting another man who wasn't what he seemed. And now Jamie is saying he still loves me. He's split from Bella, too.'

'I'm sorry to hear that. But that's a turn up.'

'Tell me. But my head is in such a muddle I actually wish he was still with her.'

'Would you ever think about going back to him?'

'Oh, I don't know. I missed him *so* much when we were apart but there was a reason we split. And if I wasn't good enough for him once, why would I suddenly be again?'

'I can't answer what your heart is feeling, Cali, but all I can say is that I realised what a terrible mistake I made with that stupid young girl. And it's made me realise that Patricia is the love of my life and the most amazing person. I was driven by desire, nothing more. I'm a weak man. I think a lot of us are when something is put on a plate.'

'But I don't want to be with a weak man. My take is, if you love someone you can look but never touch. Why would you *want* to touch someone else, anyway? I don't get it.'

'If only life and love were so simple.'

'If Patricia knew what you had done, then I can tell you your life wouldn't be simple. She'd probably be filing for divorce as we speak.'

'OK, OK. I hear you, Cali. But if you think there is any chance with you and Jamie, then don't give up on something that has such strong foundations. That's what I think I'm trying to say, anyway.'

'Trust is so important to me, though.'

'I know, but sex is sex and over in a heartbeat. Love is love and *can* last a lifetime with the right person.'

'But it's never as cut and dried as that when you're living the situation. I feel like I want to shake my head really fast and make all this confusion fly out of my ears. And as for my heart, if you were to open me up I think it would look like a bruised peach with the words "help me" written on it.'

'Cali.' Marcus got up from behind his desk and gave her a big hug. 'Well, I'm here for you whatever. At least it's the weekend tomorrow and it looks like it's going to be a scorcher.'

'Thanks, Marcus. It's so good having a boss as a friend, or a friend as a boss ... oh, you know what I mean.'

'Before you go, this is a bit awkward but HR has got wind that you're divorcing and will need to know if you'll be reverting back to your maiden name for payroll purposes. That's if you *are* getting divorced, eh?'

'I hadn't even thought about that. But I can't stay with Jamie just because I don't want to be plain old Miss Cali Gray again, can I?'

# Chapter Seventy-three

Cali parked up at her flat and put her head against the head rest. Usually, on a Friday night, she would be excited about the weekend, but her pending meeting with Jamie the next day was weighing heavily on her mind.

Getting out of her car, a Worldwide Flowers delivery van pulled up beside her.

'All right, love? Just checking number seven is in this block, save me searching for it?'

'Number Seven, that's my flat.'

'Well, that's a right result.' He opened the back doors and handed her not a bunch of flowers but a beautiful plant in a light purple ceramic pot.

'Calista? I take it that's you? It's a Peace Lily.' He nodded his head.

'Yes, very nice. Thank you, and have a lovely weekend.'

The van pulled off and, unable to wait to get inside, Cali ripped open the envelope. Expecting to see another message from Jamie, she was surprised at what greeted her.

*You've given me faith in this dating app thing. Dinner tomorrow at 7.30. I'll text you where later. H.O. X*

# Chapter Seventy-four

Bubble baths were Cali's favourite sanctuary from the outside world. With top-up hot water gently trickling in around her feet, she lay her head back on the comfy sponge pillow she had treated herself to that morning from the market. And, with a million thoughts running through her mind, she lathered herself in her favourite Prada shower cream and shut her eyes.

After five minutes, she glanced up to her little sunflower clock on the wall, and realised that in just two hours she would have made one of the biggest decisions of her life.

# Chapter Seventy-five

Cali was flustered by the time she reached Luigi's. Despite the time, it was still hot and, wanting to look her very best, had tried on many outfits before deciding on a flowery shift dress that enhanced both her curves and her eye colour.

On reaching the door, she hesitated for a second, then pushed it open with intent.

A handsome Italian waiter greeted her and she flinched slightly as a memory of Mario came to the fore of her mind.

'Oh, hello. You should have a table booked in the name of Summers for seven o'clock. Could I ask you to hand this to Mr Summers when he arrives, please?'

The waiter took the brown envelope from her and smiled.

'Of course. Can I say who it is from?'

'He will know.'

# Chapter Seventy-six

Despite it being seven forty-five, Windsor Great Park was still heaving with families, couples, cyclists and horse riders enjoying the balmy summer evening. She began to panic slightly. What if he had thought she wasn't coming and had already left? She reached the top of the hill and her face broke into a massive smile. At the foot of the big oak tree where they had chatted the other day was a small clothed wooden table and two chairs. She caught the glisten of two crystal glasses and champagne in an ice bucket.

She saw Will before he saw her, wearing long khaki shorts and a white T-shirt. He had his hands on his hips and was looking the other way.

She crept up behind him. 'Hello, handsome officer.'

Will turned round and beamed. 'Better late than never, I guess.' He kissed her on the cheek.

'I'm really sorry, I had to do something first and the taxi was late.'

He popped the cork on the champagne and poured two glasses. They clinked glasses and suddenly Cali felt shy for some reason. 'I can't believe you've done all this for me.'

'I haven't; it must be someone else's. But while

we're here …' His face was completely deadpan.

'You!' Cali laughed.

'Now, it might be a bit wobbly on the roots, but with a bit of steadying I think we'll be fine.' He winked at her as she gave him a knowing look.

'Thanks for the lovely plant, too.'

'I figured you could do with a bit of peace in your life. Even if just in the guise of a Lily.'

He went to a cool box behind the tree and pulled out egg mayonnaise sandwiches and ready salted crisps. 'Sorry it's not gourmet, but I knew you definitely liked both of these.'

Cali bit her lip. 'It's perfect, just perfect.'

They drank champagne slowly and ate their little feast, and with the sun setting, they folded up the table and chairs and lay down together on a picnic blanket.

Cali lay in the crook of the handsome officer's arm.

'This is the best dinner I've ever had in my life.'

'I think maybe that is a slight exaggeration, but as this is where we met for the first time I kind of thought it made sense to do it here.'

'So romantic. Thanks again, it is truly lovely.'

'You deserve the best, Cali, you're a beautiful lady.'

'So why didn't you want to see me again after our first date, really?'

'Crudely, because at the time I was on a Tinder trail of sex. I think I told you I'd split from my girlfriend and I really wasn't ready for anything serious. And I could tell maybe you wanted more and it wouldn't have been fair.'

'I know it wasn't that long ago, but it's a good thing something didn't happen then. Like you, I was still raw after splitting with my ex, Jamie, and I probably would have wobbled anyway. Meeting the conman made me realise I have to stop being so immediate and so trusting. I want to get to know someone first before I jump into bed with them next time.'

'Well, we're knackered already then!' Will kissed her on the forehead. 'I take it you didn't give the conman the money and you're not seeing him any more?'

'No, it's a sorry tale and I could have got done for drink driving.'

'Let's not dwell on it. Conversation closed. May the conman never ever be mentioned again. And your ex?'

'Exactly that – my ex. I'm sure of that now. I really am.'

'Good. You actually almost mirrored the little sonnet I had prepared for you by saying you wanted to take things slow in future. I have a deal for you. You can choose to accept it or I understand totally if you want to walk away.'

'Oh God, this sounds serious.' Cali propped herself up on her elbow. Taking in his chiselled features and pool blue eyes she wanted to kiss him there and then.

'God, you're handsome. Agh. Don't you just hate it when you think something and it comes out of your mouth? Bloody champagne.'

'Keep going, I love it!' Will kissed her gently, on the lips this time. 'Right, stop distracting me. Are you ready?'

'Ready for what?'

'Cali, no more champagne. OK, I'm saying it now.' Cali looked right at him. 'I … err … really do like you, Cali. I liked you the minute I set eyes on you and what I would have done to have taken you home on that first night. You are so hot.'

'I'm blushing now.'

'And then we had sex, not forgetting the best blow job ever! I was smitten. But instead of having a grown-up conversation with you, what did I do? I carried on sending you flippant requests. Let's sit up.'

They sat next to each other under the tree, which was now beginning to creak slightly in the evening breeze.

Will took Cali's hand. 'Cali, you are worth so much more than "30 minutes?" texts. I don't see you as someone who just wants random encounters, but I can see why you did it and I cannot blame you. A bit like me, really. Playing the field. Hiding the hurt with a quick bunk up. But I've realised it doesn't hide the hurt at all. It just makes, well, it makes me feel a bit shallow. I want more than that.'

Cali nodded. 'Yes, I made some stupid mistakes, but you weren't one of them. Even if we had never seen each other again, I would have held on to that wonderful, hot memory from our time at my flat.'

Will laughed. 'Now, my deal. Are you listening?'

'Loud and clear, handsome officer.'

'Let's date. Let's go on two dates a week for the next month. We can kiss and cuddle, but no touching even if we want to. Even sitting here next to you is a challenge. Anyway, on each date we have to learn at least five new things about the other. And if after four weeks, we still do like each other after knowing more than what our private parts look like, then I book a hotel, somewhere amazing with a sea view, where we can have the window open and hear the sounds of the ocean while we fuck like rabbits all weekend.'

Cali's response was a mixture of laughing and crying. 'That, handsome officer, sounds like the best deal I've heard in a very long time.'

'I'm so happy, I was worried you might not be ready. We better get going, it's nearly dark.'

'Not scared, are you, officer?' Cali got up and brushed down her dress. 'Because all of a sudden I'm not scared at all.'

# Chapter Seventy-seven

Jamie sat in his car with tears streaming down his face. As soon as he had seen the brown envelope, he knew exactly what it meant. Clipped to the signed divorce papers was a letter.

*Dear J,*

*I couldn't meet you face to face as I couldn't take the chance of you trying to make me change my mind. I'm not with Mario now. But I know I don't want to be with you any more.*

*This isn't going to be a long, drawn-out goodbye. I just wanted you to know that I truly loved you, and my love for you was always real. We were young, we taught each other a lot. We had fun. We laughed. We lived it. No one could ever say our relationship was boring. But trust. Trust is the most important thing in any relationship. You have to trust the people who are close to you. And even with time, coaching, whatever you wanted to throw at me, I never would have felt confident to trust you again.*

*I can't lie and say I don't love you because there'll always be part of you in my heart. I mean, we've spent over a third of our lives together! I'm just not in love with you any more. It died, as did a little part of me the day you walked out that door.*

*I think no contact is best for a while for us both to be able to move on properly. Lady P is settled with me now so that's all good. I don't know what else I have to do concerning the divorce but I'm sure the solicitors can handle that for us.*

*I wish you peace, happiness and love, and I truly mean that.*

*I say goodbye for now, as with life you never know if it will be forever.*

*Callerina X*

# Epilogue

'Mr and Mrs Smith, your sea view room is ready.'

'Smith?' Cali mouthed to Will, who grinned, then gently squeezed Cali's bum.

They followed the porter up the stairs to the first floor.

'Room 102.'

Cali laughed as Will put the key in the door.

'What's funny?' Will looked at her quizzically.

'Nothing, nothing. I'm just happy. Now, what were you saying about rabbits?'

**THE END**

# Nicola May

For more information about **Nicola May**

and other **Accent Press** titles

please visit

**www.accentpress.co.uk**

Published by Accent Press Ltd 2016

ISBN 9781786154934